MURDER
at the
Marquee

Eliza Thomson Investigates

Book 8

By

VL McBeath

Murder at the Marquee
By VL McBeath

For more about this author please visit:
https://vlmcbeath.com

https://vlmcbeath.com/contact/

*

Editing services provided by Susan Cunningham
(www.perfectproseservices.com)
Cover design: BookCoversbyMelody
(https://bookcoversbymelody.com)

ISBNs:
978-1-913838-33-1 (Kindle Edition)
978-1-913838-34-8 (Paperback)

Main category - FICTION / Historical Mysteries
Other category - FICTION / Crime & Mystery

First Edition

Previous book in the
Eliza Thomson Investigates
series

***Eliza Thomson Investigates*:**
A historical murder mysteries series:
A Deadly Tonic (A Novella)
Murder in Moreton
Death of an Honourable Gent
Dying for a Garden Party
A Scottish Fling
The Palace Murder
Death by the Sea
A Christmas Murder (A Novella)

Sign up to a no-spam newsletter for further information and exclusive content about the series.

Visit
https://www.subscribepage.com/eti-freeadt

Details can be found at **www.vlmcbeath.com**

CHAPTER ONE

August 1905

C onnie Appleton stood at her small dining table beating a cake mixture as her friend and neighbour Eliza Thomson let herself in. She stopped as Eliza approached.

"Here you are. I was beginning to think you weren't coming."

Eliza grimaced. "I'm sorry, the time ran away with me. Archie was complaining that Mr Hewitt doesn't trust him to judge the vegetable competitions, and before he'd finished, Henry arrived home and wanted to chat. I couldn't walk out on him."

"I should think not, given all those times he's been here and hasn't wanted to talk. Did you tell him about Dr Shaw's death?"

"How did you guess?" Eliza sat down at the table and pulled a bag of paper squares from her handbag. "Apparently, Henry spent time on his ward when he was training in children's medicine, so was keen to hear the details."

"He knew him? Gracious. What a small world."

"Indeed. Anyway, we finally satisfied his curiosity, and he went off to the Golden Eagle. He's brought some friends with him for the bank holiday and they're staying in some rooms there. I expect they'll all know about our break in Brighton by now."

"If you could call it that. We never stopped!"

"Quite!" Eliza chuckled. "It's like this fete. It's organised so the villagers can relax and enjoy themselves, but half of us are involved in preparing for it in one way or another."

Connie added an egg to her mixture and nodded towards the squares Eliza had laid out in front of her. "I presume they're for the tombola."

"They are. We've had eleven prizes donated, so I'll number fifty-nine pieces of paper to put in the barrel. Anyone picking a number ending with a five or a zero will get a prize."

"Will that be enough? If the villagers from Over Moreton join us, there could be well over a hundred people here."

Eliza sighed. "You're right. I was just trying to do it quickly. How about if I restrict prizes to numbers that end with a nought? Then I can do one hundred and nineteen."

"You'll still finish before me." Connie cracked a second egg into the mixture. "I'm hoping the scones will be cooked before this needs to go in the oven."

"I thought you'd already made a big batch of fairy cakes."

"I have, but this one isn't for sale. Not to start with, anyway. I want to enter it into the competition. I'll be able to charge more if it's a prize-winning cake."

Eliza sniggered. "The vicar will be pleased if you do, and Mr Hewitt. That leak in the church roof won't mend itself."

"I don't suppose it will make a great deal of difference, but if I can help..." She spooned some flour into her mixture but looked up when there was a knock on the door. "Come in."

"It's only me." Sergeant Cooper removed his police helmet as he joined them. "Ah, Mrs Thomson, I'm glad you're here. May I come in?"

"Yes, of course. Have you called for a cup of tea?"

"Heavens, no. I wouldn't want to be so presumptive ... and we can't have the neighbours talking." He made a point of leaving the front door wide open so he was clearly visible to those outside. "I wanted to ask Mrs Appleton, and you, of course, if you need any help tomorrow morning. Several of the villagers have been setting up the tables inside the marquee so we can move the produce in when we're ready."

Eliza shook her head. "I don't think we do. Henry and some of his friends are here for the weekend, so they can carry the tombola prizes and deliver Mrs Appleton's cakes to her stall."

"Oh."

Connie shot Eliza a glance as Sergeant Cooper's shoulders dropped. "We shouldn't impose on Henry without asking, not if Sergeant Cooper's happy to help."

Sergeant Cooper's face brightened. "I wouldn't have offered otherwise."

"I know you wouldn't, and I *would* appreciate your assistance tomorrow, but I'd like some help this afternoon, too, if you have time..."

"I've always got time for you, my dear. What would you like me to do?"

Connie's cheeks flushed. "I'm looking for someone other than Mrs Thomson to sample the scones. I can't serve out anything of poor quality."

"I'm sure you'd do no such thing, but I won't turn down the chance of a sample."

Connie glanced at the clock on the mantlepiece. "It's quarter past two now. Why don't you check whether anyone else needs you tomorrow and come back at three o'clock? I'll have a pot of tea and some buttered scones ready."

His grin grew broader. "How can I refuse an offer like that?" He replaced his helmet and gave a brief salute before he headed out of the door, pulling it closed behind him.

Eliza returned to her numbering. "I'm sorry I said no. I wasn't thinking. I'll be out of your way by three o'clock."

"You can't go! I can't be seen entertaining a man on my own, even Sergeant Cooper. You know how tongues wag around here."

"It's time you stopped worrying about everyone else. You've been walking out together for over a year now."

"Which is all the more reason people gossip. Sergeant Cooper has his reputation to think of as well as me. Now, I'd better get a move on. All the air will be out of this cake if I'm not quick."

The church bell rang out for three o'clock as Eliza stepped out of Connie's front door with a plate of scones and placed them on the small, round garden table beneath the window. Connie followed her with the tea, but stopped and gave Sergeant Cooper a broad grin as he waved to her.

"That was well timed."

He let himself in through the front gate. "I like to be prompt."

"Well, come and take a seat." Eliza took the teapot from

Connie and put it beside the scones. "Let me get the cups and saucers while you sit down."

Before Connie could object, Eliza ducked into the house, taking her time to retrieve the best crockery before going back outside. By the time she rejoined them, Connie and the sergeant were sitting on either side of the table, with the chair between them empty.

Sergeant Cooper cleared his throat. "Are you ready for tomorrow?"

"I think so." Connie offered him a plate. "I've just taken my competition cake out of the oven, so I only need to finish it off in the morning."

"If your other cakes are anything to go by, you'll have a winner." He glanced over to the marquee on the village green opposite. "I heard they had trouble putting it up this year."

"Mrs Thomson says it's bigger than last year's."

"It is." Sergeant Cooper pointed to Mr Hewitt as he hurried beneath the tent flap in the centre of the side nearest them. "He wants to attract more folks from Over Moreton this year and didn't want it too crowded. It rather hides the bowling club, though, the way it backs onto it."

Connie cocked her head to one side as she studied it. "I hadn't noticed that. Mr Steel won't be pleased."

"He isn't," Eliza said. "Archie told me he's been complaining that he's had to cancel all the matches planned for tomorrow afternoon."

"But he's the chairman of the club. It should be his decision. Who said they couldn't play?"

"Mr Hewitt. Apparently, he wants the entire village to support the fete without any distractions."

Sergeant Cooper's eyes narrowed. "He wants everyone involved in the fundraising, you mean?"

Eliza grinned. "I was trying to be polite. Still, he's in his element, ordering folk around. He collared Archie after church this morning to check he knew how to measure the vegetables for the competitions he's judging."

"He's been into the police station to make sure we know the rules of all the games, too. I had to remind him that we supervise them every year."

"He wants it to be right." Connie gazed across the table at the sergeant. "He puts a lot of effort into it."

Eliza nodded. "He does, and it's not an easy job. I wouldn't swap with him."

"I'd swap with the vicar, though." Sergeant Cooper stared at the scones. "He always gets to judge the baking competition."

Eliza grinned as she offered him the plate. "I'm sure Mrs Appleton will be happy to do more baking for you ... if you ask her nicely."

CHAPTER TWO

Henry was at the breakfast table with Archie when Eliza arrived downstairs the following morning and took her seat between them.

"You were late in last night. I didn't hear you come home."

"It wasn't that bad. We were playing dominos, and I left when the barman called for last orders. I thought you might need help to set up for this afternoon."

"That's very kind of you. Your father needs to do a surgery between nine and eleven, so I'll be on my own. The banks may get a holiday, but it doesn't stop people becoming ill."

Archie took a mouthful of tea. "Won't you be here at all? I'm only dealing with emergencies, but I'd hoped you'd be in the dispensary."

Eliza sighed. "I can give you an hour, but I had planned to help Connie set up her stall." She looked at Henry. "Do you remember how to dispense medicine?"

"I'm sure I could, if you remind me where everything is. It won't do any harm to keep my hand in."

Eliza grinned. "Splendid. You could give your father a hand with the patients, too, if he has more than he can deal with. Don't forget, he needs to practise measuring his vegetables before the fete starts."

Archie rolled his eyes. "I'm perfectly capable of laying a carrot beside a ruler, thank you very much. Still, having some help wouldn't go amiss. I don't want any unexpected amputations though, just because you know how to do it."

Henry laughed. "I'll try not to. Besides, I said I'd meet up with the chaps at midday."

Eliza stopped spreading the butter on her toast. "You know the fete starts at one? Will you try to be there to watch Lord Harrington-Smyth cut the ribbon?"

"I will if I can drag the others out with me. Not that I'm promising anything."

Eliza studied him. "What made you invite them?"

"We'd all arranged to go to Lowton Hall for a weekend party, but we got news from Lord Albert that he needed to postpone it. We were deciding what else to do when your letter arrived."

"Lowton Hall?" Eliza's heart skipped a beat as she thought back to the trouble her father had run into when they were last there. "I didn't think you saw Lord Albert any more."

"We've not seen him since we left Cambridge, but he wrote to say he's getting married and asked if we'd like to join him for a bachelor party."

Eliza's forehead creased. "If he arranged a party, why was it suddenly not convenient?"

"He didn't say." He faced his father. "I'll go on ahead. I

could do with reacquainting myself with the dispensary before the first patients arrive."

Archie stood up as Henry disappeared, but Eliza caught hold of his arm.

"He won't talk to me, but will you see what you can find out? I've a feeling he knows exactly what's going on at Lowton Hall ... and that I won't like it."

Archie tutted. "Stop worrying. Lord Lowton's still in prison."

"Are you sure? He's got friends in high places."

"It would have been in the newspaper if there was anything going on."

Eliza relaxed as his hand squeezed her shoulder. "I hope you're right. I'll follow you through to the surgery as soon as I've finished here."

Mr Hewitt was standing at the entrance to the marquee when Eliza arrived with a basket full of prizes for the tombola. Connie and Sergeant Cooper walked beside her with their first batch of cakes. Mr Hewitt raised his hat to them.

"Good morning, ladies, and to you, again, Sergeant. You look as if you've been busy."

Eliza smiled. "I'm afraid I can't take any credit. This is mostly Mrs Appleton's work, with just a contribution from my cook. Are there many people here yet?"

Mr Hewitt held open the flap to the marquee. "Most people have been over at least once. Mrs Petty was the first to arrive. She wanted her flower arrangements in prime position."

"That's no surprise. She's not won for the last three years

without reason." Eliza stepped into the marquee and ran her eyes around the rectangular walls, resting them on a large orange and white flower arrangement at the far end. "That's lovely, and the space isn't as cavernous as I'd expected with all the tables and produce in."

Mr Hewitt grimaced. "I'm concerned it won't be big enough if they all come from Over Moreton."

"It will be fine. Not everyone will be in here at the same time."

"I hope not. There's a fixing around the back of the marquee that doesn't seem very secure, and I'm worried there'll be an accident if it gets too busy."

"Oh dear. Do you have someone to mend it?"

Mr Hewitt nodded. "Constable Jenkins has gone over to Molesey to find the fellows who put it up. I'm hoping they'll be here soon."

Eliza's shoulders relaxed. "That's reassuring. Now, where would you like me and Mrs Appleton?"

Mr Hewitt directed them to two tables halfway down the right-hand side of the space that were already covered with boxes. "I saved these tables for you when several ladies brought in their contributions. Their names are on the boxes, in case you'd like to thank them."

"This looks fine. Thank you." Eliza turned to Connie as Mr Hewitt hurried over to some newcomers. "If you leave your cakes here, I'll stay with them while you and Sergeant Cooper go for the others."

"What about the rest of your prizes?"

"Henry's bringing them once he's finished with Archie."

"I'll go for the cakes now, then." Connie grinned at her.

"Don't forget, there are others doing some baking for me, so you may need to take the deliveries."

"I can manage." Eliza watched the two of them leave as Mrs Pitt, the shopkeeper's wife, arrived in the tent and headed straight for her.

"Good morning, Mrs Thomson."

"Mrs Pitt. Do you have something for the cake stall?"

"In a manner of speaking. I promised these to Mrs Appleton." She produced six jars of damson jam from her bag. "They're from last year's fruit, but I opened one from the same batch yesterday and it was fine."

"I'm pleased to hear it. Mrs Appleton is preparing some buttered scones, so these will go down a treat." Eliza took them from her and stacked them on Connie's table. "Are you closing the shop today?"

"Oh, no. It's one of our busiest days with everyone from Over Moreton being here. Mr Pitt will stay behind the counter while I help out here."

Eliza looked across to the entrance as Henry called to her.

"Oh. Will you excuse me, Mrs Pitt? I'd better not keep him waiting." She walked towards Henry and peered into the box of prizes he held in front of him. "Is that it?"

"As far as I could see. They were on the dining table."

'Yes, that's right. I must have brought more than I thought."

He walked past her and put his wares on the table. "We're all finished at the surgery. Father said he'd be over in about half an hour."

"Are you staying to help?"

Henry tutted. "I told you. I'm supposed to be having a weekend off and you've already had me working. Besides, I promised to be in the Golden Eagle for opening time. I'll see you later."

As Henry left, Mrs Petty wandered over to join her from her place by the flowers. "He's turned into a handsome gentleman. Does he have a young lady yet?"

Eliza shuddered. "That's kind of you to say, but no, he doesn't, and I hope it stays like that, too. He's only just qualified as a doctor and arranged a permanent job. The last thing he needs is a distraction."

"He's time yet. There's no need to rush these things." Mrs Petty ran her eyes over the cake boxes on the table. "You look like you'll be busy. I'll have to stay around and hope to be first in the queue when Mrs Appleton arrives."

"If you're at a loose end, I'd be delighted to have some assistance laying them out. I'm sure she would, too."

Mrs Petty's eyes twinkled. "I'd like that. It will give me an excuse to stay and watch the judges with the flowers, too."

Eliza laughed, but stopped when Constable Jenkins appeared at the door, confusion on his face.

"Is everything all right, Constable?"

"Have you seen Mr Hewitt?"

Eliza glanced around. "He was here five minutes ago. Have you checked outside?"

"I didn't see him."

"He may be around the back. He said there were some loose connections or something on the marquee, so he may be checking them."

"He'd better be. I've got a couple of men here to fix it, and I need to get to the station. The sarge will wonder where I am."

Sergeant Cooper. Where have he and Connie got to? "I'm sure he won't mind. You've been away for a good cause."

"Hmm." He turned to the two men who had followed him in. "We'll go around the back."

Mrs Petty nodded towards the men as they left. "I saw them on Saturday when they were putting up the tent. The shorter one in the black cap looked to be a strange fellow."

"Why? What was he doing?"

"Not much, by the looks of it, but that was the thing. The other three were working hard, but he was snooping around as if he was looking for trouble."

"Perhaps that's why there's a problem with the marquee. At least he's here to put it right."

"I'd say the taller one's in charge, so he must have made sure he was the one who lost out on his bank holiday. Serves him right."

"I've said before, I wouldn't like to get on the wrong side of you..." Eliza stopped when Connie and Sergeant Cooper reappeared. "Where've you been?"

Connie blushed. "We met Lord and Lady Harrington-Smyth outside and they were looking for Mr Hewitt."

"Did they find him?"

"We're not sure. Constable Jenkins was looking for him, too, so they went with him towards the bowling club."

Eliza looked at the sergeant. "Did the constable see you? He was planning on going straight to the station once he'd found Mr Hewitt, so he'll be wondering where you are."

Sergeant Cooper put the remaining boxes on the table. "I'll be going, then. I'll see you later."

Connie gave him a discreet wave. "We'd better get these laid out and nip home for a spot of luncheon. It wouldn't do to feel ravenous with all these cakes around us." She studied the boxes as their over-the-road neighbour, Mrs King, arrived and handed Eliza her contribution.

"Thank you. That's very kind."

Mrs King hesitated. "I-I can't stay. I told my daughter I'd be home..."

Eliza smiled. "That's quite all right. Will you and your daughter be coming along this afternoon?"

"Yes, we hope to."

"Then I'll look forward to speaking to you later. Now, if you'll excuse me, we've a lot to do, but not much time to do it."

CHAPTER THREE

A s the time approached one o'clock, Mr Hewitt strode into the middle of the marquee and clapped his hands to silence the stallholders.

"May I have your attention? Lord Harrington-Smyth will give his opening speech in two minutes once the church bells have sounded. Are you all ready?"

When he got a series of nods, he rubbed his hands together. "Splendid. Ah, there are the chimes now. By your tables, everyone."

Mrs Petty stood beside Connie and collected up the empty cake boxes.

"Let me put these under the table. No one will see them with the cloths reaching the ground around the front."

Connie studied the overladen stall. "There looks rather a lot. I hope we don't have to take any home."

Eliza put a hand on her shoulder. "When have you ever been left with cakes? It's the most popular stall of the fete. And don't forget, you need to save some for Sergeant Cooper and Constable Jenkins."

"Still…" She turned as Lord Harrington-Smyth's voice filtered into the tent. "Here we go." A minute later, a cheer rang out, followed by a round of applause. Connie stood to attention as Mr Hewitt pulled back the flaps to the marquee and ushered the visitors inside.

Eliza's face brightened as Henry was the first to join them. "You made it."

"Only because I told everyone about the cakes, and they sent me to fetch some and take them to the alehouse."

"Shouldn't you be encouraging them to come over here instead?"

"They will. Once they've had one cake, they'll want another. I'll mention the games outside, too. They'll want to show off their skills."

He made his selection and accepted a box from Connie as Eliza attended to several villagers from Over Moreton who were keen to take their chances on the tombola. When three tickets failed to secure them a prize, they bid her farewell. Eliza picked up the scraps of paper they'd tossed onto the table, but looked up with a smile as the soft Scottish lilt of her husband's voice reached her.

"You're here."

"I've been outside for a while, talking to Mr Steel."

"Don't you see enough of him at the bowling club?"

He raised an eyebrow. "Not as often as you see Mrs Appleton."

"Fair point. Is he still trying to persuade you to take over at the club?"

"He didn't mention it just now, but he knows I'm busy. He invited me to the alehouse later though, so he may be going for bribery next."

Eliza smirked. "I hope he doesn't try too hard. It would be nice if you could walk home in a straight line…"

"The way I always do, you mean." Archie shook his head. "You needn't worry about me. I've no intention of becoming chairman. I'm about the only man in the club who still works full-time."

Eliza tutted. "Just because Mr Steel doesn't work any more, he shouldn't assume everyone has as much time on their hands as he does. In fact, why isn't he carrying on himself? He's still fit and healthy enough."

"Mrs Steel doesn't like him being at the club for so long. I think she's rather needy. Her health isn't as good as his, either."

"That's a shame."

"It is, but I won't let him browbeat me into taking over. One of the others can do it. Judging the vegetable competitions once a year is enough for me."

Eliza laughed. "Are you ready?"

He held up a ruler and notebook. "I just need to find Mr Hewitt to get my final instructions. I'll see you later."

Once all the tombola prizes had been claimed, Eliza moved to help on the cake stall. Connie and Mrs Petty hadn't stopped all afternoon, and by the time Mr Hewitt rang a large handbell and called for attention, the cakes had all but gone.

"Ladies and gentlemen. I'm delighted to say that the judging has now finished, and we'll announce the results at half past three." He checked his pocket watch. "That's in five minutes. If you're with anyone who entered any of the competitions, and they're not already in the marquee, you may like to go and find them."

Eliza watched as half the women in the tent disappeared. "Why is it that the men always want to stay outside?"

"They'll be more interested in throwing sticks at the Aunt Sally dummy." Connie's grin froze on her lips.

"What's the matter?"

"Don't look, but Maria Hartley and her daughter are here. By the door."

Eliza risked a quick peek as Connie began collecting up the empty serving plates. "She's not often seen in the village."

"Then what's she doing here?"

"I'll ask her. She's coming over."

"Don't encourage her to stay."

Eliza smiled as the elegant, slim woman joined them. "Good afternoon, Mrs Hartley. I've not seen you for a while."

"No, I've been keeping busy in the garden, but decided I shouldn't stay locked away forever. I hated it when my husband kept me in the house, so why do the same thing to myself now he's not with us?"

"Why indeed."

Mrs Hartley glanced around. "The fete seemed as good a time as any to meet the villagers. Not that I know who anyone is. I've been talking to Sergeant Cooper, and he said you were here."

Connie glared at her. "You shouldn't disturb him while he's busy."

"I tried not to, but he was keen to talk, and I didn't want to be rude. He's such a nice man..."

Connie hissed as a knife clattered to the floor. "Excuse

me. I need to get tidied up." Connie bent down to pick up the knife before scurrying away.

Mrs Hartley grimaced as Connie left them. "Oh dear, I hope I've not upset her."

"She'll be fine as long as you stay away from Sergeant Cooper. She's rather protective of him and sees you as a threat. It's a compliment ... in a way..."

"If you say so. I'd forgotten she was fond of him."

"More so than before."

"And she doesn't want me *distracting* him. I understand that. Widows have a reputation ... it's one reason I've not ventured out. You probably don't realise, but it's three years this week since my husband's death."

"Goodness, no, I didn't."

"I try not to think about it myself, especially now the court case is over."

"I hadn't heard. That must be a relief."

She nodded. "It was when the judge came down in my favour..."

"Well, it's nice to see you out and about again."

Mrs Hartley sighed. "It may be for you, but not your friend. Would it help if I bought that last piece of Victoria sponge? It looks rather lonely by itself."

"I'm sure it would." She offered Mrs Hartley the plate. "Not that my son will be pleased. He and his friends have eaten a dozen or more already, and it wouldn't surprise me if they come for more ... although thinking about it, I've not seen them for a while, so perhaps they know their limits after all."

Mrs Hartley chuckled as she picked up the cake with a napkin. "I hope so. If they come again, we can't have them arguing over a single slice."

"Exactly! They should be grateful you're prepared to help out..." Eliza paused as Mr Hewitt rang his bell again.

"Ladies and gentlemen, your attention, please." He waited for silence to descend. "Before we give out the prizes, I'd like to thank Lord Harrington-Smyth, Mr Royal from Over Moreton, and Mr Steel, the chairman of our bowling club, for their kind donations. I'd now like to invite their lady wives to step forward to do the presentations."

Mr Steel handed his wife the prize of a silver tankard as Mr Hewitt cleared his throat.

"First, the longest carrot competition ... and the winner is ... Mr Pitt."

There was a round of applause, which gradually faded as Mrs Pitt made her way to the front.

"I'm afraid he's in the shop."

"Never mind." Mr Hewitt took the prize from Mrs Steel. "Would you take this tankard for him with our congratulations?"

"I can manage that. He'll be delighted."

Once Mrs Pitt had disappeared back into the crowd, Mr Hewitt announced the winners from a list Archie had compiled for him, while Mrs Royal, Mrs Steel and Lady Harrington-Smyth handed out the prizes. Twenty minutes later, he turned to the table of flowers against the back wall of the tent.

"Next, the prize for the best flower arrangement. I'm sure you'll all agree we've had a marvellous selection of entries this year, but according to our judge, Lady Harrington-Smyth, the winner, once again, is Mrs Petty for this delightful orange and white display!"

Mrs Petty grinned at the audience as she accepted a glass

vase from Her Ladyship. "Thank you so much. I don't know what to say."

Mr Hewitt ushered her into the crowd. "Thank you, Mrs Petty. There's no need for a speech. Now, we've only one award left, and that's for the vicar's favourite competition. The cake baking!" He studied his list. "This year, the winner is ... Mrs Appleton!"

Sergeant Cooper stood at the front of the marquee, beaming as Connie collected a china plate from Mrs Royal. Eliza patted her on the shoulder as she returned to their table.

"Congratulations. I told you, you'd nothing to worry about."

"I know, but you can never take it for granted..." She stopped as Mr Hewitt once again clapped his hands together.

"Thank you all for your attention ... and for your generosity on the stalls. The formal part of the fete is over, so if you'd like to make any last-minute purchases, now's your chance."

Connie glanced around the tent. "I suppose it's time for us to tidy up."

"I thought you were going to sell off your competition cake."

"Sergeant Cooper's offered to buy it."

"The whole thing?"

Connie flushed. "I promised to make him a cup of tea to go with it. You're welcome to join us."

Eliza smiled. "I must admit, that sounds very tempting, especially as we've nothing left to take home. Mrs Hartley took the last piece of sandwich cake."

"Did she indeed?" Connie muttered to herself as she flicked crumbs onto the grass.

Eliza sighed. "What's got into you?"

"You know jolly well what. She's no right to flash those seductive green eyes at Sergeant Cooper…"

"I doubt she did anything of the sort, and even if she did, Sergeant Cooper isn't interested in anyone but you. Not even Mrs Hartley."

"And I want to keep it that way."

Eliza shook her head. "Falling out with Mrs Hartley is hardly going to help. It's Sergeant Cooper you need to talk to."

"Don't be silly. I can't talk to him about things like that."

"Maybe you should…"

Connie stared at the floor. "I'm sorry. I didn't mean to be rude…"

Eliza's shoulders dropped. "And I didn't mean to be harsh. Now come along, you can apologise to Mrs Hartley the next time we see her."

Eliza stacked the last of the plates but straightened her back as Mr Hewitt strolled to the table with three men trailing behind him.

"Are you finished here, ladies?"

Eliza nodded. "We are, although I'm afraid we're out of cake, if that's why you're here."

"I wish I was." He indicated to the men with him. "Mr Taylor and his men are waiting to dismantle the marquee, but they've lost one of their colleagues, a Mr Hobbs. We wondered if you'd seen him recently. He's a short, plump chap who was wearing a black cap."

Eliza looked at Connie. "He was here earlier when he came to repair the problem, but I've not seen him since."

Mr Taylor, the taller man with dark hair and moustache,

groaned when Connie agreed. "Typical. I knew he'd disappear."

Eliza's eyes flitted around the group. "If he's been here all day, might he have gone to the alehouse?"

"Quite likely, knowing him." Mr Taylor turned to an older man with greying hair. "Will you go and check, seeing you're the one who he usually works with?"

Mr Hewitt pointed over his shoulder. "If you turn left out of here and walk to the road, it's on your left."

The man grinned. "We know the way. We were in there on Saturday. Thank you, anyway,"

Mr Taylor nudged the arm of a younger man who stayed with him. "We may as well make a start outside. There's no point hanging around."

As the men disappeared, Mr Hewitt bid Eliza and Connie farewell. "I offered to help Mrs Petty take her flower arrangements home, so I'd better not keep her waiting."

"She won't mind." Connie looked to the end of the tent. "She's tickled pink to have won again, and her admirers are only just leaving. She must be running out of places to display those vases."

"I'm sure she'll find room..." Eliza spun around as a scream suddenly pierced the air. "What on earth...? Mrs Petty?"

There was a moment's silence before the crowd in the tent moved towards the flower table.

"Wait, please..." Mr Hewitt held his arms out to his sides. "Everyone, stand back..."

Sergeant Cooper dashed over from the door. "What seems to be the problem?"

Mrs Petty's voice quivered as she pointed beneath the

white tablecloth. "I-I went to get m-my handbag, and ... t-there's a man. H-he's..."

"All right, Mrs Petty, calm down. It may be a workman taking down the marquee."

"While we're still in it?" Constable Jenkins strode to the table. "We need to have a word."

"And we will..." The sergeant lifted the edge of the cloth. "Whoever you are, come out of there..." He leaned forward to peer under the table, but quickly straightened up. "Right, yes. Mr Hewitt, Constable, we need everyone out. Direct them onto the village green." He ran a hand around the back of his neck. "Will one of you look for Dr Thomson while you're out there? I need him here."

"Yes, sir." Constable Jenkins glared at the crowd. "You heard the sergeant..."

As the villagers filed out, Eliza caught Connie's arm and slowly edged them towards Sergeant Cooper. Constable Jenkins didn't immediately notice, but as soon as he did, he called to them.

"Come on, ladies..."

Sergeant Cooper turned as he spoke. "Give them a minute, Constable, and they'll be with you. Make sure everyone else is out first."

Constable Jenkins' mouth tightened as he pushed the last of the guests from the marquee and marched towards the sergeant. "If you're going to tell them what's happened, you can tell me, too."

"Very well." Sergeant Cooper lowered his voice as he turned his back on the crowd. "It's the missing marquee man. He's lying under the table. Dead."

CHAPTER FOUR

"Dead!" Constable Jenkins stepped around Eliza to peer under the table. "How did that happen with so many people here?"

Sergeant Cooper wiped his brow. "That's a very good question and one we need an answer for."

"May I see?" Eliza didn't wait for a reply before she, too, lifted the cloth. A man wearing a green tweed jacket and black cap stared out at her with blank eyes. She flinched but kept her eyes on the body until she let the cloth fall. "That doesn't look like an accident. There's bleeding from the head, so he was most probably hit with something heavy."

Archie's voice echoed around the now empty marquee.

"What's going on? Mr Hewitt said you wanted to see me..."

Eliza reached her husband before the sergeant. "There's a body under the table. Another murder."

"You can't know that. It may have been natural causes."

"I doubt it, given he has blood coming from his left

temple. Besides, if it was natural causes, why would someone bundle him under the table? From the outside, too?"

"Let me see." Archie crouched on the floor and raised the cloth. "Ah, you may be right. The way the body's lying isn't natural. Sergeant, can I have more space around here? I'll need to take a closer look."

"Shall we fetch Mr Taylor? He's the one in charge of the men."

"I wouldn't recommend involving him yet. Let's see what we've got first. If you and the constable could get on either side of the table and move it out, it will shield the body from anyone coming in. Eliza, will you and Mrs Appleton stand by the door to keep people out?"

Eliza was about to object when Archie sighed. "Please ... and don't let anyone in, except Mr Hewitt, if he turns up."

By the time they reached the entrance of the marquee, the table had been moved and all they could see were the two police officers in their blue jackets staring down at a space between them. It wasn't long before Archie appeared between them. "We'll need a post-mortem, but I would say the death was due to a single blow to the head, almost certainly murder rather than an accident."

Eliza whispered in Connie's ear. "Didn't I say that ten minutes ago?"

"I think you missed out the word single ... although in fairness, Dr Thomson may not have been here at the time."

The two sniggered as Archie stared over at them. "We'll need to take the body to the surgery. Would you be able to bring the stretcher over with a sheet?"

Sergeant Cooper looked across at Connie. "Would you like me to help? It may be rather heavy."

Eliza opened her mouth to reply, but Archie interrupted.

"Actually, Sergeant, I think we should tell Mr Taylor. Could you or the constable find him while the other one of you stays by the door?"

Eliza glanced around the marquee. "Mr Taylor shouldn't be far away, because he wanted to make a start on taking this down. Not that they seem to be doing much..."

"Excuse me, Mrs Thomson." Mr Hewitt poked his head through the gap in the door. "May I come in?"

"Yes, of course." She stepped to one side.

"We've a crowd of people outside waiting to collect their produce. I was hoping we'd be able to let them in."

"Not at the moment, I'm afraid. We've a dead body to move before we can do that."

"So, Mrs Petty was right?"

Eliza sighed. "She was indeed. How's she doing?"

"She's made a remarkable recovery now she has an audience. Not that everyone believes her."

"Perhaps we should leave it that way. Have you seen Mr Taylor lately?"

"The marquee man? He's outside. Why?"

"Sergeant Cooper would like a word with him." Eliza pointed to the other end of the tent before she held open the flap for Connie. "We won't be long."

Connie groaned as they left the tent. "I can't believe this has happened again."

"I know what you mean. I hope you weren't planning on doing anything this week. We're going to be busy."

. . .

Many in the crowd had dispersed by the time they returned with the stretcher, and Mr Taylor was talking to Sergeant Cooper as they went into the tent.

"I don't believe it. Why would anyone want him dead?"

"That's what we need to find out, sir. We'll speak to you later, so if you and your colleagues would go next door to the bowling club, there'll be someone to make you a cup of tea."

"Tea ... right. Thank you." He nodded to Eliza and Connie as he passed them on the way to the exit.

Eliza took a deep breath. "He looked shocked."

"Is it any surprise?"

"Probably not, but it's worth noting when you're looking for a killer."

"Ah, yes, I'll make a note of it." Sergeant Cooper reached for his notebook. "Fortunately, Mr Steel has said we can use the bowling club to speak to people. It's less formal than taking them to the station."

"That's a good idea. Why don't we make the tea for everyone? That way, we can talk to people as well."

Sergeant Cooper nodded. "If you wouldn't mind, that would work well. Tell him I asked you to, if he's worried about women in his club." He took the stretcher from them. "Let me help Dr Thomson with the body, and I'll follow you over."

"Before we go, might I have a word with my husband? I ought to know how the victim died. And his name. Was it Mr Hobbs?"

"It was, from the marquee company. Mr Taylor has just confirmed his identity."

"Am I right in thinking there were two other men with them?"

"Yes, Mr Bedford and Mr Gilbert. Mr Bedford is the older of the two."

"Thank you, Sergeant. What a to-do this is after the events of Brighton."

"It is indeed, Mrs Thomson. Still, it should make it easier, being on home soil."

"I hope so." She left Connie with the sergeant as she strolled over to Archie. "Did you find anything of interest?"

Archie pulled the tablecloth over the body and stood up. "Not really. You were right. It was a blow to the head, the left-hand temple if that makes any difference, but we've not found what he was hit with."

Eliza scanned the edge of the marquee. "It may be outside. The fabric is loose enough for someone to have rolled him underneath. It was fortuitous for the killer that the table was up against the wall. Are you able to estimate the time of death?"

"Within the last hour, I would say. The body's still warm."

Eliza shuddered. "Poor chap. Should we ask what people were doing between three and half past four?"

"Won't Sergeant Cooper be doing that?"

"With a little help ... and we need to know we're asking the same questions."

Archie groaned. "Very well, yes, I'd say that's appropriate. It was half past three when we started giving out the prizes, and I noticed the church bell ring for four o'clock a few minutes after Mrs Appleton collected her prize. Mrs Petty must have found the body five or ten minutes later."

Eliza nodded. "Most people were in the marquee while the prizes were being given out, so the killer would have had the opportunity to act without being seen. The timing will give most people an alibi, too."

"The killer must have timed the attack to coincide with the applause ... or the church clock. We'd have heard the scuffle otherwise."

"Premeditated then?"

Archie grimaced. "Or fortunate."

"Hmm." Eliza paused before she straightened up. "I'll leave you to it. See you later."

CHAPTER FIVE

Connie followed Eliza from the marquee but stopped when she turned left.

"I thought we were going to the bowling club."

"We are ... but not straight away. I want to check around the back of the marquee first to see if we can find the murder weapon."

"What are you looking for?"

"I don't know. Something light enough to pick up, but heavy enough to do some damage."

"That could be anything."

"I know, so stay alert." Eliza picked her way over the ropes holding the marquee in place while Connie followed.

"How could anyone commit murder with all these tent pegs in the ground?" Connie glanced around. "It's a wonder they didn't trip over."

"Maybe they did." Eliza stopped to study them. "What's that over there, halfway along? There's a rope hanging loose." She continued carefully until she reached the right spot. "And the tent peg's missing ... or at least part of it is."

Connie looked at her. "Could that be what we're looking for?"

"It wouldn't surprise me. It would make a good murder weapon and would explain why the killer was able to push the body under the fabric." Eliza called through the material. "Archie, are you there?"

"What? Eliza? Where are you?"

"On the outside of the marquee. There's a tent peg missing."

Sergeant Cooper spoke. "Have you looked around the area for it?"

"Not thoroughly, but it isn't obvious. You may want to send Constable Jenkins to search for it."

"Will do. Thank you both."

Eliza studied the white picket fence that butted up to the ropes. "Now we have to get out of here. I don't know why they put it so close to the boundary."

"To give more room around the front, I should imagine. It would be more helpful if there were a gate."

"It would. We'll have to mention it to them before next year."

The lounge of the bowling club was empty when they arrived, but before the kettle was on the stove in the small kitchenette, the marquee men had arrived and slumped onto several chairs. Eliza wandered out to greet them.

"Good afternoon, gentlemen. May I get you anything?"

Mr Taylor looked up at her. "Not unless you've any brandy..."

Eliza glanced around. "There must be some here, but it will be locked away. I can make a pot of tea."

"Not for me. I need to be going. I'd hoped to get the marquee down tonight, but there's no point doing it now. I'll have an early start in the morning."

"If you wouldn't mind staying a little longer. I know Sergeant Cooper would like to speak to you before you leave. He shouldn't be long."

Mr Taylor nodded but said nothing.

"Do you have details of Mr Hobbs' next of kin? The police will need to notify them."

Mr Taylor looked at his colleagues. "I don't think he had any. If he did, he never mentioned them to me."

"He had none." Mr Bedford stared at his hands. "He never married, and his only brother died last year."

"That's sad." She turned back to Mr Taylor. "You must have been like family to him, then. Had he worked with you for long?"

"The best part of thirty years."

"Gracious. He's going to be quite a loss."

Mr Taylor gazed out of the window. "He certainly is."

"And what about you gentlemen?" She looked at Mr Bedford and Mr Gilbert. "Have you been with the firm for long?"

Mr Bedford spoke. "Me and Hobsy started together when Mr Taylor set up on his own."

Mr Gilbert grunted. "I'm the new boy. I've only been with them for twenty years."

"It's still a long time. You must have all been very close."

Mr Taylor snorted. "You'd think so, wouldn't you?"

"You mean you weren't?"

He shrugged. "We had our issues, but show me a group of men working together who don't."

"Would any of those issues be a cause for murder?"

Mr Gilbert gasped. "Of course not. We wouldn't do anything like that."

Eliza's eyes flicked between them. "Can you think of anyone who might have wished to harm him?"

"Plenty." Mr Bedford looked up. "I don't like to speak ill of the dead, but he did have a way of annoying people. I'd got used to him, but not everyone had."

"Would you mind telling me who he upset?"

"Friends, neighbours, clients. You name it."

"Could you narrow it down?"

Mr Gilbert's brow creased. "There were one or two here today who knew him. That would be a good place to start."

Eliza looked at Mr Taylor. "Sergeant Cooper might like to see your list of customers. It could help to check who they were."

"I can provide that." Mr Taylor stood up. "Do you know where the sergeant is? I need to get home."

Connie looked through the window. "He's here now." She opened the door and waved as she stepped outside. A minute later, the sergeant joined them with Constable Jenkins.

"Gentlemen. I'm sorry to keep you waiting. We had to move the body..."

Mr Bedford stood up. "What happened to him?"

"I'm afraid I can't say until we get confirmation from the coroner, but it doesn't look like an accident."

"The doctor said it was a blow to the head." Mr Taylor blew out his cheeks. "I still can't believe it."

"No, sir, it's quite a tragedy, but while we wait for the

coroner, I need to ask you all where you were between three and half past four this afternoon?"

"Us?" Mr Taylor turned to his men. "You can't think one of us did it."

"These are just preliminary questions, sir. We need to be able to place everyone." The sergeant stood with his pencil poised over his notebook. "So, where were you?"

"We were on the green, near the games."

"Can anyone confirm that?"

"You can for a start…" Mr Taylor stared at the sergeant. "You were in charge of the Aunt Sally. Didn't you see the three of us watching? Or you, Constable?"

Constable Jenkins shook his head. "There were a lot of people around."

Eliza huffed. "Was Mr Hobbs with you at any time?"

"Not then." Mr Taylor's brow creased. "I was with him when we came to secure the frame of the marquee, but when I offered him a ride to Molesey, he said there was no point if we had to come back again, so he was going to the alehouse. That must have been about half past twelve." He looked around at Mr Bedford. "He told me you'd be in there."

"I said I'd meet him at three o'clock, but when I arrived, he'd gone. That's when I came to find you."

Sergeant Cooper wrote in his book before he asked the next question. "Can anyone confirm you were in the alehouse, Mr Bedford?"

"The landlord, for one. I asked him if he'd seen Mr Hobbs."

"And had he?"

"He'd been in, but he hadn't noticed him leave."

"And this was at three o'clock?"

"Give or take five minutes."

Sergeant Cooper sighed. "I need you to be more precise. Do you remember hearing the church bells strike three?"

"Can't say I did."

"Perhaps they rang when Mr Bedford was in the Golden Eagle." Eliza looked between them. "The sound must be muffled in there."

"They are, especially on such a busy day." The sergeant turned back to Mr Bedford. "So for the sake of argument, you left the alehouse shortly after three o'clock and went straight to the front of the marquee?"

"I-I didn't take the most direct route. I walked around the road and came in from the opposite direction."

"Why would you do that?"

"I wondered where Mr Hobbs had got to and decided to look for him."

"Didn't you assume he'd be at the fete?"

"I never assumed anything with him. He wasn't one to enjoy himself. He'd have been more likely to go looking for trouble."

"Unfortunately, it looks as if he found it." Sergeant Cooper licked the end of his pencil. "Where did you search?"

"I peered into the churchyard, but only from the gate. I didn't go in. Then I called at the shop. When he wasn't there, I walked past this place, then carried on to the fete in case he'd come looking for me."

"Which he hadn't?"

"No."

The sergeant turned to Eliza. "Do you have any more questions?"

"Not for Mr Bedford, but can we check what time Mr Taylor and Mr Gilbert arrived at the fete?"

"Mr Taylor was here before me..." Mr Gilbert looked relieved when Mr Taylor didn't argue.

"I arrived shortly after three o'clock, but Mr Gilbert didn't join me until about half past."

"So, you were on your own until Mr Bedford joined you? What time was that?"

"About five or ten minutes before Mr Gilbert. I was on the village green all the time I was waiting."

"Did you go into the marquee when the competition prizes were being given out?"

"Erm ... no. We were still waiting for Mr Gilbert when they started, and when he arrived, we stayed outside discussing how to get people out of the way so we could take the marquee down."

"And were the three of you alone by that stage?"

"No. There were still people milling about. In fact, if you want to check, there were a couple of young men who carried on playing the Aunt Sally. Having a fine old time, they were, laughing and joking."

Sergeant Cooper puffed out his chest. "Were they indeed? I hope things are as I left them. Mr Hewitt will expect everything back in one piece..."

"Forgive me for interrupting, Sergeant." Eliza gave him a feeble smile. "Before you carry on, may I ask about the young men? Could any of you describe them?"

"Hmm, now." Mr Taylor looked at Mr Bedford. "There were two of them."

Mr Bedford nodded. "Both had dark hair, I think. One with a moustache and the other with a full beard."

"Yes, that's right. They looked rather respectable…"

Eliza's heart rate quickened. "You're sure they both had facial hair? There wasn't one who was clean-shaven?"

They both shook their heads as Mr Taylor spoke. "I don't think so."

She sighed. *Is that good or bad?* "And there was no one else?"

"There probably was, but I didn't notice anything about them."

"All right, thank you." Eliza looked at the sergeant. "Is that all we need for now?"

"I'd say so. Thank you, gentlemen. I'll be in touch if we need anything more."

Mr Taylor nodded. "We'll be here in the morning to take the marquee down, if that's all right?"

"I don't see why not. We'll do a final inspection of the murder site this evening. Thank you, again."

Eliza waited for them to leave. "I think we've gone as far as we can with the questions for now. Until we have a proper idea of what happened. What do you think, Sergeant?"

He checked his pocket watch. "It's turned five o'clock, so I suggest you go home. We'll do a last check of the marquee, and we can speak to the young men tomorrow."

Connie gazed up at him. "Who'd have thought we'd be doing this again after our week in Brighton? Did you find the missing tent peg?"

"No, we didn't." He looked at Constable Jenkins. "I presume you had a good look."

"I checked all around the area between the tent and the bowling club but didn't see it. We'll have to extend the search tomorrow."

"That's frustrating." Eliza stared out of the window towards the marquee. "We could do with studying one of the other pegs so we know precisely what to look out for."

Sergeant Cooper made a note. "I'll make sure we get one from Mr Taylor before they leave."

CHAPTER SIX

Dinner was ready by the time Eliza arrived home and she called to Archie and Henry as Iris placed the serving dishes on the dining room table. She looked up as they joined her.

"What have you been doing?"

Archie waited for Iris to leave. "Henry wanted to see the body."

"Ah." Eliza paused as Henry took his seat. "Did you recognise him?"

"I didn't know him, but he was in the Golden Eagle for a good couple of hours this afternoon."

"Really! I don't suppose you remember what time he got there? Or when he left?"

"Not with any accuracy. He wasn't there when I arrived, but I noticed him partway through the afternoon, when a steady stream of visitors popped in to speak to him. I joked it was like he was holding a surgery at one point."

Archie studied him. "Could they have been people he bumped into while he was there?"

"I doubt it. We were in the snug, and he had a table in the opposite corner to us. The callers all looked as if they had prearranged meetings. Not that I could hear anything that was said with all the noise."

"Did you know any of them?"

Henry accepted a dinner plate from the maid. "Most of them. All the marquee workers came in ... one at a time, though, not together. Then there was Mr Hewitt and Mr Steel. I didn't notice if there were any others. I'd lost interest by that stage."

Archie's brow creased. "Why would Mr Steel want a word with him?"

Eliza helped herself to some buttered new potatoes and placed them beside the pork chop on her plate. "Is he planning any events at the bowling club? He may want to hire a marquee."

"He's not told me, if he is. I hope he has no plans to land his successor with the job of organising an event he's dreamed up."

"He wouldn't, would he?"

"Who knows, but it would give me a reason to decline taking over from him."

"We'll need to talk to everyone else who visited Mr Hobbs, too, find out what they all wanted. At least Henry's statement should help narrow the field down a bit. Along with the list of clients Mr Taylor has promised to share with us."

Archie gasped. "You can't think Mr Steel or Mr Hewitt were involved."

"Of course not, but we need to eliminate them from the enquiries. We've already spoken to Mr Hobbs' colleagues, and they all denied having anything to do with his death. None of them mentioned they'd visited him in the alehouse, though, and I specifically asked what they were doing between three and half past four."

Henry's eyes narrowed. "That was probably because the meetings were before three o'clock. Mr Hobbs had disappeared by the time we left, and we had several games of Aunt Sally before the prize-giving. What time was that?"

Eliza laid down her knife and fork. "It started at half past three. Did you hear the church bells when you left the alehouse?"

Henry gave a gradual nod. "Yes ... we were playing a game by then, so we must have left at around quarter to three."

"Then why would Mr Taylor, Mr Bedford and Mr Gilbert tell us they weren't in the village until later?"

Henry shrugged. "You'd better ask them that, but it was definitely them."

"That's good to know. I've a question for you, too." She waited until she had her son's full attention. "Mr Taylor said they were outside the marquee while the presentations were taking place and there were two young men still throwing sticks at the Aunt Sally. It sounded like your friends. The dark-haired ones. What did you call them?"

"James Cartwright and Anthony Everett."

"That's right. Does one have a moustache and the other a full beard?"

"Yes. Why? I hope you don't think they had anything to do with it."

"Not necessarily. I just wondered where you and your other friend were. Mr Taylor was sure the others were on their own."

"We ... erm ... we called at the shop ... for some sweets."

Eliza studied him. "Hadn't you had enough with all those cakes?"

"It wasn't me, it was Toby. Dr Dunlop. He wanted a walk along the river ... so I nipped into the shop on the way."

"Why would he want to do that?"

"He didn't say, and I didn't ask."

"But you were with him all the time he was there?"

"Yes ... well, except for when I was in the shop. He went on ahead. We were only apart for a couple of minutes." Henry's mouth fell open. "You can't think he killed him. He didn't even know him."

"Maybe not, but as I've said, everyone's a suspect to start with." Eliza paused. "Were any of the marquee men in the shop when you were there?"

"No. I didn't see anyone except Mr Pitt."

"Never mind. Mr Pitt will be able to confirm who called during the afternoon. Sergeant Cooper will want to speak to you all before you leave, too."

Henry groaned. "Can't you tell him what I've told you? I've nothing more to add."

"You can't know what Mr Cartwright and Mr Everett were doing, or what they saw, if you weren't with them."

"It's Dr Cartwright, and they weren't murdering anyone, if that's what you mean."

"No, it's not. I mean, they could be important witnesses."

"As long as that's all it is."

Archie finished the last of his chop and laid his knife and fork on the plate. "I'll have a word with Mr Steel when I get to the alehouse and ask if he noticed anything."

Eliza raised an eyebrow. "You're still going?"

"Why not? There's nothing more I can do until tomorrow."

"I suppose not, but I doubt he'll have seen much. He was in the tent giving out the prizes from half past three."

"That's only half an hour, and I did suggest the murder could have taken place any time after three. If he was in the alehouse, he'll have had to walk across to the marquee at some point, so he may have noticed something."

"You're right. Don't let me stop you meeting him, then. I look forward to hearing what he has to say."

It was approaching half past seven when Archie and Henry left for the Golden Eagle, and Eliza fixed her summer bonnet and headed next door. Connie was tidying her hair when she arrived.

"I wasn't expecting you."

"Archie and Henry have left me on my own, so I thought we could make a start working out who to speak to tomorrow."

"Oh..."

"Would you rather we didn't?"

Connie's cheeks coloured. "Frank ... Sergeant Cooper ... is calling so we can take a walk."

"Ah ... you won't want me around, then."

"I'm sorry... I could put him off if you like."

"You'll do no such thing. I'm delighted for you."

"You're sure?"

Eliza sniggered. "Of course I am. It's about time you spent more time together. Besides, you can ask him if he found anything when they checked the marquee again."

"But you need help with the questions."

"I can make a start on my own ... and you can add your thoughts to it later."

"As long as you don't mind. Thank you."

Eliza turned to the door. "Come in for coffee in the morning after surgery, and we'll talk then."

Sergeant Cooper was nowhere to be seen when Eliza stepped back onto the footpath, but she stopped to wave as Mrs Petty walked across the village green.

"Good evening, Mrs Petty. I didn't expect to see you again today."

She smiled as Eliza waited for her. "I was on my way to visit you and Mrs Appleton, as it happens. I hope you don't mind."

"Not at all, although you'll have to make do with me, I'm afraid. I've been left on my own."

"I saw you nipping into Mrs Appleton's house and thought it would be a good time."

Eliza tittered as she led her into the surgery. "You never miss a trick from your wonderful seat by the window... Come on in. Cook should still be around to make us a cup of tea."

"Oh, don't worry about that, I won't take up much of your time. I just wondered if you'd be helping Sergeant Cooper with his investigations."

"I hope so." Eliza showed her into the drawing room and gestured to one of the settees adjacent to the hearth. "Take a seat while I pull the curtains across. The sun comes straight in at this time of day."

Mrs Petty ignored her invitation and joined her at the window. "It really is a wonderful view of the river. It's a shame you weren't here this afternoon with the window open."

Eliza looked at her. "Are you too warm?"

"No, not at all. It's just that your son's friend was out there earlier, talking to the victim."

"Henry's friend? One with dark hair or fair?"

"The fair one."

"He spoke to Mr Hobbs? When?"

"Around three o'clock. I went to the shop for Mrs Appleton and saw them on my way back to the fete."

"Henry was here at three o'clock?"

"No, he wasn't with them. I assumed he was with his other friends."

Eliza stared at the older woman. *He told me he was with his friend Dr Dunlop all afternoon.* "Was he in the shop?"

"No."

A sinking feeling hit Eliza's stomach. *Where on earth was he? And why did he lie to me?*

CHAPTER SEVEN

E liza hadn't joined Mrs Petty on the settee before Iris knocked on the drawing room door and let herself in.

"Good evening, madam. I thought it was you. Would you like a pot of tea?"

"Oh, yes, please, but before you go, might we have a word?"

The maid took a step backwards as her eyes flicked between Eliza and Mrs Petty. "A word?"

"Don't look so worried. I'd just like to ask you about this afternoon."

"I-I was here all the time. I didn't leave the house ... I polished the silver in the dining room... I'll fetch it if you want to check..."

Eliza tutted. "You'll do nothing of the sort. I've absolute faith in you. The thing is, Mrs Petty says Dr Dunlop, one of Henry's friends, was by the river earlier, talking to another gentleman. I wondered if you'd seen them."

"You mean the fair-haired one?"

"So you did?"

"I-I think so. I nipped in here for the candlesticks ... there was no point doing the silver without cleaning them, too, but..."

"But, what?"

"When I came in, the window was open. I heard voices outside, so I took a peek to find out who it was ... I-I didn't mean to listen. I couldn't help it..."

Eliza smiled. "There's no need to worry. I was hoping you'd overheard what they said."

The maid's eyes widened. "You were?"

"Did you hear that a man was found dead at the fete this afternoon...?"

"Y-yes... Cook told me..."

"Well, if my guess is right, the victim was the man you saw talking to Henry's friend. He was short and plump, and wore a black cap."

"That's him. He's dead?"

"I'm afraid so. That's why we're keen to learn what he said to Dr Dunlop."

"I didn't hear much, but Dr Dunlop seemed angry with him and said he owed them fifty pounds for the damage..."

"What damage?"

"He didn't say. The older man's face was red, and I thought there'd be a fight... That's when I left. I didn't want to get involved..."

"I'm sure you wouldn't have, but thank you, anyway. We'll have that cup of tea now, but if you remember anything else, will you let me know?"

"Yes, madam."

Eliza took a seat opposite Mrs Petty. "What do you think of that?"

"I'd say someone's got some explaining to do. Were you acquainted with this friend of your son's?"

"Not really. Henry introduced us earlier when they came for some cakes, but that's it."

"So, you can't vouch for him?"

"No, but more worryingly, I don't understand why Henry didn't say anything. He must have known about the meeting."

"He wasn't with them, though, so that must be good … mustn't it?"

"I suppose, but why would he lie about it unless he hoped to give his friend an alibi?"

"I can't answer that, but don't forget, I found the victim in the marquee, not by the river."

Eliza nodded. "You're right, of course, but if Dr Dunlop had a grievance with Mr Hobbs, he may have followed him back to the marquee. Did you notice any noises while you were by the flower stall or when you received your prize?"

"I can't say I did. There was a lot of chattering in the marquee, though, and once the presentations started, the crowd applauded every minute or so."

Eliza sighed. "They did. It's going to be impossible to place everyone at the fete, too. Is there anything else we should follow up on?"

Mrs Petty sat back in her seat. "I've been thinking about that, but I've not come up with anything other than your son's friend."

"All right, why don't we start at the beginning? Can you tell me everything you did after about two o'clock this afternoon?"

"Well, as you know, I was on the cake stall for most of the

afternoon. It felt as if half the village called for a cake... Not that I had a chance to talk to many of them."

"Me neither." Eliza nodded. "Remind me why you left to go to the shop. Were we out of butter or jam by then?"

"No, we'd run short of paper napkins, so Mrs Appleton asked me to see if I could get any."

"And that was around three o'clock?"

"A few minutes before, because the church bells sounded as I was walking."

"And while you were at the shop, did you meet anyone?"

"No, it was quite empty. Most folk were either in the marquee or on the village green. Two of your son's friends were playing on the games when I left, and one of the men who put up the marquee was watching. I've a feeling Mr and Mrs Royal were there, too ... although, no, thinking about it, that was when I got back."

Eliza held up a hand to stop Mrs Petty. "Was the marquee worker still there when you got back?"

"Yes."

"Can you remember which one?"

"The man in charge..."

"Mr Taylor." Eliza paused. "That makes sense. He confirmed he was the first to arrive, and that Mr Gilbert didn't join him until turned half past three. Mr Bedford was more vague. What time did you get back to the stall?"

"I was gone for about ten minutes, maybe fifteen, so around ten past three."

"Mr Bedford told us he'd been in the Golden Eagle at three o'clock but had walked up past the church and gone into the shop before he joined Mr Taylor. It must have been more like a stroll if you didn't see him."

"He may have stayed for a drink before he left the alehouse."

"He may. I'd better check." Eliza reached into her handbag for her notebook. "Let me write this down." *Speak to Mr Bedford about when he left the Golden Eagle.* "Good. So, going back to when you went to the shop, when did you first notice Dr Dunlop?"

"Not until I was on my way out of the shop. That's when I heard voices by the river and wondered who it was. They were behind the surgery, which would be why your maid overheard them."

"And there's no possibility of Henry being with them?"

Mrs Petty's cheeks coloured. "I can't say for certain, but I took a good look and didn't see him."

Eliza grinned. "Good for you. I wish everyone was as observant as you." She paused as Iris returned with the tea tray. "Thank you. Just set it on the table. I'll pour."

Iris did as she was asked. "Will that be all?"

"Just one more thing before you go. When you saw the men outside, was Henry with them?"

"No ... I don't think so. Not that I had a proper look."

"All right. Thank you." Eliza re-dipped her pen into the ink. "I need to ask Henry where he was, because he told me he and his friend were together for the whole time except when he went to the shop." She looked up at Mrs Petty. "Was Mr Pitt there when you went in?"

"Yes, why?"

"I just wanted to check. I'll need to ask who else called, and whether he served Henry."

Mrs Petty stared at her. "You can't suspect your own son of murder?"

"Of course not, but I'm afraid I can't speak for his friend."

"But they're both doctors. Surely, they wouldn't hurt anyone."

"You'd hope not given they swore an oath promising to do no harm." Eliza stood up and offered Mrs Petty a cup of tea. "There must be a perfectly simple explanation."

CHAPTER EIGHT

The surgery was coming to an end the following morning, when Connie let herself into the dispensary.

"I hope I'm not too early."

"Not at all. Take a seat and I'll be with you shortly." Eliza spooned the contents of her mortar bowl into separate sachets and folded the tops carefully. "There we are, Mr Johnson. Dissolve each sachet in water and take one in the morning and one in the evening for the next five days. That should sort you out."

The man picked up his medicine and bid them farewell as Eliza wandered to the corridor to see Archie's surgery door open.

"He was the last one. Let me just put this lot away and we can go through to the morning room. Did you have a nice evening with Sergeant Cooper?"

"I did, thank you. We took a walk along the river to Over Moreton."

Eliza paused and studied her friend. "You didn't find our murder weapon by any chance, did you?"

Connie's cheeks reddened. "I-I'm afraid we weren't looking."

"No. I don't suppose you were. Did Sergeant Cooper find anything near the marquee after we'd left him?"

"No. He said they'd done a thorough search and counted up all the tent pegs, but there was still one missing."

"That doesn't surprise me." Eliza reached up to put a jar in the cupboard. "Why don't we walk along the river ourselves this afternoon? I won't be such a distraction as Sergeant Cooper."

Connie stood up and turned to face the window. "I'm sorry. I should have paid more attention."

"There's no need to be. I was the same when I first met Archie ... and Sergeant Cooper *is* entitled to some time off."

"I doubt he'll get much of that until we find our killer." She nodded towards the village green. "There he is now, talking to the marquee men."

"Let me see." Eliza hurried to her friend's side. "They've not wasted any time taking that down. I'd like to speak to them before they leave again." She glanced at the clock on the wall. "Are you desperate for coffee or can you wait half an hour? I don't want to miss them."

"Then we'd better go. It will give me an excuse to say good morning, too."

Eliza grinned. "Come along then. I'll tell you what I found out later."

Sergeant Cooper wore a big smile as he waved across the green to Connie, and she blushed as she waved back.

"Good morning, ladies. I thought I might see you. Not that I've got much to tell you since yesterday."

"Don't worry, Sergeant." Eliza strode towards him. "I may have something of interest for you. Or rather, the marquee men may. Do you mind if I ask them a few more questions?"

Sergeant Cooper watched Mr Taylor as he removed a section of wooden supports. "He should be finished soon. He just unties the rope and lets them all fall."

Eliza watched. "I had wondered how they'd got it down so quickly. It's not as precise as putting it up."

"No indeed. Do you want to speak to him now? He looks as if he has a minute."

Eliza nodded and followed the sergeant across the grass.

"Mr Taylor. Do you have a moment? Mrs Thomson would like a word."

"Now? I need to get this down and over to West Molesey by this afternoon. I'm late as it is."

Eliza cleared her throat. "I'm sorry, but I need to check on something you told us yesterday. You said that once you'd fixed the broken part of the marquee, you returned to Molesey, but came back to the fete at around three o'clock."

"That's right."

"So..." She held his gaze. "How do you explain the fact that you were seen in the Golden Eagle with Mr Hobbs shortly after two o'clock?"

"T-two o'clock?" He glanced at Sergeant Cooper. "I-I ... you must be mistaken."

Eliza shook her head. "I don't think so. Someone recognised you, and Mr Hobbs had left the snug before three o'clock, so it must have been before then."

"Who's someone...?"

"Shall we just say I have connections? Now, if you wouldn't mind answering the question."

"Oh, yes. I ... erm ... I needed a word with him. His work had become shoddy, and I wanted him to know I wouldn't stand for it."

"Why didn't you tell us you'd spoken to him?"

Mr Taylor shrugged. "It didn't look good, did it? I'd been to reprimand him and an hour later, he's found dead ... but it wasn't me..."

"Don't you think it looks more suspicious that you didn't mention it?"

He scratched his head. "I suppose it does, but I wasn't thinking straight. You must believe me. Why would I harm him? I'm a workman down now."

"A workman you didn't rate..."

"It's still no reason to kill him."

"Not on the face of it." Eliza studied him. "May I speak to your colleagues while I'm here? I'd like to ask them the same question."

"You would?" His mouth fell open as he looked across the tent. "I suppose... Mr Bedford. A word."

Mr Bedford ambled over to them. "What can I do for you?"

Eliza smiled. "We just need to confirm your whereabouts yesterday afternoon. You said you were in the Golden Eagle at about three o'clock to meet Mr Hobbs, and then took a walk around the top end of the village looking for him. You didn't tell us you'd paid him a visit earlier."

"No ... well, you asked where we were between three and half past four. I didn't think seeing him earlier was relevant."

"I don't remember mentioning a time when we first spoke."

"I'm sure you did. I would've said something otherwise."

Eliza's eyes narrowed. "May I ask what you wanted to see him about?"

Mr Bedford sighed. "If you must know, he owed me money. Twenty pounds. He'd borrow a little here and a bit extra there. For ale and the like. He was always promising to pay me back, but he never did, and I was getting desperate for it."

"Did he give it to you on Monday?"

"No. I spoke to him about it, and he said he'd have half of it if I went back at three."

Eliza's forehead creased. "Where would he get ten pounds from at such short notice?"

"I didn't ask and was stupid enough to believe him, but when I got back, he'd gone. He probably only said he'd give me the money to stop me going on about it."

"You must have been angry."

"I was furious." Mr Bedford huffed. "It wasn't the first time he'd let me down, and I wanted to find him..."

"So you could take a stick to him? Or should I say, a tent peg?"

"A tent peg?"

"We believe the one that's missing may have been the murder weapon."

"No." He shook his head. "An old tent peg wouldn't kill a grown man."

"It wouldn't?"

"Not on someone like Mr Hobbs. It would snap before his head split."

"If they're so delicate, how can they be strong enough to hold up a marquee?"

"Because you use dozens of them and knock them in properly."

"Oh." She looked at Connie, then back at the men. "Could you suggest anything that might have killed him, then."

"Me? How would I know?"

"You were angry with him."

His eyes widened. "Not enough for me to harm him. I won't get my money now he's dead. I needed him alive."

Eliza nodded. "What about your friend, Mr Gilbert?"

"What about him?"

"Do you know why he would have visited Mr Hobbs in the alehouse?" Eliza didn't miss the look that passed between the two men. "Does that mean you do?"

Mr Taylor sighed. "Not at all. We're as surprised as you. He told us he didn't arrive in Moreton until about half past three."

Eliza glanced around the remains of the marquee. "Is Mr Gilbert here?"

"He should be." Mr Taylor called his colleague. "Gilly!" When he got no reply, he shouted again. "Where's he got to? He was here five minutes ago."

"He was indeed." Sergeant Cooper stepped forward. "I saw him with my own eyes when I arrived. Leave it to me. I'll find him."

Connie yelped as he stepped away. "You will be careful. He may be our killer..."

"Don't be daft..." Mr Bedford tutted, causing Sergeant Cooper to stop.

"Why is it daft? You told us Mr Hobbs had a way of annoying people. Did that include Mr Gilbert?"

"No..."

"So, they had a good working relationship?"

"As far as I know."

Eliza studied the boss as he stared at the ground. "Mr Taylor? You've gone rather quiet."

He sighed. "I don't want to get anyone into trouble, but Mr Hobbs lived close to the Gilberts in Molesey. Unfortunately, he'd developed a soft spot for Mrs Gilbert and would visit her uninvited. That's why Gilly didn't like to leave her unless Hobsy was working."

"Did he confront him about it?"

"I couldn't say for sure, but he said he was going to."

"Might that be why he called into the Golden Eagle yesterday?"

He shuffled his feet. "You'd better ask him."

"And we will. If we can find him. Have you any idea where he may be?"

"None. Now, if you don't mind, we need to get on with this."

Eliza looked at Sergeant Cooper. "Do you have any more questions?"

"Only for Mr Gilbert ... if we can find him."

CHAPTER NINE

Archie was already at the table when Eliza returned home and strolled into the dining room.

"Where've you been?"

"Talking to the marquee men."

"Again? Does Sergeant Cooper know?"

"Yes, he was with us. Why?"

Archie grunted as she took her seat opposite. "As long as he knows what you're doing. Did you find much of interest?"

"Not really. Mr Taylor and Mr Bedford admitted they visited Mr Hobbs in the alehouse, but we can't find Mr Gilbert."

Archie raised an eyebrow. "Can't find him?"

"No. Sergeant Cooper was sure he was around when we arrived, but we suspect he overheard our conversation with the others and skedaddled. Sergeant Cooper's gone in search of him."

"Running away doesn't look good. Does he have a motive?"

Eliza nodded. "Of sorts. It appears that Mr Hobbs had

taken a shine to his wife, and Mr Gilbert wasn't happy about it."

"I don't suppose many men would be … although whether it's enough reason to kill a man…"

"Exactly." Eliza glanced at the door. "Have you seen Henry lately? I thought he was joining us for luncheon before he left."

"He was meeting his friends, but he said he'd be back at one o'clock. He won't be long."

"I wish he'd hurry up. I need to be out again for two."

"Why?"

"I'm calling for Connie."

Archie rolled his eyes. "Of course you are!"

"Don't be like that. Anyway, tell me about your evening with Mr Steel. Did you ask why he called on Mr Hobbs?"

"I did." Archie grinned at her. "He said it wasn't planned, but Mr Hobbs had been a customer of the bank when he worked there, and he'd recognised him."

"Mr Hobbs had a bank account?" Eliza's forehead creased.

"There's no reason why he shouldn't. He may have had savings."

"I suppose so, although you still wonder why he would have needed to speak to his bank manager. I'm surprised he knew who he was. Did you ask?"

"Of course I didn't."

"Never mind. Will you, next time you get the chance?"

"No, I won't. A man's banking details are private. I hope you don't think he's our killer."

Eliza sighed. "Not really, but he was one of the men who spoke to Mr Hobbs in the alehouse, so we need to eliminate him from the enquiries." She stopped as the front door opened and Henry joined them.

"Sorry I'm late. We took a walk along the river and went further than I planned."

"I thought you wanted to get away."

"We do, but we decided the three o'clock train would get us back to London in time."

"That's all right, then." Eliza cocked her head to one side. "You didn't mention that your friend Dr Dunlop had met Mr Hobbs by the river yesterday."

Henry stared at her. "How do you know that?"

"That doesn't matter. What does, is why you didn't tell me..."

"I-I didn't know."

"You told me you'd spent the afternoon together."

"We did ... but I called in at the shop on the way."

"You said you'd only left him for a couple of minutes."

"And I did."

"Then where did you go? The people who saw Dr Dunlop with Mr Hobbs said they didn't see you near the shop or the river. Are you hiding something from me?"

"Of course, I'm not. Why would I?"

"I was hoping you'd tell me." Eliza studied him. "Has your friend been up to no good?"

"Like what?"

"I can't imagine, but I heard he was angry with Mr Hobbs and told him he owed someone fifty pounds..."

Henry's eyes widened. "Who told you that?"

Eliza held his gaze. "Why won't you tell me what's going on?"

"There's nothing to tell."

"But you disappeared."

"I didn't. Check with Mr Pitt. He'll vouch for me." He pushed himself up from the table. "I need to go. I'll send for my bags later in the week."

"Henry ... come back..." Eliza groaned as the front door slammed and she slouched in her chair. "That didn't go according to plan." She remained silent as Iris placed a casserole in the middle of the table. "That will be all, thank you. I'll serve."

"I've the vegetables to bring..."

"Yes, of course..." She tapped her fingers on the table as she waited for the second bowl to arrive. "What's he hiding?"

Archie studied her. "Can there be any doubt it was his friend by the river?"

"Two people told me independently that it was him."

"And he was definitely with Mr Hobbs?"

"Yes." She paused as Iris placed the vegetables in the centre of the table. "Thank you. Will you close the door on your way out?"

"Certainly."

Eliza waited for the click of the latch. "Did you meet Henry's friends?"

"I sat with them last night until Mr Steel arrived. They seemed nice enough."

"What were they talking about?"

Archie shrugged. "Nothing of any consequence. They reminisced about Cambridge, the parties they delighted in ... the women they knew."

Eliza's eyes narrowed as she handed Archie his dinner plate. "I've just remembered. He was due to go to Lowton

Hall last weekend. Did you ever ask him what was going on there?"

Archie shook his head. "I completely forgot. It didn't seem important after yesterday."

"I suppose not. I still think he's up to something. Will you walk up to the railway station later and see if you can get anything out of him ... or Dr Dunlop? Henry won't talk to me."

"He won't want to talk to me, either, if I ask him too many questions."

Eliza took a deep breath. "All right. Ask about him and his friend first. The antics at Lowton Hall can wait."

Connie was plumping the cushions on her armchairs when Eliza called after luncheon.

"Are you ready?"

"Give me a minute." She took off her apron. "Are you still planning to walk along the river?"

"I think so, but before we do, I'd like to check whether they've found Mr Gilbert."

Connie peered out of the window. "It looks as if the others have gone."

"Perhaps we should go to the police station and see what Sergeant Cooper has to say, then."

"I won't argue with that." Connie's hat was still in place from the morning, and Eliza held open the front door as she fastened her summer cape around her shoulders. "How did you get on with Henry?"

"Don't ask." Eliza groaned. "He got very defensive when I asked where he'd been, and left without eating luncheon."

"Oh dear. That's not like him. What did he say?"

"Nothing much, but he was surprised when I told him what I knew. He said he was taking the three o'clock train back to London, so I've asked Archie to walk up there and have a word with him. I just hope he asks the relevant questions. Not like he did with Mr Steel..."

"Mr Steel? What's it got to do with him?"

"He met with Mr Hobbs in the Golden Eagle on the afternoon of the fete, so I asked Archie to find out why. Apparently, Mr Steel had recognised him from the bank and gone to talk to him."

"Why would he do that?"

Eliza sighed. "That's the bit Archie didn't ask. If Mr Steel's at the bowling club, we can speak to him."

"Should we go now? There's a chance Sergeant Cooper could be there. Especially if he's found Mr Gilbert."

"We could do." Eliza linked Connie's arm as they headed across the road. "At least it's on the way to the station, so we can carry on if he's not there."

As they approached the door, Eliza pointed to the lounge area. "There's Sergeant Cooper. Who's he talking to?"

Connie gazed through the window. "It looks like Mr Hewitt."

"You're right. That's fortunate. I was thinking we should talk to him as well."

"You don't think he did it?"

"Not at all, but he may have seen something. He was in and out of everywhere yesterday."

"Let's go, then."

Sergeant Cooper and Mr Hewitt stood up as they entered.

"Good afternoon, ladies." Sergeant Cooper beamed at

Connie. "Mr Hewitt popped in to ask about the murder weapon."

"Have you found it?"

"I'm afraid not, but after what Mr Bedford told us about the tent peg, we're not really sure what we're looking for."

Eliza nodded. "You're not alone there."

"It must have been something light enough to pick up easily, but heavy enough to ... you know." Mr Hewitt mimicked the action. "I must admit, I did wonder if a tent peg was strong enough to kill someone."

Eliza's eyes narrowed. "What did they use to knock the pegs into the ground? Would that be strong enough?"

"A mallet, and it may have been, but it would still be made of wood."

"It would be more solid than a tent peg." Sergeant Cooper looked at Eliza as she raised a finger to the side of her head.

"And he was struck on the temple, which is one of the weakest parts of the skull."

Sergeant Cooper reached for his notebook. "I'll write that down."

Eliza nodded. "There's a chance the murder weapon will have blood on it, too."

"You're right." Sergeant Cooper looked up from his notes. "Did you call in for anything in particular?"

"Yes. We wondered if you found Mr Gilbert."

"There's no sign of him. I even sent Constable Jenkins to Molesey to check whether he was there, but he wasn't."

Eliza sighed. "That doesn't bode well. Will you be contacting Inspector Adams? We may need to ask for help finding him."

Sergeant Cooper grunted. "I'd hoped to have it all

wrapped up before I involved New Scotland Yard, but it looks like I've no choice."

"He's not so bad now he knows us, and we can still do what we can before he arrives."

Sergeant Cooper puffed out his cheeks. "Maybe he's no trouble to you, but I'm the one he gives all the orders to. Let's see what we can find out this afternoon, and I'll send a telegram later."

CHAPTER TEN

There was a warm breeze as Eliza and Connie strolled along the bank of the River Thames towards Over Moreton. They'd both taken walking canes from a selection in the bowling club cloakroom, and Eliza swiped the square ivory handle of her cane through the grass to her left, while Connie ran her curved wooden handle closer to the river. They hadn't gone far before Connie shrieked and jumped backwards.

"What's the matter?"

Connie's cheeks coloured. "A couple of frogs. They frightened the life out of me."

Eliza giggled. "I wondered why there was a splash. I don't suppose they were expecting you, either."

"No, especially not the way I was hitting the grass. I need to be more careful."

"Not too careful. We're not doing this for fun, remember."

"It is rather enjoyable, though, don't you think?" Connie resumed her sweep of the grass. "And it gives the walk more purpose."

"Are you suggesting we do this more often?"

"It depends what we find. You never know, we could come across something valuable."

"I doubt it. I've not seen much at all, so far."

"Me neither, and after seeing the frogs, I'm wondering if the weapon could have been thrown into the river."

Eliza sighed. "That's quite possible, if the murderer came down here. It's what I'd do if I wanted to get rid of something I didn't want finding."

"Is there any point going on?"

Eliza stared along the river bank. "We probably should, just to be thorough, although my arm will be worn out by the time we get back. This cane is heavier than it looks."

"You should have chosen a wooden one like me."

"And miss out on carrying something more glamorous..."

Connie chuckled. "It's hardly glamorous when you're carrying it upside down."

"I'll use it properly when we get back to the village."

By the time they reached the end of the village, the path narrowed, forcing them to walk in single file.

"How much further are we going?"

Eliza placed a hand on her hips. "As far as Over Moreton? If anyone was going to hide the weapon by the river, it's more likely to be in the less-walked section."

"Very well." Connie led the way. "It's quiet here this afternoon. I was expecting to see more people."

"They're probably still recovering from the fete ... or staying indoors until the killer's found."

Connie shuddered. "I hadn't thought of that. I hope he isn't hiding along here."

"You're not the only one."

They were almost at the boundary to Over Moreton when Connie stopped abruptly.

"Who's that?" She stepped to one side, disappearing behind a large rhododendron, before pointing a little way in front.

"I-I don't..." Eliza peered into the distance. "Wait a minute. It's Mr Gilbert."

"No!"

Eliza nodded but didn't take her eyes off him. "Let's approach him slowly. I don't want to scare him away. Turn your stick round so it looks like we're using them to help us walk..."

Connie did as she was told and followed Eliza as she crept forward. They were within ten feet of Mr Gilbert before he jumped up.

"Ladies!"

Eliza held up a hand. "Don't be alarmed. We're just out for a walk."

"All the way down here?"

"Why not? It's a nice day and you seem to like it here."

"Yes." He sat down again and stared at his hands. "I suppose you've been wondering where I got to."

"It had crossed our minds. We were hoping to talk to you."

He nodded. "I wasn't ready to talk. I'm still not."

"But you must see that disappearing during a murder investigation doesn't give a good impression."

He looked up at Eliza. "I didn't kill him."

"Then why disappear?"

"I needed time on my own..."

"Why? Do you know who the killer is?"

"No." He ran a hand through his hair. "The thing is, he

was upsetting my wife. That's why I called to see him in the alehouse. To tell him that if he didn't leave her alone, he'd regret it…"

"So, you wanted him dead?"

"No! It wasn't like that. I'd have cheerfully taught him a lesson, but that was it…" His face reddened as he clenched his fists. "I wouldn't have killed him … just stopped him from coming to work for a while…"

Eliza studied him. "Surely if you'd done that, he'd have had more time to spend with your wife."

"Not by the time I'd finished with him. He'd never set foot in our street again."

Eliza grimaced at Connie. "So, you wanted to maim him, but not kill him?"

"Yes."

"But you didn't want to tell us?"

"It doesn't look good, does it, when the man was found dead shortly after?" He pushed himself up. "If you'll excuse me."

"Actually, I'd rather you didn't leave. If you're telling the truth, I suggest you accompany us to the village and give Sergeant Cooper your statement. We need to find out if you saw anything that may help with our enquiries, too."

"What like?"

"We can talk about that on the way back."

Mr Gilbert stared in the direction of Over Moreton before he nodded and turned towards them. "If I must. Let's get this over with."

Eliza waited until they could walk three abreast before she spoke. "Do you remember what time you got to the Golden Eagle?"

"Not exactly, but probably about quarter past two."

"And how long did you stay?"

He shrugged. "Not long. I might have throttled him there and then if I'd stayed longer."

"Were you angry when you arrived at the alehouse?"

"I wasn't best pleased."

"And what did Mr Hobbs have to say for himself?"

Mr Gilbert's eyes narrowed. "It wasn't what he said. If I could have knocked the smirk off his face there and then, I would... Ten pounds he wanted from me to stay away from her..."

"Ten pounds?" Eliza glanced at Connie. "That's the amount he'd promised to Mr Bedford."

Mr Gilbert stopped. "What for?"

"He owed him some money and told him that he'd have half of it if he went back to the alehouse at three o'clock."

"So, he'd planned this all along..." Mr Gilbert's face turned puce as Eliza continued.

"Did you pay him?"

"Of course I didn't." Mr Gilbert gasped as they resumed walking. "Where would I get that sort of money at such short notice?"

"Did you promise to pay at a later date?"

"No, I did not. I wouldn't give him a penny. I told him that the next time I saw him near our house, I'd knock his head off."

"What did he say to that?"

"He laughed." Mr Gilbert's fists clenched as he stared into the distance.

"It sounds like you had a lot of provocation."

"It doesn't mean I killed him. As much as I may have liked to. Mr Taylor had as much reason as me to want him dead."

"Mr Taylor! Why would he want anything to happen to him?"

"Hobsy was a troublemaker. Mr Taylor was desperate to get rid of him, but for some reason, he wouldn't sack him."

"Do you have any idea why?"

"Not a clue."

Eliza took a deep breath. "Very well. What did you do when you left him?"

"I went to the marquee."

"Straight away?"

"Yes."

"Which way did you walk?"

"I couldn't tell you." Mr Gilbert stared at her. "Look, I was angry ... furious ... I wasn't thinking straight. I may not have taken the most direct route..."

"Hopefully, we can refresh your memory when we reach the village. We'll go to the bowling club first..."

"The bowling club?" Mr Gilbert stared at her. "That was behind the marquee, wasn't it?"

"Yes, why?"

"I walked around it on the way back from the alehouse."

"What time would that have been?"

He shrugged. "I've no idea. I told you, I only had one thing on my mind."

"Did you notice anyone near the club as you went past?"

"I didn't notice anything..."

"So, you didn't see anyone around the back of the marquee?"

"With a hammer, you mean...?"

"A hammer?"

"He was hit over the head, wasn't he?"

"Yes, but we've never mentioned what he was hit with. What made you say that?"

"There'd been a couple lying around, so I just assumed... We use them to knock in the tent pegs when the ground's hard."

"Did you have your hammer with you in the alehouse?"

He shook his head. "It's too heavy to carry around. Our tools were tucked away round the back."

"So, anyone could have helped themselves to them?"

"I suppose they could, but nobody usually touches them."

"People aren't usually murdered." Connie didn't turn her head as she carried on walking, but Mr Gilbert looked at her.

"No. I'm sorry, but I'm afraid I can't help. I was so mad with Mr Hobbs I wasn't paying attention to what was going on around me. You can ask Mr Taylor. He had to grab my arm to stop me storming past while he was waiting for me."

Eliza studied him. "You told us on Monday that you only got to the marquee at about half past three. That's over an hour after you left the pub. What did you do in the meantime?"

"I-I don't know. I must have misjudged the time I left the alehouse."

"Or done more than walk to the marquee."

He sighed. "If you must know, I sat in the churchyard for a while. It must have been for longer than I thought. I wasn't watching the time. You could check with Mr Taylor. He always has his eye on his pocket watch ... making sure we're not taking too long to put a marquee up or take it down. Time is money. That's what he always says."

"He said people had already gone into the marquee for the prize-giving when you arrived. That was at half past three. Going back to the churchyard. Did you see anyone while you were there?"

"Not that I remember, but then I had my head in my hands for most of the time."

"All right. What about your tools?"

"What about them?"

"Have you noticed any of them missing since the attack?"

"I've not looked. Mr Taylor's in charge of them, given he paid for them. He always likes to account for everything."

"All right. When we get to the village green, we can check if any of them are missing. It would be helpful to know what we're looking for."

"Mr Taylor will have taken them to the next job at Molesey."

"Ah." Eliza glanced at the back of the surgery as they approached the entrance to the village. "We're almost here."

Once they reached the road, Eliza pointed a little further ahead of them. "When you walked from the alehouse, was there anyone at the shop?"

Mr Gilbert stopped to stare at it. "There was, as it happens. A younger man, who was just leaving. I nearly bumped into him."

"Could you describe him?"

"Only that he was smartly dressed. Not a worker."

Eliza hesitated. "Did you notice if he had a beard or moustache?"

"He had a beard."

"That narrows it down a bit. Did you see if he was with anyone?"

"Can't say I did."

She feigned a smile as they crossed the road. "Never mind. I need to speak to Mr Pitt, the shopkeeper, so I'll check with him. Going back to your tools, do you know where we'd be able to find Mr Taylor so we can confirm their whereabouts?"

"He'll be putting the marquee up in West Molesey now, but he'll be in the Bell Inn tonight."

"What about tomorrow?"

"I've no idea. He only tells us where we're going the night before, and as I've not seen him..."

"All right. I'll ask Sergeant Cooper to pay him a visit." Eliza noticed the droop in Connie's shoulders. "Or Constable Jenkins. He'd probably like an evening out on business."

"I hope so." Connie led the way into the bowling club, and she called out as Mr Gilbert held open the door for them. "Sergeant Cooper, are you here?"

When they got no response, Eliza approached the office at the end of a short corridor. "Anyone here...? Oh, Mr Steel. I'm sorry to disturb you."

"Mrs Thomson. What are you doing here? You're well aware that women aren't allowed..."

"I am, but we're looking for Sergeant Cooper. Has he been in this afternoon?"

"Not since about three o'clock. He went off to look for this murderer ... Gilbert, was it?"

"Yes ... no ... I mean, that's who he was looking for, but he must have gone to the station. We'll look for him there. Good day..."

Mr Steel stood up and walked to the door. "Are you with someone?"

"Erm, Mrs Appleton ... and a possible witness ... or suspect."

"Another woman..." He pushed past her, but stopped as he reached the lounge. "Well, well, if it isn't the disappearing man." He grabbed Mr Gilbert's arm and twisted it up his back as he spoke to Eliza. "Go and fetch Sergeant Cooper at once. I'll keep the killer here until you find him."

Mr Gilbert swung his free arm round to connect with Mr Steel's face. "You'll do no such thing."

Mr Steel instinctively released his grip, and Mr Gilbert pushed him away. "I'm off." He turned to Eliza as he stepped into the vestibule. "I'm going home. If the sergeant wants to speak to me, he knows where to find me. I'm not being accused of something I didn't do by simpletons like him."

"No, Mr Gilbert, come back..." Eliza chased to the door, but he was well ahead of her before she reached the steps. She watched him leave before she went back inside.

"Thank you, Mr Steel. He'd walked here, without any complaint, and you go and do that. You can't assume someone's guilty before there's any evidence."

Mr Steel rubbed the red mark on his chin, his eyes like slits. "I don't need any lectures from you in my own bowling club. Now get out. As I've already said, this club is for men only."

"Perhaps my husband should become chairman so he can change that. Good day, Mr Steel. We'll see ourselves out."

CHAPTER ELEVEN

Sergeant Cooper was behind the dark mahogany counter when Eliza and Connie arrived at the police station.

"Good afternoon, ladies."

Eliza closed the door. "You sound weary."

"Only because I need to contact New Scotland Yard. I can't make any sense of what's happened."

Connie grinned. "We may be able to help. We found Mr Gilbert."

"Oh, well done!" His broad smile lasted for no more than a second before he looked at Eliza. "Where is he?"

Eliza joined them at the counter. "I'm afraid he's gone again. We found him by the river, outside Over Moreton, and persuaded him to come back here to give you a statement. Annoyingly, we made the mistake of calling at the bowling club in case you were still there, and as soon as Mr Steel saw him, he assumed he was the killer and put him in an armlock."

"But you said he'd gone." Sergeant Cooper looked between the two of them as Connie shook her head.

"Mr Gilbert didn't like the accusation and punched Mr Steel before he escaped. We've not seen him since."

"What did Mr Steel do that for if the man had come here of his own accord?"

Eliza sighed. "He assumed Mr Gilbert was our killer."

"He may well be right, but he should leave it to the police. As should you. As grateful as I am for your help, you shouldn't have been on your own with him."

"What else could we do? We stumbled upon him quite unexpectedly. Besides, once we'd assured him we were no threat, I didn't feel there was any danger. I'm not convinced he's our murderer."

"He's not?"

"No. He was furious with Mr Hobbs for being too familiar with his wife, but he seemed genuine when he said he didn't kill him."

"Then why disappear?"

"He was still angry and realised his visit to Mr Hobbs in the alehouse didn't look good. When he left us, he said he was going home and suggested that if you want to speak to him, you call on him there."

"He'd better not be lying. I don't want another wild goose chase."

"I don't think it will be. He also told us you'll find Mr Taylor at the Bell Inn in Molesey later."

Sergeant Cooper's forehead creased. "Why do we need to talk to him again?"

"Mr Gilbert had the idea that the murder weapon was a hammer—"

"How does he know that?"

"He assumed it was because the murderer hit Mr Hobbs over the head."

"What's that got to do with Mr Taylor?"

"I wanted Mr Gilbert to check if any of his tools were missing, but he said Mr Taylor would have taken them with him when he left. We hoped you could speak to him."

"Ah. Let me write this down. Is there anything else I need to ask if I see either of them?"

"Actually, there is. Two things." Eliza waited for the sergeant to finish writing. "First, I remembered on the way here that Mr Taylor promised to show you his client list so you can check if there was anyone at the fete who may have held a grudge against Mr Hobbs."

Sergeant Cooper's pencil scratched on the page of his notebook. "C l i e n t – l i s t. I doubt he'll have it with him at home, but I can arrange to see it tomorrow. Did Mr Gilbert give you his address?"

Eliza groaned. "I assumed you had it, so I didn't ask. If you find Mr Taylor, I'm sure he'll point you in the right direction."

"I'd better go, then. Once I've told Constable Jenkins what I'm up to…"

"Oh, before you do, there's one more thing. While we were talking to Mr Gilbert, he told us that Mr Taylor was angry with Mr Hobbs for poor workmanship, but that he wouldn't sack him. We need to know why."

"Yes, right. I can do that."

Connie lowered her eyelids. "I had hoped you'd send the constable instead of going yourself."

He patted her hand as it rested on the counter. "I wish I

could, but this is important, and I need to do it myself. I'll leave now and be back as soon as I can."

"Will I see you later?"

"I hope so..."

Eliza cleared her throat. "We should let Sergeant Cooper get on."

"Yes, of course." Connie straightened up as she gave a small wave. "Be careful."

Archie was in the sitting room when Eliza got home, and he immediately stood up and offered her a glass of sherry.

"Ooh, yes, please. It's been quite an afternoon."

"I thought you were only going for a walk."

"We were, but Mr Gilbert was on the river bank as we approached Over Moreton."

Archie stared at her with the sherry decanter in his hand. "Are you all right? He didn't try anything...?"

"We're fine. I suspect he was more worried about seeing us than the other way around."

"What did you do?"

Eliza waited for him to pour their drinks and hand her a glass. "We persuaded him to come to Moreton to give Sergeant Cooper a statement."

"That was rather foolish. I hope the police have him behind bars."

"Actually, no. Things didn't quite go according to plan."

Archie took a seat opposite her. "What do you mean?"

"We called in at the bowling club looking for Sergeant Cooper, but Mr Steel was there."

"Why do I get the impression you're not happy with him?"

"Because I'm not. As soon as he saw Mr Gilbert, he grabbed him, but before he secured his hold, Mr Gilbert gave him a swift blow to the jaw and escaped."

"So, we've a killer on the loose?"

Eliza shook her head. "I don't think he's a murderer. Not after talking to him on the way back from Over Moreton."

"You can't say that. The man disappeared as soon as he heard about Mr Hobbs—"

"Not straight away, he didn't. It was the next day. Besides, I've spoken to a lot of suspects over the last few years, and my gut feeling isn't often wrong. What did you say to Mr Steel that made him think Mr Gilbert was guilty?"

"Nothing ... other than to tell him he disappeared before Sergeant Cooper could question him."

"Is he usually that impulsive?"

"Not that I've noticed, although, to be honest, most of us assumed that Mr Gilbert running away was an admission of guilt."

"I suppose so." Eliza paused before she continued. "I wonder if Mr Gilbert had a bank account. Maybe Mr Steel knew something about him, too."

"If he did, he didn't mention it."

"That doesn't mean anything. We need to ask one or other of them next time we see them." Eliza reached for her notebook. "Did you speak to Henry?"

"After a fashion. He wasn't best pleased to see me and told me to tell you that you're looking for trouble where none exists."

"What about Dr Dunlop?"

Archie grimaced. "Much to Henry's annoyance, I asked him why he was talking to Mr Hobbs, but he just shrugged and said he remembered passing the time of day with someone but didn't know who it was."

"But Iris overheard Mr Dunlop say Mr Hobbs owed someone fifty pounds..."

"Maybe she misheard."

"How do you mishear something like that? She said their voices were raised."

"Then I can't help. The four of them seemed to support each other."

"So, we're back to square one, unless we can find the murder weapon. It may give us something to go on. I can't believe it's disappeared. I'm beginning to think the killer threw it into the river."

"We can't rule it out."

"I know. I don't suppose you've heard from the coroner yet?"

"They only collected the body after luncheon."

She sighed. "How long will it be before you get the report?"

"A few days at least, by the time he's done the post-mortem and put the letter in the post. Even then, we might not find out much about the actual weapon other than whether it was a blunt or sharp object."

"Sergeant Cooper's gone over to Molesey to search the marquee men's tool bags in case it was in one of them. I should have gone with him. It will need a keen eye to see if there are traces of blood on any of them."

"I'm sure he can manage. Did you ask him to look at Mr Taylor's list of clients?"

"I did, although I'm not hopeful he'll have them with him in the alehouse."

"Even if he does, I doubt it will be anyone around here. Nobody has the land to erect a marquee. Other than the Hartleys at Oak House."

"Mrs Hartley..." Eliza's mouth fell open as she stared at Archie. "She was at the fete!"

"That's hardly a surprise. She lives here."

"But she never usually leaves the house. Why would she choose Monday to reintegrate herself into village life? Might she have come because she knew there'd be a marquee and she wanted to speak to Mr Hobbs ... or worse?"

Archie's forehead creased. "Could a woman really kill a man with a single blow?"

"It depends on the weapon, I suppose. I'll speak to her tomorrow."

"You can't just wander over there and accuse her of murder."

"I'm not that insensitive." Eliza rolled her eyes. "As luck would have it, Connie upset Mrs Hartley yesterday ... something to do with her speaking to Sergeant Cooper ... and Connie wanted to apologise. It will be the perfect excuse to invite her for afternoon tea."

CHAPTER TWELVE

E liza was tidying the dispensary when Connie called the following morning and she put the last of the jars onto the top shelf of the wall unit before she wandered around to the other side of the counter.

"That was well timed. Did you see Sergeant Cooper last night?"

"Eventually." Connie took a seat. "It was turned eight o'clock before he called, so we only had time for a quick walk around the village before it went dark."

"Oh dear. Did you ask if he found out anything of interest?"

Connie's cheeks coloured. "We didn't get around to that."

"Never mind. We can call at the station on our way to Oak House."

"Oak House!" Connie shot to her feet. "What are we going there for?"

"Don't look so worried. I want to invite Mrs Hartley to afternoon tea."

"Today?"

"If she's available."

"But why? You know she's not my favourite person."

"First of all, if you remember, you said you wanted to apologise for being rude to her on Monday, so I thought we should strike while the iron's hot."

"D-does she need to come for afternoon tea? I was only hoping to bump into her in the shop or something like that."

"If you don't mind, I'd prefer it to be more formal. I need a reason to speak to her about Mr Hobbs' death."

Connie's eyes widened. "You think she did it?"

Eliza took a deep breath. "I don't know, but I can't help thinking how strange it is that we had another murder in the village on the day she reappeared."

Connie shuddered. "I hadn't considered that."

"Neither had I until last night. As a ruse to get her here, will you join us for tea and apologise?"

"If I must, but I'll wait at the gate while you make the invitation. Seeing her once is more than enough for me."

Eliza grinned. "I can manage that, but before we go out, I suggest we have our morning coffee."

Constable Jenkins was leaning on the counter at the front of the police station half an hour later when Eliza held open the door for Connie.

"Good morning, Constable."

"Ladies!" He jumped to attention. "Sergeant Cooper isn't here."

"That's annoying. Do you know where he is?"

"He's gone back to Molesey to talk to Mr Taylor."

"Didn't he find him last night?"

"He did, but they had more business to attend to."

"Ah. Hopefully, that means he's going through the list of clients who've ordered a marquee over the last few years. What time did he leave?"

Constable Jenkins' brow creased. "Shortly after nine o'clock. I'm expecting him back any time now."

Eliza turned to Connie. "Shall we go to Oak House while we wait?"

"We may as well." She looked at Constable Jenkins. "Will you tell him we called if he gets back before we do?"

"I can certainly do that. I'll see you soon."

Once they were outside, Eliza checked for Sergeant Cooper's carriage before she linked her arm through Connie's and turned left to walk to the other side of the village.

"This shouldn't take long. I only want to extend the invitation."

"It's to be hoped the maid answers the door, then. Mrs Hartley might invite you in there and then."

"Even if she does, I'll decline and tell her I need to get back to the surgery."

"What if she won't join us?"

"We can cross that bridge if it comes."

Connie was subdued as they turned into the cul-de-sac towards Oak House, and Eliza held her tongue as they walked to the gate.

"At least it's not locked. That's a good sign."

"I'll wait here, then."

"And don't worry. It will all be fine."

The gravel path leading to the attractive sandstone building crunched under Eliza's boots and she took a deep breath as she rapped on the brass door-knocker. She didn't wait long before Mrs Hartley opened the door.

"Mrs Thomson."

Eliza was relieved to see a smile on her face. "I'm sorry to disturb you. I expected the maid to answer."

Mrs Hartley shook her head. "We let most of the staff go after my husband died. We don't get so many visitors that I can't greet them myself."

"That's a shame ... that you don't have more callers, that is. Perhaps when you get out and about in the village, there'll be more."

Mrs Hartley grimaced. "That's what I'm worried about ... not you, of course. You're always welcome."

"Thank you, I'm glad. I've called to ask if you might be free this afternoon. Mrs Appleton's been riddled with guilt these last few days over what happened on Monday, so I'm hoping you can both join me for afternoon tea at the surgery. She'd like to apologise."

"Oh, well, I don't know ... I'm not used to socialising." She glanced down at her handsome blue dress. "I'll need to change."

"Not at all. It won't be anything formal, just the three of us with tea and cakes."

Mrs Hartley nodded. "Very well, thank you. I'll look forward to it."

"Splendid. Shall we say four o'clock?"

Connie had wandered to the main road by the time Eliza returned to the gate and she waved to attract her attention.

"I wanted to watch out for Sergeant Cooper. His carriage went past a couple of minutes ago."

"Excellent. Shall we go?"

Connie fell into step beside Eliza as they turned right towards the station. "Did you pass on the invitation?"

"I spoke to Mrs Hartley herself. She says she has so few visitors, she can answer the door herself if the need arises."

"Or she likes to flaunt herself..."

"Connie!"

"I'm sorry, I can't help myself."

"You must. I told her you'd been feeling guilty about the way you spoke to her and that you wanted to apologise. She really isn't as bad as you make out."

"That's because you're married."

"We've been through this."

Connie held up her hands. "All right. I promise I'll be on my best behaviour."

"I'm pleased to hear it. Now, a big smile for Sergeant Cooper."

"You don't need to tell me to do that."

Sergeant Cooper beamed at them from behind the counter when they arrived at the police station. "What good timing, I've just come back from Molesey."

Connie's cheeks coloured. "We know. We called earlier and then I saw you arrive."

"I didn't see you..."

Eliza interjected. "We were on the other side of the village green. Constable Jenkins told us where you'd gone, so we took a walk."

"Well, I'm glad you came back. I wouldn't like to miss you."

"How did you get on with Mr Taylor?"

"Very well, as it happens." He pulled a sheet of paper from his pocket. "The clients he's worked for over the last two years."

"Excellent, but before we go through it, did you speak to him about why he was unhappy with Mr Hobbs?"

"I did." Sergeant Cooper beamed at her. "He said that Mr Hobbs' mistakes were costing him money he couldn't afford."

"Did he admit he wanted to get rid of him?"

"He did but said that when you've worked with someone for thirty years, it's not easy."

"Hmm."

"Don't you believe him?"

"I've no reason not to, but if Mr Hobbs was causing him so much trouble, wouldn't you think he'd try harder to sort something out?"

Sergeant Cooper puffed out his cheeks. "He might, but killing him seems a bit harsh."

"You're right. I'm getting carried away. Let's look at this list of names." Eliza spread the document out on the counter. "Is there anyone here of interest?"

"There is." Sergeant Cooper placed his index finger halfway down the second column.

"Dunlop!" Eliza's eyes were wide as she stared at him. "That's the name of Henry's friend."

"That's what I thought. According to Mr Taylor, he erected a marquee for the man's father. He said he looked familiar when he was in the alehouse with young Dr Thomson, but he hadn't been able to place him. It only came back to him when he saw the name."

"Good grief. That explains a lot. I wonder if Henry knew."

"I'm sure you'll find out easily enough."

Eliza gave a wry smile. *I wouldn't bank on it.* "What about the rest of the list? Is there anyone else of interest?"

"Not that I can see, but they certainly have a distinguished set of clients." He moved his finger down the page. "Look here. Lord Harrington-Smyth from Over Moreton and even Lord Albert of Lowton."

"Lord Albert?" Eliza gasped as she looked at Connie.

"It's not that unusual. They had a marquee when we visited for Lady Alice's ball."

"But it means they may have known Mr Hobbs."

Sergeant Cooper shook his head. "You can't think he had anything to do with the murder. Lord Albert wasn't even in Moreton on Monday."

"Not that we know, but what if he's the reason Henry's behaving so strangely?"

"We'd have noticed if a carriage had arrived with the Lowton family crest on the side."

Eliza sighed. "I suppose so. It just seems strange that his name has cropped up several times this week. Maybe it's a coincidence."

"Of course it is." Connie rolled her eyes. "It's only because Henry was here. If he hadn't been, this would have been the first you'd heard of him, and you wouldn't have batted an eyelid."

"No." Eliza straightened up as she turned back to the sergeant. "What about Lord Harrington-Smyth? He's on the list."

"And I doubt he was on his own for long enough to catch his breath."

"That's true. Did you look at the tools while you were in Molesey?"

"I did, but Mr Taylor thought that everything looked to be present and correct."

"Did you check for signs of blood?"

"We did, but there was nothing. If one of them had been our murder weapon, the killer must have washed it ... but none of them looked as if they'd ever been cleaned."

"So, we're none the wiser. We'll need to broaden our search, including the river."

"That could take weeks, and we might not find anything anyway with the current being as it is."

"We should leave it as a last resort, then. We've still a few people to speak to." She looked at the sergeant. "Did you find Mr Gilbert?"

"I did, last night. He was at home when I called."

"Did he have much to say?"

"Nothing you hadn't told me already. His wife seemed a nervous type, so I can imagine Mr Hobbs' affections could have been difficult for her."

"Did you speak to her as well as him?"

"Should I have?"

Eliza shrugged. "She may have been able to confirm when her husband was at home, or whether he'd been agitated on the evening of the fete."

"No." His shoulders slumped. "I didn't think of that."

"Never mind. If you thought Mr Gilbert was telling the truth, it probably wasn't necessary. How about Mr Hewitt,

Mr Steel and Mr Pitt? Have you had formal statements from any of them?"

"I've not had chance yet."

"I suspected as much. We really should talk to each of them." Eliza bit her lip. "If we visit Mr Pitt and Mr Hewitt, would you be kind enough to have a word with Mr Steel? We didn't exactly leave him on the best of terms yesterday, so I doubt he'll want to tell us what he and Mr Hobbs spoke about in the alehouse."

The sergeant's eyes widened. "They met in the alehouse! Why is this the first I'm hearing of it?"

"I'm sorry, there's been so much going on, it must have slipped my mind. The thing is, Mr Steel told Dr Thomson that Mr Hobbs had once been a customer of his at the bank, but I can't help thinking they wouldn't have had much to talk about."

"What time did they meet?"

"We don't have an accurate time, but probably between half past one and half past two."

Sergeant Cooper made a note. "I'll see what he says."

"Could you also ask if any of the other marquee men had accounts with the bank? We could do with knowing whether it was just Mr Hobbs, or if they all did."

"You think Mr Steel may have known all of them?"

"Not necessarily, but it might explain why he was so hostile to Mr Gilbert."

"Right you are." He closed his notebook. "I said I'd call on Mrs Petty, too, so I'd better get a move on."

Eliza nodded. "We've already spoken to her, but it would help to get her statement in writing. She was the one who told us about Dr Dunlop and Mr Hobbs."

"Ah. I wondered where you'd heard it from. I'll call on her first."

"Excellent. We'll aim to speak to everyone this afternoon." She looked at Connie. "It must be time for luncheon. Are you ready to go?"

"I certainly am. Good day, Sergeant Cooper. I'll see you later."

CHAPTER THIRTEEN

Eliza positioned her knife and fork on her empty plate and sat back in her chair as Archie finished his luncheon of liver and mashed potatoes.

"Mrs Hartley accepted my invitation to afternoon tea."

"That's nice. Is she calling today?"

"Yes. Four o'clock. Will you be here?"

He grinned. "I'll try my best to be out."

"You don't need to."

"Perhaps not, but I've several home visits, so I doubt I'll be here, anyway. Did Sergeant Cooper ever see the list of clients from Mr Taylor?"

"He did. He went over to Molesey this morning and brought a copy back with him."

"Is there anyone on there of any interest?"

"There is. A Mr Dunlop. The father of Henry's friend."

Archie raised an eyebrow. "Do you know that for sure?"

"Mr Taylor recognised Dr Dunlop once he saw the name."

"So Henry's friend must have known Mr Hobbs after all."

"That's what it sounds like, but it makes me wonder why both he and Henry denied it."

"Is the sergeant going to speak to Dr Dunlop about it?"

"He didn't say, but I expect he will. We need to talk to Henry again, too."

"Don't you think you should leave it to the police? I doubt you can have a calm conversation with Henry about this."

"It shouldn't stop me from trying."

Archie sighed. "It will only build up resentment between the two of you."

"Why should it? If his friend's been lying to him, he needs to be told."

"It may have been something completely innocent."

"In which case, why not tell us?"

"I've no idea, but at least let Sergeant Cooper have a word with the Dunlops before you mention anything to Henry. We can speak to him once we know what's going on." Archie paused as Iris came in to collect their plates.

"Cook's made an apple crumble for dessert. Would you both like some?"

Eliza nodded. "Please, but only a small portion for me. Mrs Appleton and Mrs Hartley are joining me for afternoon tea. Tell Cook I'll be in to see her about it soon."

"Very good, madam." Iris pulled the door closed behind her as Archie studied his wife.

"Have you anything else planned for this afternoon?"

"Sergeant Cooper's asked us to speak to Mr Pitt and Mr Hewitt about Monday. We probably should have done it sooner, but with everything else that's been going on..."

"Mr Pitt may give you some answers about Henry."

"That's what I'm hoping."

. . .

Mr and Mrs Pitt were both in the shop when Eliza and Connie arrived, and they smiled as they greeted them.

"What can we do for you, ladies?" Mr Pitt moved to his place by the till as Eliza answered.

"Sergeant Cooper has asked us to talk to you about Monday afternoon. I hope you don't mind."

"Not at all." Mrs Pitt joined her husband. "You're good at this detecting work. What a terrible end to the fete, though. I've still not got over it."

"No, it was shocking. Did you speak to the police while you were there?"

She shook her head. "Not in any meaningful way. I mean, I had nothing to say. One minute I was watching Mrs Appleton receive the prize for baking the best cake, and before I'd had a chance to congratulate her, Mrs Petty was shrieking at us."

"Where were you when you heard Mrs Petty?"

"I'd gone to the vegetable table to collect Mr Pitt's carrots. You can't let prize- winning vegetables go to waste."

"Certainly not, and congratulations, Mr Pitt. It's a shame you couldn't be in the marquee to receive the prize yourself."

He glanced around his small square shop. "Somebody had to stay here. Just because the fete was on, doesn't mean people don't need provisions."

"That's a shame." Connie huffed. "If they knew the shop would be shut, they'd have to be more organised and do their shopping in the morning."

"I don't mind..."

Eliza studied him. "Were you busy on Monday

afternoon?"

"Not really. A lot had planned ahead like Mrs Appleton suggested, but there was the crowd from Over Moreton to consider, and I'd rather not let people down."

"Tell me, did my son come in here at any time during the afternoon?"

"Young Dr Thomson? Yes, he called to send a telegram."

"A telegram! Do you know who to?"

"I'm afraid I can't say. He swore me to secrecy ... and gave me half a crown, which he said he'd be back for if anyone found out."

Eliza gasped. "I could give you a crown..."

"No." Connie put a hand on Eliza's arm. "You can't put Mr Pitt in a difficult position. Besides, do you think Dr Thomson would be happy if you asked him for so much money?"

"No. I just want to know what he's up to." Her shoulders dropped. "Do you remember what time that was?"

Mr Pitt puffed out his cheeks. "Probably close to three o'clock. Mrs Petty called while he was here, so you could check with her."

"I already have. She said it was about that time, but she didn't see Henry."

"That would be because we went into the back room to send it."

"Ah, I see." *At least that explains what he was up to, if not why.* "What about any of his friends? Were they with him? There were three of them, all of a similar age..."

Mr Pitt gazed at a spot somewhere above Eliza's head. "There was a young man with dark hair and a full beard who came in about half an hour later. Might that be one of them?"

"Possibly." *Dr Cartwright, wasn't it?* "Was he alone?"

"Yes. He only wanted a quarter of aniseed balls, so he was in and out."

Eliza scowled. "Did you notice which way he went when he left?"

"Most people who called turned right, towards the green, and I don't remember him being any different."

"Thank you, that's helpful." She looked at Mrs Pitt. "Did you see any of the young men at the fete?"

"I saw them buying cakes at Mrs Appleton's stall. At one point, they never seemed to be away. You must have made a healthy profit."

Connie beamed. "They certainly kept us busy, but I just gave the money to Mr Hewitt, so I've no idea how much there was. I've no doubt he'll tell us all once he has the final figures."

"I imagine so." Mrs Pitt chuckled but Eliza's forehead remained furrowed.

"Going back to my son's companions, did you see them anywhere other than the cake stall?"

"Hmm. I'm not sure I did ... other than perhaps... Were they playing on the games outside the marquee?"

Eliza nodded. "I've been told they played several games. Do you remember how many of them were there?"

"No, I'm sorry. I'd say there were at least two, but whether there were any more... I wasn't paying a lot of attention. I was keen to tell my husband he'd won with his carrots. Not that he was here..."

"Excuse me." Eliza looked at Connie as she gasped but didn't miss the colouring of Mr Pitt's cheeks.

"I was out at the back of the shop. A supplier was making a delivery..."

"But ... you said somebody needed to be here. Shouldn't you have let Mrs Pitt know?"

"Oh, he never tells me anything, deary..."

"But he didn't mention it to us, either. May I ask why?"

"I didn't think it was important."

Eliza took a deep breath. "And it may not be, but, for example, my son or his friends could have called while you were out, and you wouldn't have known."

"Ah, well ... if you put it like that..."

"It really wasn't a problem." Mrs Pitt squeezed her husband's arm. "He doesn't like to admit that I arrived to save the day. He never gives me any credit for helping out around here."

Eliza reached into her bag for her notebook. "All right, let me get this straight. Sergeant Cooper will want to know who you saw and when. What time did you meet your supplier, Mr Pitt?"

"I couldn't rightly say."

"Hadn't you planned it with him? After all, it was a bank holiday."

"W-we said half past three, but he was late."

"Five minutes, ten?"

"Something like that."

"How long were you outside?"

Mr Pitt stared at his feet. "Fifteen, twenty minutes..."

"And you planned on leaving the shop open and unoccupied for all that time?" Eliza shook her head. "Mrs Pitt, if I remember rightly, the award for the longest carrot was the first to be made, so that would mean you were in the shop shortly after half past three."

"Not that quickly. I didn't come here straight away. Mr

Pitt had entered the largest onion contest, too, and so I waited in case he'd won that ... but he hadn't."

Eliza looked at Connie. "Do you remember when that was?"

"The third or fourth, maybe."

Mrs Pitt nodded. "It was fourth."

"So, assuming it took a couple of minutes per award, you would have left the marquee around twenty to four?"

"I suppose so."

"And that was when you saw at least two of Henry's friends, and when Mr Pitt was *otherwise engaged*. How long had you been in the shop before he reappeared?"

"A good ten or fifteen minutes, because as soon as he appeared, I went back to the marquee. I was only just in time to see Mrs Petty receive her award."

"So, between ten to and five to four?"

Eliza turned her attention to Mr Pitt. "That means you were with your delivery driver from approximately twenty-five to four."

"Something like that."

"Was there any suspicious activity around the bowling club while you were outside?"

"I can't say I noticed anything, but then I wasn't looking."

"Very well. Could you give me the name and address of the man you met?"

"His name?"

"We'll need to confirm your alibi."

"Ah. Yes, actually, I-I didn't catch his name. He just arrived from the company..."

"Which is?"

"I-I'll check."

Eliza cocked her head to one side. "You don't know the name of the supplier you were dealing with?"

"It will be on the top of the invoice. I'll find it for you."

Eliza let her gaze linger on him. "I need to report this to Sergeant Cooper. Shall I tell him you'll drop the details off at the station?"

"Y-yes. You do that."

Eliza raised an eyebrow at Connie as they left the shop on their way to the church. "What do you make of that?"

Connie's cheek creased. "I really don't know. Surely Mr Pitt can't be our killer."

"I'd hope not, but unless he can give us some names so we can check his alibi, it doesn't look good for him. He was out of the shop right in the middle of the estimated time of death."

"You'd think someone would have seen him if he'd gone far. Or the delivery carriage."

Eliza looked at her. "You're right. Come with me." Eliza turned back to the shop but stopped at a narrow driveway that ran to the rear of the property. "I've never been down there before, but there isn't a lot of room."

"Carriages usually stop on the road at the front of the shop. I doubt they'd get in and out of there."

"Yet Mr Pitt said he met the driver around the back. Why would this delivery be different? We need to send Sergeant Cooper to look further into this."

"Then I hope Mr Pitt isn't our murderer. I don't want there to be any more trouble."

Eliza nodded. "We'll suggest he take Constable Jenkins with him. It's better to be safe than sorry."

CHAPTER FOURTEEN

The church door was open when Eliza and Connie reached the end of the path through the churchyard, and Eliza pushed it further before stepping inside.

"Vicar, Mr Hewitt, are you there?" She blinked her eyes to adjust to the candlelit interior. "Mr Hewitt..." She looked at Connie. "I don't think they're here."

"It doesn't sound like it. Shall we go? It's so eerie in here when it's empty."

"Let me check the office in case they didn't hear us."

Connie stayed close to Eliza but spun around as a door creaked behind them. "Oh, Mr Steel! You gave me a fright. What are you doing here?"

"I could ask the same of you."

"W-we're looking for Mr Hewitt." She flinched again as Mr Hewitt joined them.

"Did someone call?"

Eliza smiled at him. "We did. May we have a word with you about Monday afternoon?"

"I expect so. Would you like to take a seat?"

She turned to Mr Steel. "Are you here to speak to Mr Hewitt as well? I don't want to delay you."

"Not at all. I can wait." He sat in the pew closest to Eliza and folded his arms.

"Oh." She looked at Mr Hewitt. "I'd hoped we could talk in private."

Mr Steel groaned. "That's a shame. I was hoping to find out what's been going on."

"There's not much to tell, other than to say that Mr Gilbert is no longer a suspect."

"Ah, that's unfortunate. If you don't mind me saying, you seemed rather out of your depth the other day."

"Not at all. These things take time."

"I'm sure they do, but if it all gets too difficult, I'm happy to help."

Eliza bit her tongue as she glared at him. "We can manage, thank you. Now, if you'll excuse us, we're here to ask questions on behalf of Sergeant Cooper, and would prefer to speak to Mr Hewitt alone."

Mr Hewitt's eyes flicked from one to the other. "Was it me you came to see, Mr Steel?"

"No." He pushed himself up. "It was the vicar. Will you tell him I'll call again?"

"I will." Mr Hewitt watched him leave. "He seemed to be in a strange mood."

Eliza sighed. "I'm afraid that's our fault. We disagreed over an incident at the bowling club, so I suspect he was being deliberately difficult."

"I see. Now, how may I help?"

"We'd like to go over the events of Monday in case you

noticed anything of importance. You were in and out of the marquee more than anyone else."

"I suppose I was. Not that I was paying too much attention to things that weren't a direct concern to me."

"I understand, but you never know. You may have seen something without realising. Shall we go back to three o'clock? That was about half an hour before the prize-giving started, and the earliest we believe Mr Hobbs was killed."

Mr Hewitt nodded. "I remember hearing the church bells strike three, because they gave me quite a start."

Eliza tittered. "They still do that to me, but I'd expect you to be used to it by now."

"I didn't mean it that way. I was amazed it was three o'clock already. The afternoon flew by."

"Yes, it did. Do you recall what you were doing when you heard the bells?"

"I was outside talking to some of the villagers and then I made my way over to Constable Jenkins to find out how the games were going. I must confess, I was mainly concerned about how much money we were bringing in." He glanced up at the roof. "I'm praying it doesn't rain for the next few months."

Connie followed his gaze. "Sergeant Cooper told us they were busy all afternoon."

"They were, and the money they took proves it."

Eliza interrupted. "Do you know what time it was when you were with Constable Jenkins?"

He shook his head. "Probably about ten past, but I couldn't be sure. It was a while after I'd heard bells."

"And do you remember who was near the games at the time?"

He laughed. "I do, as it happens. Lord Harrington-Smyth was pitching sticks at the Aunt Sally. Can you believe it? It stopped me in my tracks when I saw him."

"That's a surprise. Was Lady Harrington-Smyth with him?"

"I don't think so. She was doing a lot of circulating with the stallholders, though, so was likely to be inside."

"Was there anyone else?"

"Mr Royal and Mr Steel were watching His Lordship. They may even have been waiting their turn, and there were others, presumably from Over Moreton, that I didn't recognise. Oh ... and two of the marquee men. Mr Taylor and Mr Bedford."

Eliza studied him. "Were either of them agitated when you saw them?"

Mr Hewitt's eyes narrowed. "I can't say I noticed. If I remember rightly, I don't think they were doing much at all. They weren't even standing together."

"How strange. Did it look as if they'd had a falling-out?"

"I can't help you there. You'll have to ask them."

Eliza nodded. "We will. Can we move on to my son and his friends? Did you see any of them over the course of the afternoon?"

Mr Hewitt's brow creased. "They were there at one point, but whether it was close to three o'clock... No, thinking about it, it was later when I called everyone in for the presentations."

Eliza nodded. "That seems to agree with what others have told us. What about inside the marquee? Were the stallholders always present and correct when you were walking round?"

"I'd say so. Having said that, most of those with stalls were women, and I doubt they'd have been able to kill a man with a single blow."

"You're probably right, although it's not beyond the realm of possibility." Eliza made a note in her book. "Did you go around the back of the marquee at all once the fete had started?"

"I did beforehand, when I took Mr Taylor to show him the damage, but then not again until after we'd found the body."

Eliza sighed. "What about when you visited the alehouse?"

Mr Hewitt stared at her. "The alehouse?"

"I believe you called on Mr Hobbs while he was in there, sometime between half past one and half past two."

"Ah, yes. I'd forgotten about that. I didn't stay for a drink, you understand."

"No?" Eliza raised an eyebrow.

"No, the thing was, I'd noticed a tent peg was missing, and I asked him to come and replace it."

"But you said you hadn't been around the back."

"Not at the time of the murder, but before the fete started, some of the material was loose, so as soon as everything was up and running, I went to ask him to repair it before the end of the fete. I didn't know he'd take my meaning literally and turn up at the end."

"Hadn't you noticed the missing tent peg when they were fixing the other problem?"

Mr Hewitt shook his head. "I'd swear everything else was in order. That must have come out later."

"How did you know Mr Hobbs would be in the alehouse?"

"He'd mentioned it earlier, when he was mending the other problem."

"So, the first issue was different?"

"It was. A knot had come loose on that occasion. Mr Hobbs secured it, but when Mr Taylor offered him a lift to Molesey, he said it wasn't worth the effort, and he was going to the alehouse."

Eliza nodded. "Thank you, Mr Hewitt. You've been very helpful." She paused as the clock struck the half hour. "Is that half past three? We'd better go. We've a visitor calling at four o'clock."

Eliza and Connie sat on opposite sides of the fireplace in the drawing room as they waited for Mrs Hartley to arrive. Connie fidgeted with her fingers as Eliza rearranged the cushions beside her.

"Do you think she's changed her mind about coming?"

"I hope not." Eliza glanced at the clock on the mantlepiece. "It's still a couple of minutes to four, so there's time yet. Don't look so worried. She won't bite."

Connie twisted her hands in her lap. "I can't help it. What do I say to her?"

"Why not tell her the truth?"

"The truth?"

"That you and Sergeant Cooper are officially walking out together. I'm not aware that she knows."

"I doubt that would stop her from getting her claws into him..."

"Stop that. She's not even looking for another husband."

"That's beside the point. I wasn't expecting to walk out

with anyone until I started seeing Frank. These things creep up on you."

"That's as may be, but if you tell her you're walking out together, I'm sure she'll take the hint."

"I don't know. She might hate me..."

"Don't be silly..." Eliza paused as the knocker sounded on the door. "She's here. Why don't you just get the apology out of the way? I'll do the talking after that."

"I can do that."

The lounge door opened behind Connie, and Eliza stood up to welcome her guest. "Mrs Hartley. How good of you to come."

"Mrs Thomson. Mrs Appleton." She gave Connie a curt nod.

"Mrs Hartley." Connie forced a smile as she got to her feet. "I'd like to apologise for being abrupt with you the other day ... and on all the other occasions we've met."

"Apology accepted. I presume Sergeant Cooper is the root of the problem."

"Y-yes..." Connie looked at Eliza. "We're walking out together."

"Good for you. I wish you well. Let me reassure you that even if I was considering another husband, which I'm not, he's really not my type."

Connie glared at her. "What's wrong with him?"

Mrs Hartley gave a gentle shake of the head. "Nothing, I'm sure, but ... how shall I say this? I prefer older men."

"Older?"

"Those with more money ... and influence." Mrs Hartley tutted. "Don't look so shocked. How do you think I'm able to live in Oak House?"

Connie stood with her mouth open as Iris carried a large tea tray into the drawing room. "Here you are, ladies. Cook made a fresh batch of scones, and she's whipped some cream to go with the jam."

Eliza smiled as Iris set down the tray. "Thank you. That looks lovely."

"I'll tell Cook, madam. I hope you enjoy it."

Eliza offered Mrs Hartley a seat beside her. "There's a lot to be said for marrying into money. My father wasn't happy for years that I'd married a doctor."

"From what I've seen of your father, that doesn't surprise me, but I suppose if you find someone you enjoy being with, that's just as important. I may have money, but my husband was hardly the affectionate type. Especially not after his accident."

Connie sat up straight. "Sergeant Cooper's affectionate."

"Then I'm pleased for you." She turned to Eliza. "I hear you've been helping the police with this murder."

"Who told you that?"

"I ventured to the shop yesterday morning and met Mrs Petty while I was out. There doesn't seem to be much she doesn't know."

Eliza chuckled. "You're right. She has a marvellous view from her front window and a chair at the right angle to see most of what's going on in the village. It's a shame she wasn't sitting there on Monday afternoon. She'd have seen our killer."

"She told me she'd been so busy helping you and Mrs Appleton, she barely looked up."

Eliza nodded. "We were all in the same boat." She

handed Mrs Hartley a plate. "Please help yourself. And you, Connie."

Once Eliza had poured the tea and helped herself to a cucumber sandwich, she studied Mrs Hartley. "Did you recognise the men who put up the marquee?"

"I don't remember seeing them. Why?"

"I wondered if they were the same ones who'd organised the one in your garden when you had your party."

"I couldn't tell you, to be honest. My son arranged it..."

"Ah." Eliza's stomach churned as Mrs Hartley stared down at her plate. *Change the subject.* "Were you at the fete all afternoon?"

"No, I popped in and out. I was there for the opening, but it got rather busy and so I left after about half an hour."

"Did you go home?"

"I didn't, actually." She gave Eliza a discreet smile. "It had been such a long time since I'd been into the village, I took the opportunity to look around, while everyone else was otherwise engaged."

"How lovely. Did you go anywhere nice?"

"First, I visited the churchyard to pay my respects to my husband. I was there for a while, just thinking about what might have been, and once I'd finished, I walked past the shop to the river. I ended up in Over Moreton, but the village was deserted, so I came back."

"You walked to Over Moreton? Did you see my son with one of his friends?"

"I can't say I did, but then I wasn't paying attention. I'm not certain I'd recognise him, either, after all these years."

"But you'd have noticed two young men?"

"Probably. But I don't recall passing anyone matching that description."

"Never mind. How long did your walk last?"

"I really don't know. It was such a lovely day that I wasn't worried about the time."

"But the fete was still going on when you arrived back. Is that when you came to the cake stall?"

"It was. As I said, I stayed outside talking to..." She paused as Connie bristled. "I was outside talking for several minutes and then I came in. That was just before the prize-giving."

"Did you stay to the end?"

"Not quite. I watched Mrs Petty receive her award but realised that there'd be a rush to leave once the final prize was given out, and so I left early."

Eliza cocked her head to one side. "You must have gone past the bowling club on your way home."

"I did. I walked along the footpath."

That would have been around the time Mr Hobbs was attacked. "Did you see anyone at the back of the marquee?"

"Only Mr Steel, but he was in the bowling club doing something."

Eliza's forehead creased. "Mr Steel? Are you sure? He would have still been at the prize-giving with his wife."

"You're right. I thought it was strange at the time, but I didn't see his face, so I was clearly mistaken. It looked like him from a distance, but he didn't wave when I called to him. Whoever it was probably thought I was rather eccentric."

"I doubt it, but I wonder who it was. They were obviously near the scene of the murder at around the right time."

Connie leaned forward and selected half a scone. "Did you go anywhere near the shop before you went home?"

"I'm afraid I didn't. Should I have?"

"No, but I wondered if you'd seen Mr Pitt. Could it have been him you saw by the bowling club?"

"I don't think so. I only spoke to him yesterday, so I doubt I'd get the two mistaken."

"They both have greying hair and moustaches."

"I suppose so ... but doesn't Mr Pitt carry more weight than Mr Steel?"

Eliza nodded. "He's a little chubbier, and slightly shorter, but would you notice that if he was at a distance?"

"Possibly not, and I don't know either of them terribly well, so maybe you're right."

Eliza looked at Connie. "We need to check Mr Pitt's alibi. Something about it doesn't add up."

CHAPTER FIFTEEN

Sergeant Cooper was standing on Connie's doorstep when she stepped out of Eliza's front door and he waved as he wandered over to them.

"Good evening, ladies. Have you any news for me? Did you speak to Mr Pitt and Mr Hewitt?"

Connie grinned. "We did. And to Mrs Hartley. That's why I'm late getting home. She's not long since left."

He glanced at the small table and chairs positioned outside Eliza's dining room window. "Might we sit down so you can tell me what you've found? I need to contact Inspector Adams, but I'd like to know as much as possible before I do."

"Certainly ... as long as you don't mind tongues wagging." Eliza studied the surrounding houses before indicating to the chairs. "Did you call on Mr Steel and Mrs Petty?"

"I did but I'm afraid there's not much to report. Mrs Petty's disappointed that she was so busy on the cake stall she missed everything, and Mr Steel claimed that between three and four o'clock, he was either outside the marquee watching the games or handing out prizes. We can't really argue with that."

"No. Did he mention meeting Mr Hobbs in the pub?"

"Not until I asked him, but he said the same to me as he had to Dr Thomson. That he hadn't mentioned it because it wasn't near the time of death, so he didn't think it was important."

"It probably isn't, but it clearly shows he knew the victim. Did you ask if he knew the other men?"

"He didn't, but he said it was no surprise because there are several banks in Molesey."

"That's true."

Sergeant Cooper took out his notebook. "Shall we cross Mr Steel off our list of suspects?"

"I think so, although it's still confusing that Mrs Hartley said she saw a man resembling him by the bowling club when Connie was receiving her prize. Not that she saw his face."

Sergeant Cooper rubbed his chin. "Who could she possibly confuse for Mr Steel?"

"She'd only seen him during the prize-giving, so it would be easy to confuse him with another grey-haired man."

"Hmm, then we need a list of all the men with grey hair who attended the fete. That could take a while."

"It could but we wondered about Mr Pitt."

Sergeant Cooper's brow creased. "He was in the shop, wasn't he?"

"Not for the twenty minutes that happen to coincide with the time of Mr Hobbs' death."

"No! Did he tell you that?"

"Not exactly." Eliza pulled out her notebook and shared the details of their discussion with Sergeant Cooper.

"So, he has an alibi?"

"Of sorts, but we need to confirm it. We asked him to get the name of the man he'd met, and the company, and pass them to you, but if he hasn't called by midday, I suggest you pay him a visit."

"I most certainly will. I don't like the sound of what he's been up to."

"Neither do we. Mrs Pitt seemed oblivious to what he was doing, though, so I doubt she had any part in it."

"I'm glad to hear it. What about Mr Hewitt? Did he say anything of interest?"

"Not directly, but he mentioned something that's had me thinking."

Connie was as intrigued as Sergeant Cooper. "You didn't say anything."

"It only occurred to me when we were talking to Mrs Hartley. Do you remember, before the fete started, Mr Hewitt was looking for Mr Taylor because there was a problem with the marquee that needed mending?"

"I do, because it delayed Constable Jenkins when he had to fetch them."

"Exactly. Well, little more than an hour later, Mr Hewitt noticed a tent peg was missing, so he called at the alehouse to ask Mr Hobbs about it."

Connie nodded. "He was sure it had been there when they'd tightened the knot on the frame."

"So...?"

"So..." Eliza chose her words carefully. "What if someone had deliberately sabotaged the marquee ... to get Mr Hobbs away from the crowd ... and from prying eyes."

Connie squealed. "Ready to murder him?"

"It's a thought."

"And not a very pleasant one." Sergeant Cooper shook his head. "What's the world coming to? That would mean the same person was around the back of the marquee before the start of the fete, and then again shortly afterwards."

"The trouble seems to be that no one else was there to see them."

Connie looked at Eliza. "We should ask Mr Steel what time he arrived at the fete. If he was at the bowling club before he joined us, he may have seen our killer."

Sergeant Cooper made his own notes. "It's something to ponder for sure. Is that all you have for now?"

Eliza checked her book. "It is. Shall we come to the station again in the morning when we've had a chance to think everything through and decide what to do next?"

Sergeant Cooper huffed. "You can, but I'd better send a telegram to Inspector Adams tonight. Hopefully, he'll have other things on his plate and won't be able to join us straight away." He patted Connie's hand before he stood up. "I'll call by later, if you don't mind."

She smiled. "I was hoping you would. I'll be ready for seven."

Archie was in the drawing room when Eliza returned to the house, and he looked up from his newspaper.

"That took a long time."

"Sergeant Cooper called and wanted to know how we'd got on with Mr Pitt and Mr Hewitt, so we sat in the front garden."

"And how did you get on? Do you have any suspects yet?"

"Not as such, but Mr Pitt confirmed that Henry went to the shop ... to send a telegram."

Archie's brow furrowed. "Where did he get the money from for that?"

"Is that all you can say? Don't you want to know who he was messaging?"

"You know as well as I do, that's none of our business. If he wants to tell us he will."

"But he won't..."

"Then leave it. Is that what you spoke to the sergeant about?"

"No. We were telling him about our meetings with Mr Pitt and Mr Steel. It looks like we need to speak to both of them again."

"Mr Steel? You can't think he did it?"

"No, but we have to ask if he saw anything. I'd say it's a good job he was in the marquee helping with the awards or he'd have a lot more questions to answer."

"That's preposterous. What possible motive could he have?"

"There isn't one, as far as we're aware." Eliza looked at him. "How well do you know him, though? Other than when you meet him at the bowling club."

"As well as anyone, I suppose. He's given his life to the bowling club since he retired, and when he's not there, he's in his garden or caring for his wife. You won't find a milder-mannered man."

"Why does he need to do that? She seemed in reasonable health on Monday."

"Her heart's failing. Apparently, she was exhausted when

they got home after the fete and spent the rest of the evening and most of the next day in bed."

Eliza's head furrowed. "She doesn't visit the surgery."

"It's only recently become a problem, and I usually call at the house to check her over and give her some digitalis."

"I don't suppose there's much else you can do, but it's a good job Mr Steel has an alibi. He was behaving strangely in church when we called on Mr Hewitt."

Archie cocked his head to one side. "In what way?"

"It's difficult to describe other than he was rather annoying."

"That doesn't sound like him."

"It does with women. I put it down to our disagreement earlier in the week. Mr Pitt, on the other hand... He's been strange in another way. He said he was with a delivery driver at the time of the murder but didn't know the man's name or the name of the company. He has to be a prime suspect unless he comes up with a bit more information."

"Goodness. You wouldn't credit that."

"No, but then, many of the murders we've been involved with have taken us by surprise, so we can't rule him out."

"Is Inspector Adams likely to turn up? I doubt he'll be pleased if he finds out you haven't told him what's going on."

"Sergeant Cooper's probably sending him a telegram as we speak."

"So, we can expect him tomorrow?"

"I would say so."

CHAPTER SIXTEEN

E liza was in the dispensary the following morning when the postman called with a handful of letters.

"Here you are, Mrs Thomson. There's an important-looking one on the top for the doctor."

Eliza took them from him. "So there is, thank you. I'll take it through once he's finished with this patient."

She hovered by the dispensary door until an elderly gentleman hobbled towards her and handed her a piece of paper.

"Take a seat and I'll get this made up as soon as I can. I need to see my husband first." She didn't wait for a reply before darting down the corridor to the surgery. "May I come in?"

Archie looked up. "Have we finished?"

"No, there are another couple waiting, but the postman's brought this. It looks like the results of the post-mortem."

"It does indeed." He sliced the top of the envelope with the letter opener and pulled out several sheets of thick, cream writing paper. "Let me see. Yes, as we thought. He died of a fracture to the skull near the left temple."

"Just the one blow?"

"No. The report says there were at least three, but only one was thought to be fatal. He was attacked with a blunt implement, which left bruising on the skin."

"So, Mr Hobbs didn't go down as easily as we thought."

"Looking at this, any one of the blows would have knocked him unconscious. If it was the first, it would have made it easier for the killer to finish the job."

"It sounds like a rather frenzied attack."

"In which case, why did no one hear anything?"

"That's a good question. Unless it coincided with the ringing of the church bells."

Archie grunted. "That would make sense, and it would fit with the time of death. The coroner agrees it most likely happened between half past two and when the body was found shortly after four o'clock."

"But Mr Hobbs was still alive at three o'clock. That was roughly when he was seen with Dr Dunlop."

"You're sure?"

"Yes, Mrs Petty and Iris both confirmed it."

"Then it must have been between three and four o'clock."

"He can't have been at the marquee before ten past at the earliest, and then he must have spoken to someone who asked him to go around the back to look for the missing tent peg."

Archie studied the report. "If there was a scuffle, the church bells may have covered the noise. Not that those on the quarter hours would have been long enough."

"The chimes at quarter *to* might have been."

"I suppose so."

"I'll count how long they last next time I hear them." Eliza rested her chin on a hand. "When you first examined the body, you said it was still warm. Was it warm enough to have been dead no more than ten minutes or so?"

Archie puffed out his cheeks. "I'd say so, but it was a hot day, so even if Mr Hobbs had died earlier, he wouldn't have cooled down as quickly as he would in the winter."

"That's true. It also means I'll need to go back through my notes to see what everyone was doing around quarter to four and four o'clock."

"Don't forget, it may not be at either of those times. The noise in the marquee may have masked any disturbance, if there even was any. If the first blow came as a surprise and knocked him unconscious, he wouldn't have had chance to put up a fight."

"I'll bear that in mind, but we've got to start somewhere. Let's see what we come up with."

Connie was preparing coffee in her small kitchen when Eliza joined her half an hour later.

"Ah, I'm glad you didn't wait for me. I thought I was late."

Connie took a second cup from a hook under the shelf. "I'm running behind myself today. I wanted to wash my navy dress."

"On a Thursday?"

"It's ideal to walk out in of an evening, and I didn't want to wait until Monday before I wear it again. What delayed you?"

Eliza smiled. "Archie got the results of the post-mortem. Three or four blows to the side of the head, although only one was fatal. As we suspected, we're looking for a blunt object."

"So not a hammer?"

"We can't say that for certain. Some hammers are blunt, but it's unlikely to be a wooden mallet. They'd be too big. It sounds like it was quite a nasty attack, and given no one heard anything, Archie and I wondered if it happened when the church bells were ringing."

"At what time?"

"That's the thing. The report says the death occurred after half past two, but given we know Mr Hobbs was alive at three o'clock, it's more likely to have been quarter to four or four o'clock."

Connie carried the coffee to the table. "So, Mr Pitt could be a suspect if it was quarter to. Mrs Pitt said he was in the shop by four."

"But she left him to go back to the fete, so he could have sneaked out again."

"Do you think he would?"

"He did it once…" Eliza pulled out her notebook. "We'd better go over everyone's alibis while we drink this to see who we can rule in or out before we walk to the police station. If Inspector Adams is here, we don't want him asking questions we can't answer."

Constable Jenkins was behind the counter when they arrived at the station, and he looked up with a scowl.

"Sergeant Cooper doesn't want to be disturbed."

"Good morning, Constable." Eliza exaggerated her smile. "Is Inspector Adams here?"

"Oh, sorry, good morning. No, not yet, but he's sent word to say he'll be here this afternoon."

"Then why's Sergeant Cooper so preoccupied?"

"He wants to go through all his notes and do a report before he arrives."

"Ah, then we may be able to help. Mrs Appleton and I have done the same thing. Would you tell him we're here?"

Constable Jenkins grunted before he turned on his heel and popped his head into the office behind. He hadn't returned to his post before Sergeant Cooper joined them.

"Ladies. Am I glad to see you. I'm trying to make sense of everything before Inspector Adams arrives, and I could do with your help."

Connie bounced on her toes. "We've gone through our notes, too."

"Splendid. Come on through."

Constable Jenkins glared at them as Sergeant Cooper lifted the flap on the counter to let them in.

"Take a seat." Sergeant Cooper offered them chairs on the opposite side of the desk to his. "Do you know who our killer is yet?"

"If only it were that simple." Eliza reached into her bag for her notebook. "We have the results of the post-mortem, though."

Sergeant Cooper sat in silence as Eliza updated him. "So we can eliminate all those in the marquee between about twenty to four and four o'clock."

"Not completely, but we should prioritise those with no alibi for those times."

"Who should we focus on, then?"

Eliza paused. "In no particular order, we should speak

again to Mr Bedford, Mr Taylor, my son's friends ... oh, and Mr Pitt."

"And what do we ask them?"

"Let's start with Mr Bedford. He said he was due to meet Mr Hobbs in the alehouse at three o'clock, but when he wasn't there, he decided to look for him."

Connie interrupted. "Mr Hobbs was by the river talking to Dr Dunlop."

"Exactly. Not that Mr Bedford was aware of that."

Sergeant Cooper flicked through his notes. "Did he find him?"

"Not as far as I'm aware. He told us that once he reached the marquee, he stood outside with Mr Taylor, but we need to check whether that covered the period between quarter to four and four o'clock. We should also ask him about the arrival of Mr Gilbert and whether he seemed angry or agitated."

"Why not just talk to Mr Gilbert?"

"We need to confirm he's telling the truth. He admitted he was angry when he got to the marquee and that Mr Taylor had to stop him from storming straight past them. I've been wondering how true that was. And if it is, where Mr Gilbert had been. He said he got to the marquee shortly after half past three, but that means it took him over an hour to get from the Golden Eagle."

The sergeant flicked back several pages in his notebook. "I've written here that Mr Taylor agreed with the time."

"He did, but we need to make sure there's no mistake about when he arrived. Or whether he arrived up at the marquee and disappeared again."

Connie's eyes widened. "Do you think he was involved, after all?"

"I don't know, but it would help if Mr Bedford confirmed what the other two told us. We also need more information from Mr Taylor. He wanted Mr Hobbs out of the company but couldn't sack him. Would that be a motive for murder or is a thirty-year working relationship a good enough excuse to put up with someone who's costing you money?"

"You think there's another reason?"

"It wouldn't surprise me ... whether Mr Taylor is the murderer or an innocent bystander."

Sergeant Cooper found a fresh page in his notebook. "I'll send Constable Jenkins over to Molesey."

"Splendid. If enough of us talk to them, they may tie themselves up in knots ... if they're lying, that is." Eliza turned over her piece of paper. "Now, others we should speak to are my son's friends, Dr Cartwright and Mr Everett. They left the Golden Eagle around three o'clock and were on the Aunt Sally when the rest of the folks went inside for the prize-giving."

The sergeant wrote their names in his book. "Are you suggesting they nipped around the back of the marquee once we'd all gone inside?"

"It's possible, but we haven't found a motive for why they would."

"What about your son? I don't remember seeing him with them."

"No ... he and his other friend, Dr Dunlop, went to the shop..."

"Did you ask what they were doing at the time of the murder?"

"I-I did, but ... well, we hadn't confirmed the precise time of death, so the conversation was rather vague. They all left for London on Tuesday afternoon, so we've not been able to follow up with them." Eliza sighed. "Henry didn't know Mr Hobbs, so there's no reason why he'd harm him."

"Then we'll get an alibi from him and move on to his friend, Dr Dunlop. What do we know about him?"

"Dr Thomson spoke to him, and he admitted meeting someone matching the appearance of Mr Hobbs, but claimed he didn't know who he was. Not that we believed him, given the Dunlops were on the list of customers who'd had a marquee erected."

Sergeant Cooper paused. "Why would he lie?"

"We've no idea, but he was overheard telling Mr Hobbs that he owed someone fifty pounds."

Sergeant Cooper sucked air through his teeth. "That's a lot of money."

"It is, but as with Mr Bedford, would Dr Dunlop want him dead if he was owed money from him? He won't get it now."

"No, he won't. Is there anyone else?"

"Mr Pitt. He told us he was in the shop at four o'clock, but so far, we've no one to confirm that. Has he brought in details of the delivery driver he was supposedly with between half past three and four o'clock?"

"Not yet." Sergeant Cooper glanced at the clock above the door. "If he hasn't arrived in the next half an hour, I'll go over and speak to him. Should we concentrate on anyone else?"

"Not at the moment ... assuming we can discount all the women. I doubt any of them would be able to deliver such a blow."

"I'd say you're right. A man's done this, and we need to find out who."

"Actually, for completeness, we should probably talk to Mr Royal, too."

"Mr Steel said he was with him while they waited for the prize-giving and then they were together in the tent."

"He did, but we should check the times. It would confirm Mr Steel's alibi, too."

Connie interrupted. "Don't forget, we want to ask Mr Steel if he saw anything suspicious near the bowling club before he joined us."

"We do." Sergeant Cooper reread his notes. "We've a lot to do here. I'd better travel to London with Inspector Adams when he leaves. We need answers from all these gentlemen. And fast."

CHAPTER SEVENTEEN

Once luncheon was over, there was a knock on the door of the surgery before Connie let herself in.

"Are you ready?"

Eliza appeared in the hallway. "Nearly. I've been going over my notes again. Come in for a moment." She led Connie into the dining room. "Let me collect these up."

"Have you worked anything out since this morning?"

"I'm afraid not. I've just added Sergeant Cooper's information to ours. Have you seen Inspector Adams arrive?"

"No, but I may have missed him. Should we walk up to the police station, anyway?"

Eliza glanced at the clock. "Let's leave it for an hour. He won't be leaving in a hurry, so we should give Sergeant Cooper time to tell him what we know."

"What about walking along the river, then?"

"I thought we should stay on the road so we could see when he arrived..."

Connie pointed to the window. "There's no need. He's here now."

"Splendid. Let's take that walk to Over Moreton, then, and we can call on Mr Royal. Sergeant Cooper won't have a chance this afternoon."

They walked out of the back door to the surgery, through a small gate at the bottom of the garden and onto the path beside the river. Connie looked up at the sky.

"It should stay nice, and there are just enough clouds to keep the sun off us."

"That would be why there are more people out."

"The panic over Mr Hobbs' death will have died down a little, too."

"I expect so. Not that we're any closer to finding the killer."

"Don't you have any gut instincts?"

"Not really. There are too many who had a motive, even though most are weak. We didn't eliminate anyone when we tried to fit their alibis to the probable time of death, either. All we did was show that we need to speak to everyone again."

"That's true. It's as well Inspector Adams has arrived. At least he should be able to help with the London side of the investigation."

"Not on his own."

Connie looked up at her. "What do you mean?"

"If anyone's going to visit Henry and his friends, it should be me, not the police. Imagine what it will do to his standing at the hospital if anyone sees him being questioned."

"He's only helping with their enquiries. It doesn't make him guilty."

"You know how tongues wag. No, I need to speak to the inspector and ask if we can join him and Sergeant Cooper."

"Won't Dr Thomson be cross with you?"

"I'll make sure he isn't. We'll stay with Father for a few days and tell him we're going shopping. He's used to that by now."

"As long as your father doesn't mind."

"Don't be silly, he'll be delighted. We should invite Henry for dinner, too, to make up for our falling-out the other day. And to find out more about that telegram."

"Will you invite him on his own?"

Eliza stared into the distance. "Yes, I'd say so. He may be more open than if he was with his friends. It would look more suspicious if we invited them, anyway."

"He didn't want to talk on his own on Monday."

"No ... I'll need to be more tactful. Tell him what we've learned so far. He's usually interested."

"Will we do some shopping, too?"

"Definitely!" Eliza grinned. "I can hardly tell Archie that's what I'm doing and then come home with no bags."

The walk to Over Moreton took less than half an hour and after strolling down the high street, they arrived at the forecourt of Royal's manufactory.

"My, they've given it a lick of paint since we were last here. That's better." She studied the single-storey red-brick building. "I don't suppose they've done much with the inside."

"I doubt they could with that large furnace dominating the space."

"Let's find out, shall we?"

The heat that bellowed out as the door opened caused Eliza and Connie to take a step backwards before they both took a deep breath and went inside.

Eliza pointed to the left. "That's his office." With her

head down, she headed for the glazed door without waiting for assistance from any of the soot-covered men. She'd no sooner knocked than a tall man with dark hair opened the door.

"Mr Royal."

His brow creased. "Mrs Thomson? What are you doing here?"

Eliza could feel the perspiration settling on her forehead. "May we come in?"

"Yes, of course, I'm sorry. I'm just surprised to see you."

"Apologies we didn't warn you in advance, but it was a bit of a last-minute decision."

"Then how may I help?"

"We're helping Sergeant Cooper with the investigation into the murder on Monday afternoon, and he asked us to call while he's preoccupied with Inspector Adams. He arrived from New Scotland Yard about an hour ago."

"Ah. He needs to take him through the evidence, does he?"

"He does. He's spoken to a lot of people, but we realised that nobody had been to Over Moreton."

"I suppose you want to know my whereabouts at the time of death."

"There is that, but we're also here to ask if you saw anything suspicious or noticed a scuffle outside the marquee … at the back, behind the table with the flower displays."

"A scuffle? I can't say I did, but it was rather noisy with all the applause and cheering."

"Yes, it was. We suspect that's why nobody heard any commotion, but we need to make sure."

"Quite right, too."

"What about seeing anything suspicious? I understand

you were outside the marquee near the games before you awarded the prizes."

"I was, with Mr Steel, if you must know. We were discussing who would present each prize."

"What time was that?"

"Oh, now. Let me see. My carriage left here shortly before three o'clock, so I expect I arrived between five past and ten past."

"And your wife was with you?"

"She was, and the coachman will confirm the timings if you need to be more precise."

"Did you meet with Mr Steel immediately?"

"No, he joined me at quarter past three. I remember hearing the church bells."

"But then you stayed together until the prize-giving started?"

"We were together pretty much until the end. He gave Mrs Petty her prize and then I ended the fete once my wife had presented Mrs Appleton with hers."

"The most prestigious prize of the day." Eliza grinned at Connie. "Did you have a battle on your hands over who did what?"

Mr Royal laughed. "Not at all. Mr Steel wasn't unduly troubled by the order. He and his wife gave out more prizes than Mrs Royal, which is what it was all about. Being seen to support the villages."

"And I'm sure it was appreciated." Eliza glanced around. "Is there anything else of relevance while we're here?"

"I don't think so. I was on my way from the marquee when the body was discovered, so can't comment on that."

"Were you still outside?"

"I was. Looking for Mr Steel as it happens, to say cheerio, but I suspect he'd already gone to the bowling club."

"And he didn't say farewell before he left?"

"There wasn't much need. We'd said all we had to, and he'd told me he wanted to get back to open up."

Eliza cocked her head to one side. "He was planning on opening the club? I thought Mr Hewitt had asked him not to."

"He told me it was only while the fete was on."

Eliza nodded. "I hadn't realised that. Right, well, if that's all, I'll let you get on."

The clouds had disappeared before they returned to Moreton, and after stopping at the surgery for a glass of lemonade, they continued on to the police station where they were greeted by the scowl of Constable Jenkins.

"They're busy."

Eliza took a deep breath. "Good afternoon, Constable. Are you not involved in their discussions?"

"It's always the same. You turn up here, and the sarge is happy to talk to you. Inspector Adams does the same, but if *I* ask any questions..."

Eliza nodded. "It must be frustrating for someone in your position, especially when you could have some relevant information."

"He seems to forget I'm a police officer, too. How will I ever reach sergeant if he won't share anything with me?"

"I'm sure he will when he's less preoccupied..."

"I might have seen something that was important, but he hasn't even asked..."

Eliza glanced at Connie. "What did you see?"

"I saw a lot of things, but whether there's anything that might be useful, I don't know, because I'm being kept in the dark..."

"Oh dear." Eliza gave him an encouraging smile. "I imagine Sergeant Cooper will talk to you soon. Is it right that you were at the front of the marquee all afternoon?"

"I was taking money for the games while the sarge acted as referee."

"You were busy, too, by all accounts. Was there anyone from the village who didn't have a go on at least one game?"

"There were not so many ladies, but it felt like all the men did. Even Mr Pitt came out of the shop for a go when he was quiet."

"He did? When was that?"

"It's difficult to say, but probably about halfway through the afternoon, maybe a little later."

"So, you started at one and finished at four..."

"No. We had to finish by half past three so we weren't a distraction while they gave the prizes out."

"Of course. So around halfway would be ... between two and half past. Would that be right?"

The constable screwed up his eyes. "Probably ... although it may have been a little later. I'm trying to remember which church bells I'd last heard, but I'm not sure."

"Did you see him come out of the shop?"

"No, but then I wasn't watching."

"Did you notice him leave again?"

Constable Jenkins' brow creased. "I did, actually. He was so poor on the Aunt Sally, he had a crowd cheering him on, but when he missed with all three shots, he disappeared into the marquee."

"He went inside?"

"He did."

"Did you see him leave again?"

"No, I'm afraid I didn't."

"I understand. There were a lot of people milling around."

"Some more than others. Mr Steel must've walked past me half a dozen times before he finally paid for a game."

Eliza raised an eyebrow. "What time would that have been?"

"Shortly after Mr Pitt left. He didn't settle until Mr Royal joined him."

"Mr Steel was there first?"

"He was, but he kept disappearing. I heard the three o'clock bells while he was hovering."

"That's very helpful, thank you, Constable. Is there anything else?"

He chuckled. "Lord Harrington-Smyth came for a game. He had a remarkably good throw, once he got going. He missed with his first shot."

"I imagine that pleased everyone watching."

The constable smirked. "Oh, it did. Brought him down a peg or two. He rallied after that, though."

"I'm glad you enjoyed it." Eliza grinned. "Did he play the same game as Mr Royal and Mr Steel?"

"No, he said he wanted to show them how it was done."

"Well, I'll make sure Sergeant Cooper gets a full statement from you, too."

Constable Jenkins slipped back into his sullen state. "He shouldn't need telling..."

Connie huffed. "He has been busy."

"He has, but..." Eliza paused as Sergeant Cooper opened the door.

"I thought I heard voices. Would you like to come in?"

Eliza held back as Connie followed the sergeant into the room.

"I probably shouldn't say this, but I suspect Sergeant Cooper could do with some help."

Constable Jenkins' eyes narrowed. "What sort of help?"

"There were plenty of people at the fete who we've not had chance to talk to but who may have seen something. When you're out on your beat, could you make some enquiries? Ask if anyone saw anything. Especially around the back of the marquee between half past three and four o'clock."

"Without the sarge telling me to?"

"It would show some initiative."

A smile settled on his face. "It would, wouldn't it?"

"And while you're working out who to talk to, keep it to yourself. Sergeant Cooper doesn't need to know I suggested it."

CHAPTER EIGHTEEN

E liza extended a hand to Inspector Adams as Sergeant
Cooper showed them into the cluttered office behind
the reception desk.

"Inspector. How nice to see you again."

"Mrs Thomson, Mrs Appleton." He briefly accepted
Eliza's hand. "You've been assisting Sergeant Cooper, I hear."

"You know us, Inspector. We like to help if we can."

Sergeant Cooper pulled up two more chairs. "And I'm
very glad you do. Please, take a seat."

Once she was settled, Eliza looked across to the sergeant.
"I presume you've taken Inspector Adams through the
information we have so far."

"I have indeed."

The inspector nodded. "And very impressive it is, too.
You've been busy."

Eliza smiled. "That's not all. We've just come from Over
Moreton and spoken to Mr Royal. We chatted to Constable
Jenkins, too."

"Constable Jenkins?" Sergeant Cooper's face reddened. "If he had something to say, he should have told me."

"I-I erm... He said you'd been busy, and he hadn't had a chance..."

"Nons... Ah, yes, he's right. I've not been here much. I've been meaning to get a statement from him..."

"Not to worry. He'll be ready when you are."

"Good." Inspector Adams shifted in his seat as he eyed the sergeant. "Mrs Thomson, perhaps you could summarise what they both had to say."

Sergeant Cooper wrote up the notes while Inspector Adams interrupted with questions.

"So, Sergeant, this Mr Pitt, has he brought in the information you asked for about his supplier?"

"No, not yet. I was planning on calling this afternoon..."

"What kept you?" Inspector Adams stood up and pulled on the door. "Constable!"

"Yes, sir." Constable Jenkins almost fell through the door as it swung open.

"We need details of the man Mr Pitt met with on Monday afternoon."

"What? Now?" He glanced around him. "What about the desk?"

"I'm sure it can look after itself for quarter of an hour, and if it can't, Sergeant Cooper's here. Now, be quick about it."

"Y-yes, sir, but what precisely am I asking for?"

The inspector looked exasperated. "Mr Pitt left the shop for about twenty minutes on Monday afternoon. Go and find out what he was up to and tell him I want the name of the man he met with, as well as the company details."

"Yes, sir." Constable Jenkins clicked his heels together. "Leave it to me. I'll find out what he's playing at."

Inspector Adams groaned. "If you could use a little tact..."

"Yes, sir. I'll get onto it."

The inspector glowered at Sergeant Cooper as the front door of the station closed behind the constable. "Why haven't you involved him in the case?"

"I've not had time..."

"Nonsense. You've managed to speak to the ladies. Your constable should be the first person you turn to."

Sergeant Cooper shuffled his feet. "Yes, sir."

"Now, where were we? Mr Royal."

"Actually..." Eliza took a deep breath "...before we move on, I've just realised that Mrs Pitt told us she nipped back to the shop while her husband was out. She didn't seem unduly concerned that he'd left it unattended, which I thought was odd. Constable Jenkins also mentioned that he'd seen Mr Pitt at the games around half past two. Do you remember that, Sergeant?"

Sergeant Cooper spoke through gritted teeth. "I do."

"Yet you didn't think to mention it?" Inspector Adams stared at him until the sergeant ran a finger around his collar.

"I was about to when Mrs Thomson joined us."

"And is there anything else you were *about to* tell us?"

"No."

Eliza interrupted. "You were going to ask Constable Jenkins to go to Molesey tonight to confirm what Mr Bedford was doing after he left the Golden Eagle."

"I mentioned it to him earlier, but I'll remind him again..."

"See that you do." Inspector Adams turned to Eliza. "Shall we continue?"

"Yes, now..." Eliza flicked through her notes. "Going back to Mr Royal, he said he arrived at the fete shortly after three o'clock and left once all the prizes had been awarded."

"And there are people who can vouch for him?"

"He travelled with his wife, and he's given me the name of the coachman, should we need it."

Inspector Adams nodded. "Sergeant, make a note of that. Did this Mr Royal see anything while he was here?"

"Not really, but he confirmed the whereabouts of Mr Steel for the duration of his visit, although according to Constable Jenkins, Mr Steel was hanging around the games area a good quarter of an hour before the Royals arrived."

"So, nothing of any consequence." Inspector Adams stroked his recently grown moustache. "I suppose that's helpful, but, Mrs Thomson, we need to talk about your son and his friends. I believe they have questions to answer."

Eliza pursed her lips as the heat rose in her cheeks. "They do. It was a shame they had to leave on Tuesday before I had a chance to speak to them. They had to go to work."

"All doctors, aren't they?"

"Three are; the fourth, Mr Everett, is a dentist. They all work at the Middlesex Hospital, though, near Mayfair."

"Do they live in Mayfair?"

"No, unfortunately for them, doctors don't earn Mayfair wages. They're in Soho."

The inspector raised an eyebrow. "Really. Once we've found out what's happening with this Mr Pitt, I'll take a carriage there. I'd rather be in and out before those nightclubs open. I'll travel back tomorrow."

"Oh ... I'm sure there's no need to call tonight. Henry said he was working late shifts all this week..."

"I'm afraid they've already had three days to come up with a group alibi. We can't afford to wait."

"One more day shouldn't make any difference. Besides, if you wait, Mrs Appleton and I can help. We're planning to travel to London tomorrow to visit my father. We'd be happy to pay them a visit if you're busy…"

Sergeant Cooper's mouth fell open as he looked between Connie and Eliza. "No!"

Inspector Adams swivelled in his seat. "I'm sorry, Sergeant. Did you say something?"

"No … yes … I was just surprised the ladies were going to London. I thought they were helping here."

Eliza smiled. "We won't be gone for long and if we can speak to Henry…"

"Mrs Thomson." Inspector Adams held her gaze. "May I remind you, this is a police investigation, and either I or one of my officers need to do the talking?"

"But he's my son."

"And you may be tempted to give him more information than I'd like."

"He won't have done it…"

"And that's my point exactly. You're making assumptions."

Eliza sighed. "All right, but may I join you? Please. I'll let you do the talking, but I'd like to know what's going on as much as you."

It took several seconds, but eventually, the inspector nodded. "Very well, but I'll be travelling tonight so I can make an early start in the morning."

Early. Eliza groaned. "What time?"

"Nine o'clock sharp at the hospital."

"We'll be there..." She paused and turned around as the door opened. "Oh, it's you, Constable."

"Look what I have..." He waved a piece of paper at them. "Mr Pitt's alibi."

"So, he did meet with someone?"

Constable Jenkins nodded. "A driver from the local flour mill."

Eliza glanced at the paper as the constable handed it to Inspector Adams.

"It's unusual they were working on a bank holiday."

Inspector Adams dropped the paper onto the desk. "Maybe they didn't want to lose the business."

"A flour company? He's hardly likely to go anywhere else."

Connie cocked her head to one side. "It's strange that he didn't tell us who he'd met when we first asked. He wouldn't have forgotten he'd taken in an order of flour."

Eliza nodded. "That's a good point. We'll have to find out more about it when we get back from London."

"Sergeant Cooper can do it while we're away." The inspector glared at her. "It's his job."

"Ah, yes." Eliza's cheeks coloured as she pushed herself up. "Right, well ... if you'll excuse us, we'd better go and pack an overnight bag. I'll write out the questions we need to ask Henry and his friends before we meet in the morning."

Sergeant Cooper escorted them to the door and Connie turned to give him a discreet wave before joining Eliza on the footpath.

"Poor thing, Inspector Adams wasn't very nice to him."

"He wasn't very nice to anyone."

"No. I wish you hadn't mentioned Constable Jenkins while he was there."

"I'm sorry, I didn't think, but we had to share what he told us."

"I suppose so. What will you tell Dr Thomson when you get home?"

"About going to London? I'll just say with everything that's happened, I'd like to see Father ... and that I could do with a new dress."

"And he'll believe you?"

"Probably not, but he won't object." She linked Connie's arm. "We'd better call in at the shop on the way so I can send Father a telegram to let him know to expect us later."

"Tonight!"

Eliza huffed. "We're meeting Inspector Adams outside the hospital at nine in the morning. Do you really want to be out of bed so early?"

"Not particularly, but I was seeing Frank later."

"What time?"

"He said he'd call at six o'clock so we had time for a walk."

If he can get away. "Then why don't you take a shorter walk, and we'll leave at seven? If we catch the train, we'll be there for eight ... and tell him that Father will send a carriage to pick us up. I know he worries..."

"He won't be very pleased."

"He can't stop you from going out. Not when you're not even married."

Connie's cheeks coloured. "Don't say that."

"It's true. If he wants to tell you what to do, he should make an honest woman of you." *Not that a wedding band made a jot of difference when I married Archie.*

CHAPTER NINETEEN

E liza suppressed a yawn as the carriage that had collected them from her father's house in Richmond approached The Middlesex Hospital. She looked up at the clock on the front of the building.

"Five to nine. I'd no idea it would take so long. We'd have been quicker taking the train."

"If anyone would have let us. Frank was in a right panic when you told him we were travelling on our own."

Eliza tutted. "He should know better by now. We've travelled together before."

"Not while he's been my *gentleman friend*. He doesn't want me to come to any harm."

"And you won't. At least Archie understands. Sergeant Cooper will too, one day."

"I hope so."

Inspector Adams was outside the building as their carriage pulled up, and he wandered over to them as the coachman helped them down the steps.

"Good morning, ladies. I wasn't expecting Mrs Appleton."

Eliza rolled her eyes. "Good morning, Inspector. When did you ever see me travel alone?"

"I don't suppose I have." He checked the clock. "Shall we go in? I don't want this to take all morning. Do you have the list of questions?"

Eliza patted her handbag. "I do."

"May I have it? If you remember, I'll be the one doing the talking."

"Yes, of course." She stopped to find the piece of paper. "You won't mind if I ask a few questions of my own, will you? If the need arises..."

"Only when we've finished with each suspect."

"Suspect!"

"Mrs Thomson, may I remind you...?"

"All right, I'm sorry. Lead the way."

The long whitewashed hospital corridors were already full of waiting patients as the inspector followed the instructions he'd been given to Dr Dunlop's ward. Once they arrived, he barged through the door and sought the nurse in the black dress and white hat. "Good morning, madam. I presume you're Matron."

"I am indeed. And who, may I ask, are you?"

"Inspector Adams from New Scotland Yard. I'm looking for Dr Dunlop. Has he arrived for work yet?"

"Oh." The matron glanced at Eliza and Connie, who stood slightly behind him. "No, not yet. He should be here any minute if you'd like to wait."

Inspector Adams nodded. "We will, but before you go, has Dr Dunlop been on duty all this week?"

"He has. Every day except Monday."

"And has he been his usual self?"

Matron's eyes widened. "Yes. Why?"

"Just a routine question. Will you tell me when he arrives? I don't have all day."

"Yes, sir." Matron stepped back to her station, but stopped as the door opened and a young man with fair hair and a dark suit strode through. She hurried to him. "Dr Dunlop."

Their voices dropped, and after a few glances in their direction, Dr Dunlop joined them. "Inspector." He offered him a hand before he looked at Eliza. "Mrs Thomson, isn't it? Henry didn't say you were in London."

"No, he wouldn't. It was a last-minute decision, so he doesn't know. Does he work near here?"

"He's in surgery today." Dr Dunlop checked his pocket watch. "He's probably started already."

"Oh. He said he was on late shifts this week."

"He had the chance to change and jumped at it. Would you like me to tell him you were here?"

"There'll be no need for that." Inspector Adams indicated to a side room. "I'd like a word with you."

"Certainly." He led them into the office and closed the door. "What can I do for you?"

The inspector glanced at the paper Eliza had given him. "I believe you were at the fete in Moreton on Monday afternoon."

"Yes, that's right. What of it?"

"As you presumably know, a man was murdered, so we're

speaking to everyone who may have seen anything suspicious."

"There were dozens of people there. Why come all the way to London when you have your work cut out questioning the locals?"

"There are some attendees we suspect have more information than others."

"Like me, you mean?" He put a hand to his chest. "I was hardly at the fete ... except to indulge in the treats on Mrs Thomson's cake stall."

Eliza sensed Connie stiffen. "It was Mrs Appleton's stall. I was only helping out."

"Ah. Apologies. The cakes really were delicious."

Inspector Adams took a deep breath. "If I could bring you back to the murdered man. We understand he was in the Golden Eagle while you were in the snug, and then you met with him later by the river."

"I admit I saw a man while we were there, and by the river, but I didn't know who he was. Are you telling me he was the one who was murdered?"

Didn't Archie tell him? Eliza bit her lip as Inspector Adams responded.

"Don't insult my intelligence. You know very well who he was. Was your meeting prearranged so you could talk where you wouldn't be overheard?"

Dr Dunlop's forehead creased. "Why would I do that? If you must know, I believe he followed me..."

"What makes you think that?"

"Just a feeling." He glanced into the ward. "I saw him in the alehouse, as you said, then as soon as Henry nipped into the shop, he appeared, as if by magic."

"Did he say anything of interest?"

"Not really. He told me he'd put up the marquee and was waiting to take it down again."

"But I suspect you already knew that."

"Why...? What's going on?"

"We have a witness who overheard you talking. Apparently, you accused him of owing someone fifty pounds. Would you care to elaborate?"

Dr Dunlop's mouth opened and closed several times before any words came out. "It was nothing, really. Just a silly disagreement."

"Go on."

"Well ... once he told me he was part of the team who erected the marquee, I admit I realised who he was. He'd put up a similar contraption for my father earlier in the summer."

"And the fifty pounds?"

"Yes. He ... erm ... he'd broken a statue in the garden by climbing up it. Father was furious and sent a letter to the boss demanding money for the repair."

"Fifty pounds sounds rather excessive."

"It was a big statue."

"If he owed your father money, why would he follow you to the river? I'd have thought he'd have wanted to keep out of your way."

Dr Dunlop snorted. "You clearly didn't meet him. He liked nothing better than causing trouble..."

"And what trouble was he threatening you with?"

"It wasn't like that." Dr Dunlop let out a deep sigh. "He said he'd seen me in the alehouse and wanted me to pass a message to my father to the effect that he'd be suing us for the injuries he'd received when the statue fell, and that we wouldn't get a penny out of him or his boss."

Inspector Adams held his gaze. "It must be very convenient that he's no longer with us..."

Dr Dunlop's eyes suddenly widened. "You can't think I killed him? I'm a doctor, for goodness' sake. I wouldn't harm anyone."

"Can you tell me what happened next?"

"I told the gentleman he wouldn't be getting a penny from us and that if he sued us, we'd file a counterclaim against Mr Taylor. He was about to object when Henry reappeared and caused him to hurry away."

"Then what?"

Dr Dunlop rubbed a hand over his face. "Henry and I went for a walk along the river. We'd planned it before the altercation and decided to carry on. He wanted some advice and said it was the best place to avoid being overheard."

Eliza interrupted. "Did it have anything to do with the telegram he sent?"

"Telegram? I'm sorry, I know nothing of that."

"I thought that was why he went to the shop."

Dr Dunlop shook his head. "As far as I'm aware, he went for some sweets. He came back with some barley sugars."

"Oh. What did he want advice on, then?"

"That's for Henry to tell you, if he chooses to, but I can assure you, it has no bearing on your murder investigation. We strolled to Over Moreton, had a sit-down by the church, then walked back again. The fete was over by the time we reappeared and everyone was outside the marquee listening to an elderly lady convinced she'd found a dead body."

Eliza sighed. "She had."

"Ah, well then. I can't tell you anything about what happened, because I wasn't there."

"Can anyone confirm that?"

"Apart from Henry?" He flapped his arms by his sides. "I've no idea. We walked past a few people on the river bank, and there were several more in Over Moreton, if that's what you mean. I didn't know any of them."

"I don't suppose you would. Well, thank you for your honesty."

Inspector Adams closed his notebook. "Are we finished here, then?"

Eliza nodded and let the inspector out of the office first. Once he was halfway to the exit, she turned back to Dr Dunlop. "If you see Henry before the end of the day, will you ask him to join us for dinner at his grandfather's house? I'd like to talk to him."

CHAPTER TWENTY

Connie walked in silence beside Eliza as they followed the inspector up a flight of stairs, but as they set off down a slightly less congested corridor, she linked Eliza's arm.

"Do you expect Henry will come to the house tonight?"

"I doubt it, but I had to ask."

"Of course you did. I won't say a word to the inspector."

"Thank you. I'm just worried that he's hiding something."

"It can't be anything shocking. More than likely, he's met a young lady and wanted advice on how to approach her."

Eliza grimaced. "I've never known him to lack confidence before."

"Maybe she's special. Before I started walking out with Frank, I found it harder to talk to him than to any of the other men in the village. I suppose I didn't want to make a fool of myself."

"You could be right."

"And if I am, it may be why he doesn't want to mention her."

"Probably with good reason." Eliza groaned. "He's too young..."

"He's twenty-three. Older than you were when you met Dr Thomson. I was married by then."

"It still seems wrong..."

Inspector Adams was dodging patients at the entrance to another ward as they approached him. "I was beginning to think you'd got lost."

"I'm sorry. We were musing over what Dr Dunlop said."

"Did you come up with any more questions for Dr Cartwright while you did?"

"Not really, although I'd like to know what was on Henry's mind."

"That has little bearing on the murder."

"There's no harm in checking, though." Eliza held her breath as the inspector stared at her.

"Very well. We still need to speak to Henry, though, to confirm that he and Dr Dunlop were indeed out of the village. And why."

"He may be reluctant to tell me..."

"Then I'll interview him alone. He and his friend have a strong alibi, if it's true."

Connie nodded. "I wonder if either of his other friends took things into their own hands to help Dr Dunlop."

"What like?"

"I don't know. Perhaps they suggested he disappear while they had a word with Mr Hobbs."

Inspector Adams studied Connie. "That's a good thought. I'll ask while we're here."

.   .   .

Dr Cartwright was making his way around the ward when they arrived, but after Inspector Adams had spoken to the matron, she ushered them into an office and went to inform the doctor that his presence was required. They didn't have long to wait before he joined them.

"Inspector Adams? And Mrs Thomson?"

The inspector extended a hand to him. "Forgive the intrusion, but we need to ask you a few questions about the events of Monday afternoon."

"Monday? Oh, when we were in Moreton, you mean? Gosh. I hope you've not travelled all the way here just to speak to me. I doubt I'll be much help ... assuming you're here about the murder."

"We are, sir, but don't worry, we'll be asking your friends the same questions."

"Ah, good." His rosy cheeks were barely visible behind his dark beard and moustache. "How may I help?"

"Would you give us your precise whereabouts while the fete was ongoing?"

"Let me see. We met Henry in the snug of the Golden Eagle around midday and stayed there for two or three hours."

Inspector Adams nodded. "I believe there was a man sitting in the opposite corner who had a stream of visitors while you were there. Can you tell me anything about him?"

"Not really. He must have arrived after we were settled, and I had my back to him. Henry was the one who seemed most interested. I presumed he knew him..."

Eliza raised an eyebrow at Connie. "I wouldn't think so."

"Thank you, Mrs Thomson." Inspector Adams glared at her before he turned back to Dr Cartwright.

"I'm sorry about that. What made you think Dr Thomson knew him?"

"It was just a feeling I had when he kept watching him."

"And did you recognise the man?"

"Me? No. I'd never seen him before in my life."

"Very well." Inspector Adams checked his notes. "Did you notice him leave the snug?"

"I can't say I did, although he wasn't there when we left."

"And what time was that?"

Dr Cartwright shook his head. "I don't know for sure, other than it was before three o'clock. In fact, thinking about it, one of the other workmen was looking for him when we left. Henry told him the chap in question had gone, which didn't please him. Apparently, he'd arranged to meet him at three o'clock and was angry that the man had left when he'd made an effort to be early."

Inspector Adams scrawled in his book. "What happened after that?"

"We all headed to the marquee. Henry had told us we had to buy our own cakes if we wanted any more so the fete looked busier."

"And you walked there by the most direct route? Past the bowling club."

"I presume so."

Eliza interrupted. "Excuse me, Inspector, but before you go on, may I ask Dr Cartwright a question?" She continued as the inspector nodded. "Did you see anyone around the back of the marquee when you passed?"

"Not when we were going to the fete."

"But you did at some other time?"

"When we were walking back. There was an older man,

with grey hair, messing with the fence ... or at least, that's what it looked like. It was difficult to tell."

"Could you describe him to us?"

"Only that he wore a light-coloured jacket and a hat of a similar colour."

The inspector looked at Eliza. "Does that ring any bells?"

"It sounds like Mr Steel, but he runs the bowling club, so it wouldn't be a surprise if he was there. What time would it have been?"

"I couldn't say for sure, but it was after the body was found."

"That makes sense. Mr Royal told us that Mr Steel had planned to open for the evening. We should check with him, though."

"We will." Inspector Adams added the instruction to his notes. "Now, where were we?"

"Walking to the marquee..." Eliza smiled as the inspector grunted.

"Yes, thank you. So, Dr Cartwright, when you arrived at the marquee, did you go straight to the cake stall?"

"We did. We all bought our own selections, but as we were heading back outside, Henry and Toby, Dr Dunlop that is, said they were going to take a walk by the river. When we said we'd join them, they asked if we wouldn't mind staying behind as they had something to discuss."

The inspector's mouth was open to speak when Eliza interrupted.

"Do you have any idea what they wanted to talk about?"

"Not a clue. They were both tight-lipped about it, even when they came back."

Inspector Adams sighed. "So, when it was just the two of you, what did you and Mr Everett do to fill the time?"

"I nipped over to the shop for some sweets and then we played on the games."

"Didn't they finish before the prize-giving started?"

Dr Cartwright grinned. "They did in theory, but once the sergeant went inside the tent, we carried on."

"For how long?"

"Until they'd finished in the marquee. We had to put everything away quickly in case the sergeant caught us."

Inspector Adams bristled. "While you were outside, did you see anyone acting suspiciously?"

"I don't think so."

"Did you see anyone once the prize-giving started, or were you on your own?"

"It was just us and the marquee workers."

"So, you saw them? How many were there?"

"Two or three, depending on the time. We asked if they'd like a game, but they declined."

"Was the man who'd been in the alehouse there ... while you were on the games?"

Dr Cartwright's eyes narrowed. "Only briefly. He sidled up to the taller man, muttered something to him, then disappeared rather sharpish as soon as the older man noticed him. I assumed he fled to the Golden Eagle."

Or was he going to his death?

"The older man was Mr Bedford. Did he try to follow when the other man disappeared?"

"I can't say for certain, but I saw the taller one grab his arm as if he was trying to stop him."

"And Mr Bedford stayed where he was?"

"He did."

Eliza turned to Inspector Adams. "So, Mr Hobbs spoke to Mr Taylor, but he disappeared when Mr Bedford saw him. I'm not surprised, if Mr Bedford was still angry with him. Dr Cartwright, was the third man with them at that point?"

"No. He came later."

"What time was that?"

He shrugged. "At a guess, I'd say around twenty to four. Most of the guests had gone into the prize-giving long before he arrived."

"Was he agitated when you saw him?"

"He looked ready for a fight, if that's what you mean."

Eliza's heart was pounding. "Did he stay at the front of the marquee, or did he disappear again?"

Dr Cartwright glanced at the ceiling. "I don't remember him leaving."

"And you were there until Mrs Petty came out of the marquee to tell everyone about the body?"

He nodded. "We were."

"That's very helpful, thank you."

The inspector made another note. "Dr Cartwright, what time would you say Drs Dunlop and Thomson returned to the village green?"

"Shortly after the body was discovered. I saw them emerge from behind the surgery, and Mr Everett and I walked over to tell them what had happened."

"Did they seem surprised?"

"Toby did, Henry less so."

Eliza's mouth fell open. "He wasn't?"

"He said you seem to attract murder victims, so why would the village fete be any different?"

"Oh." Eliza's cheeks burned as the inspector studied her.

"Had the two of you had words?"

Not at that stage. "No, not at all. He's always aggrieved if he's not around when they happen."

"He should get a job in the police, then. Now, Dr Cartwright, is there anything else you'd like to add? Anyone at the fete acting suspiciously?"

"I don't think so. Once Henry and Toby rejoined us, we wandered back to the Golden Eagle and, except for Henry nipping home for dinner, we all stayed there for the rest of the evening."

Inspector Adams closed his notebook. "Thank you, sir. I'll let you get on, but before I do, could you point us in the direction of Mr Everett? We need to check that he didn't see anything you may have missed."

CHAPTER TWENTY-ONE

Eliza smiled at the housekeeper who opened the door of Mr Bell's large detached house in Richmond upon Thames.

"Good evening, Mrs Wood."

"Ladies." The woman stepped aside to let them in. "My, you've been busy."

Eliza grinned as she looked down at their bags. "I've only bought a dress with a hat and matching pair of shoes."

Connie followed her in. "And I only got a hat."

"Well, let me take them from you. Your father's waiting in the drawing room."

"Thank you."

Once they'd taken off their outdoor clothes, Eliza led the way to the large, but comfortable, room at the back of the house.

Mr Bell struggled to his feet. "Here you are. I was beginning to wonder what was keeping you."

"The fact you live an hour's drive from Harrods, for one."

"I'm afraid I can't do much about that. Have you had a good day?"

"We have, thank you ... with one exception, which I'll tell you about shortly."

"Did you meet Inspector Adams?"

"We did and spoke to all three of Henry's friends. They were very nice, but we didn't learn anything new about the murder."

"Did they at least confirm your suspicions?"

"They did. So, it wasn't a waste of time. We'd finished by midday so took a carriage into London for luncheon, and then did a spot of shopping. I couldn't go home empty-handed when I'd told Archie that was why we were coming."

"As if he'd believe a word of it. You wouldn't leave Moreton during a murder investigation without good reason."

Eliza grinned as he offered Connie a sherry. "You know me too well."

"So, how's Henry?"

"Ah, that was the setback. He wasn't available."

"Why not?" Mr Bell stopped as he was about to hand her a glass. "Have you two fallen out?"

"In a manner of speaking, but that's not why. His friend said he was in surgery, so we could hardly disturb him. We did send word that we were staying here, and I took the liberty of inviting him for dinner."

Mr Bell glanced at the clock. "He'd better get a move on, then. Cook said it would be ready for six."

Eliza sank into her chair and accepted her sherry. "I don't expect he'll arrive. We had words before he left Moreton, so he won't be in a hurry to see me."

"What about now?"

"He was being rather evasive about what he was up to around the time of the murder, and when I pushed him to be more precise, he left."

Mr Bell shook his head as he sat down. "Will you never learn?"

"I try, and I didn't think I was too harsh with him. He just seemed more sensitive than usual."

"Shall I invite him here and see if he'll talk to me? Once you go home. He's more likely to be cooperative if he's not irked."

"You could. I just wish he wouldn't act as if he has something to hide..."

"Maybe he does. A young lady, perhaps."

"Not you as well." Eliza looked between Connie and her father. "Do you both know something I don't?"

"No!" Connie's voice was shrill. "How would I possibly know if you didn't tell me? I was only guessing."

"As was I." Mr Bell studied her. "It had to happen sooner or later."

"I'd rather it was later." Eliza pouted as she put down her glass. "The thing is, if he has met someone, why hide it from me?"

"He may be worried that you won't like her and try to end the relationship."

"Of course I wouldn't."

"Really? I seem to remember you weren't happy when he wanted to walk out with Lady Alice."

Eliza gasped. "That was different." She paused as a wave of nausea washed over her. "You don't think he's seeing her again, do you? He was supposed to be going to Lowton Hall last weekend..."

Connie tutted. "To join a bachelor party for Lord Albert. Lady Alice was hardly likely to be there. She may even be married by now. It has been four years since her debutante ball."

Eliza gave a sigh of relief. "You're right. I'm being silly."

Mr Bell stood up. "If he's met someone, it could explain why he's reluctant to talk to you. Now, it's approaching six o'clock. I suggest we go through to the dining room and Henry can join us later, if he arrives."

It was almost noon the following day when Eliza and Connie arrived back in Moreton, and once Eliza had instructed the coachman where to leave her bags, she wandered through the surgery to Archie's office. He looked up from his place at his unkempt desk.

"You're here. I wasn't sure when to expect you."

"I said I'd be home for luncheon."

He checked his pocket watch. "That's still an hour away." He paused as he studied her. "Is everything all right?"

She sighed as she took the seat opposite. "It's Henry."

"Did you see him?"

"No, but that's the point. I invited him to have dinner with us last night, but he didn't turn up."

"It is a long way from Soho to Richmond."

"I'd hoped that being with Father would help." Eliza fidgeted with a pen nib that was lying on the desk. "Do you think he's met someone?"

"A young lady, you mean?"

She nodded. "Connie suggested that he may have done, and then Father did, too."

"It's possible, I suppose. It would also be normal if we were the last ones to find out. I didn't tell my parents about you until shortly before we became betrothed."

Eliza closed her eyes. "That's what I'm worried about. What if he's known her for months, but has put off telling us? When he was here on Monday, he walked to Over Moreton with his friend Dr Dunlop so he could ask his advice on something."

Archie cocked his head to one side. "How do you know that?"

She kept her head bowed as she fought a smile. "We bumped into Inspector Adams while we were in London."

"I knew it." Archie banged a hand on the table. "I thought it was out of character for you to disappear at a time like this."

"I did need a new dress..."

"Which could easily have waited. Did he have any news?"

"Not when we met him, but we accompanied him when he took statements from Henry's friends."

"What did they have to say?"

"Not a lot except to confirm that Henry and Dr Dunlop went for a walk to Over Moreton, so weren't in the village at the time of the murder."

"That's a relief, then, surely."

"It is, but I never expected Henry to be involved. I think I'd know if my son was a killer."

"I'd hope so, but what about his other two friends? Did they have alibis?"

"They did, and on all major points they pretty much agreed with each other. They were together for the whole time and always in the company of others, so it's unlikely they had anything to do with Mr Hobbs. Both said they'd never met him before."

"Did you find out whether Dr Dunlop knew him?"

"We did, and he did. He admitted they'd argued when they were by the river, but if we can confirm Dr Dunlop's alibi, and by implication, Henry's, there could be no way either of them are our murderers."

"So, you're no further on, even though you left me for two nights under false pretences."

"I'm sorry, I didn't want to mislead you, but I suspected you wouldn't like me *interfering*."

Archie grinned at her. "And you wonder why Henry won't talk to you."

Eliza and Archie were still at the dining table finishing luncheon when there was a knock on the door and Connie was shown in.

"Oh ... I expected you to be finished by now."

Eliza smiled at her. "We've been too busy talking. Take a seat and I'll get you a cup and saucer."

"There's no need. I've only just finished a cup of tea. I came around because Inspector Adams' carriage arrived about ten minutes ago. I thought we should hurry up."

"Oh, yes, we should. I'd like to see how Constable Jenkins got on while we were away, too."

"Constable Jenkins?" Connie stared at her.

"It's nothing." Eliza brushed some imaginary crumbs from the tablecloth. "I only suggested he could ask some questions himself when he was on his beat."

"Isn't that Sergeant Cooper's job?"

Eliza grimaced. "It is, but he's been very busy lately, and I didn't want Inspector Adams to criticise him for missing anyone."

Connie huffed. "I wish you'd mentioned it to Frank. The last thing he needs is to look foolish in front of the inspector."

"Of course he won't. Sergeant Cooper was with Inspector Adams all Wednesday afternoon, so there was no chance to speak to him alone. If there's any trouble, I'll apologise when the inspector leaves."

"Hmm."

Eliza's shoulders slumped. "And I'll apologise to you now. I'm sorry. I didn't mean to undermine him."

Connie nodded but kept her eyes on the table.

"Come along. Let's go and see Sergeant Cooper. I expect he'll be pleased to see you safe and sound."

"He will have been worried sick." Connie wiped the back of a finger over her eyes. "I shouldn't have left him."

Eliza patted her hand. "Don't upset yourself. He'll be fine."

"I hope so, but please don't say anything to make him look bad."

"Don't worry, I won't."

CHAPTER TWENTY-TWO

Inspector Adams was at the counter of the police station when Eliza and Connie arrived, but he didn't turn round or stop the tirade he was directing towards the sergeant and constable.

"What do you mean you've not spoken to Mr Pitt again? That was the most pressing thing I told you to do."

Constable Jenkins looked indignant. "I was going to pay him a visit, but the sarge told me not to."

"Because it required a more senior officer."

Inspector Adams glared at him. "And what, precisely, was the *more senior* officer doing all day?"

Sergeant Cooper's face turned crimson. "I went to Molesey to speak to the marquee men. We needed to check what time Mr Bedford arrived in Moreton on Monday afternoon."

"And that took all day!"

Eliza gave a delicate cough and stepped to the desk. "Good afternoon, Inspector."

He spun round and stared at her. "This isn't a good time, Mrs Thomson."

"No... we'll go..." She took a step backwards, but the inspector huffed.

"I'm sorry, I didn't mean to be rude, but this investigation is floundering..."

"I'll tell you what, why don't we all sit down and share what we learned yesterday? If we put our heads together, we may work out what to do next."

"Before we do, I want someone to speak to the Pitts to find out precisely what was going on with the delivery. Sergeant..."

"Yes, sir, right away. I'll get the invoice, shall I? That should be more use than the scrap of paper we got the other day." He glared at Constable Jenkins.

"At least I got something out of him..."

Eliza held up her hands. "Gentlemen, please. This isn't getting us anywhere. Why don't Mrs Appleton and I go to the shop with Sergeant Cooper while the inspector sorts himself out?"

"Good idea." Inspector Adams stormed into the office as Connie and Sergeant Cooper left by the front door, leaving Eliza with Constable Jenkins. She leaned over to him.

"If you spoke to anyone yesterday, I suggest you tell the inspector while we're out."

"Right you are. I've a few bits of interest..."

"Excellent. I'll speak to you later."

Connie was struggling to keep up with the sergeant when Eliza spotted them rounding the bend outside the church and she slowed her pace as Sergeant Cooper reached the shop and turned to utter a few words to Connie before disappearing inside. Once Connie was alone, she turned to look for Eliza.

"Is he all right?"

"No, he's not." Connie's cheeks were red. "We should never have come with him. He needs to show his authority."

"I'm sorry. I thought that being with you would have helped."

"After the way the inspector spoke to him? Being humiliated was bad enough, but in front of me!"

"In fairness, the inspector didn't know we were there."

"He shouldn't speak to people like that even if they're on their own."

"No, but I'm afraid that's how they operate in London."

"We're not in London. The sooner he goes back and leaves us alone, the better."

Eliza squeezed Connie's arm. "Come on, cheer up. Hopefully, Sergeant Cooper will get the information he needs, and all will be forgiven."

"I doubt he'll forget something like that so easily."

"No, well... Does he want us to follow him into the shop or wait here?"

"Wait. Hasn't he been embarrassed enough without needing us to help him?"

"All right. We'll let him tell us what Mr Pitt has to say."

The sun was warm as they stood out of sight of the window, and Eliza pointed to the bench outside the church. "Shall we sit down?"

Connie nodded. "He won't be able to miss us when he comes out. The poor thing. I hate seeing him like this."

"Once he's calmed down, he'll be glad you're here."

"I hope so."

They hadn't been there long when Mr Steel approached,

his distinctive beige jacket and hat highlighted by the sun. "Good afternoon, ladies."

Eliza managed a smile. "Good afternoon."

"I must say, I'm pleased I bumped into you. How are you getting on with this investigation? I've not seen much of the police to ask them these last few days."

Eliza sighed. "They've all been rather busy, but hopefully, they're making progress. In fact, there were a few questions they had for you. Would you mind if I put them to you now?"

"Not at all."

"Excellent." She reached into her bag and pulled out her notebook. "Let me see what they were. Ah yes. Mr Royal said he couldn't find you at the end of the afternoon to say farewell. Did you rush off?"

"I did, as it happens. Your husband may have told you I wasn't pleased when Mr Hewitt declared that the bowling club couldn't open on Monday. Eventually, we compromised, and he agreed to it opening at five o'clock. I needed to get back and make sure the place was ready."

"Do you usually attend to the outside when you open?"

"Not as a rule, but I'd painted some of the fence that morning, and wanted to check it was dry."

Eliza's brow creased. "Forgive me for saying, but wasn't that a strange time to paint, given the marquee was so close to the boundary?"

"It was *because* it was there that I had to do the repairs. The men had damaged some of the wood."

"That's annoying."

"It is. They'll be reimbursing me for the paint, I can tell you."

"So, you rushed to the club straight after the prize-giving

and inspected the fence on the way. Was that while the body was still there?"

"Oh, I couldn't tell you. I saw nothing suspicious, if that's what you mean."

"Was there anyone else showing any interest in the marquee at that time, possibly even tampering with it?"

He shook his head. "Not that I noticed."

"All right, thank you." She studied her notes as she chose her next words. "This may sound like a strange question, but the prize-giving obviously took place between half past three and four o'clock. Did you nip outside at any time during the presentations?"

"Not at all. How could I? My wife isn't a well woman, and she needed my help."

"That's what I thought, but we've had a report of a man who looked like you, around the back of the marquee while the prizes were being given out."

"Someone thinks they saw me?" Mr Steel's face paled. "Who? I was in the marquee..."

"Don't worry. The witness isn't overly familiar with the men of the village, so I'm sure it was a case of mistaken identity."

"You're sure?" Mr Steel's brow furrowed. "I can't think of anyone who looks like me. It must be someone from Over Moreton."

"The only person we came up with was Mr Pitt."

"Really?" Mr Steel pulled on the lapels of his jacket. "I suppose I should be flattered. He's younger than me, although he's slightly shorter, too."

"You both have similar hair colouring."

"So do many men in this part of the world. I'll ask around

to see if anyone can come up with any more names for my look-alike. If there are any suggestions, I'll let you know."

"Thank you, Mr Steel."

"Or, why don't you tell me the name of the witness and I'll go and get more details from them? I don't want rumours spreading about me."

"I'm sure they won't. Our lady is very discreet. Ah, we need to go..." Eliza stood up as Sergeant Cooper left the shop. "Good day to you."

They stepped away from the bench as Sergeant Cooper walked towards them, leaving Mr Steel gaping after them.

"How did you get on?" Connie looked up at him, expectantly, but he hesitated until Mr Steel turned to leave.

"Not very well. All he did was repeat what he'd told Jenkins: that he'd had a delivery of flour, shortly before four o'clock."

Eliza sighed. "Did you ask about him coming to play on the games at the fete?"

"Nobody told me to."

"I'm sorry, that was my fault. We just need to know why he didn't mention it when we asked him what he was doing that afternoon. We probably should find out..."

His shoulders rounded as he turned back to the shop. "Is that it?"

"I think so."

Connie watched him leave. "I don't suppose he'll want to take a walk this evening. He'll think I've gone right off him."

"Don't be silly."

"But I'm not. I know how important this job is to him, and he wants to do it well... He's even spoken of being an inspector one day."

"Really? That's good."

"Not if Inspector Adams doesn't think he's up to it. The way he looks now, I doubt he'll mention it again."

"Now might not be a good time, but that doesn't mean he won't ever get a promotion."

"I hope not. He had his heart set on it."

Oh dear.

The bells rang for half past two and Connie stood up and strolled towards the shop before stopping a little short. Sergeant Cooper spotted her as soon as he stepped out the door and gave her a brief smile. Eliza waited for them to rejoin her.

"Did he have much to say for himself?"

"Not really. He just said he'd felt left out with everyone else at the fete and decided that one game wouldn't do any harm given he could keep an eye on the shop while he was there. He said it was before the time you asked about, so he didn't think to mention it."

"I suppose it was. Did he have anything else to say?"

"No. He said he'd had a quiet time in the shop. There'd been a few visitors, Mrs Petty and young Dr Thomson among them, and Mrs Pitt had been there while he was dealing with the delivery."

Eliza took a deep breath. "That sounds comprehensive enough. Well done, Sergeant. Shall we go to the station? Hopefully, the inspector will be in a better mood when we arrive."

CHAPTER TWENTY-THREE

Constable Jenkins was at the counter when they arrived at the station, and he smiled as they walked in.

"The inspector's waiting for us."

"Us?" The sergeant glared at him. "You need to stay where you are."

"The inspector said we can manage if we leave the door open; we'll hear if anyone comes in. Besides, he'd value my input as well as yours."

Eliza walked between them. "Shall we go through while it's quiet?"

The two officers locked eyes until Constable Jenkins stepped back to let the ladies pass. Inspector Adams looked up as they joined him.

"You're here. Good." He didn't wait for them to sit down. "What did Pitt have to say?"

Sergeant Cooper retrieved his notebook. "He confirmed what he'd told Constable Jenkins, that he'd received a delivery from the flour mill some time before four o'clock."

"Did you get a receipt?"

"He doesn't have one."

"Curious." The inspector looked to Eliza. "Don't they do book-keeping around here?"

"Usually they do..."

"Very well. We'll need to follow up with the flour mill. Was there anything else?"

Sergeant Cooper stood up straight. "I asked about his visit to the games stall at the fete, and why he'd failed to mention it previously. He said he'd been feeling left out in the shop and had come over to the fete while he was quiet. He reckoned he could see the shop from where he was standing."

The inspector again looked to Eliza. "Is that right?"

"I would say so."

"Good. Is that it?"

Sergeant Cooper nodded. "Yes, sir."

"Right, now, what about this chap Bedford? You spoke to him yesterday..."

"Not quite. I went to Molesey to speak to him. But he wasn't there."

Inspector Adams dropped his pen. "You spent a whole day over there for nothing?"

"Not exactly, sir. Mr Taylor, the man in charge of the marquee company, hadn't seen him for a few days."

"He's run off?"

"It looks like it."

Inspector Adams glared at him. "Why didn't you say!"

"I..."

"Never mind. Is the other chap still around? What's his name? Gilbert?"

"Yes, sir. He was with Mr Taylor. He hadn't seen Mr Bedford either."

"Did they have any idea where he might be?"

"No, sir."

"Did you get an address for him? I'll send a request for someone locally to look out for him."

Eliza breathed a sigh of relief when Sergeant Cooper produced a piece of paper and handed it to the inspector. "We called at the house yesterday, but there was no answer."

"Good. Well done, Sergeant. Constable Jenkins, what have you been up to?"

"I've been talking to the villagers, sir, asking if they saw anything out of the ordinary."

Sergeant Cooper's mouth fell open, but the inspector ignored him.

"Did they?"

"The majority didn't. Most of them arrived across the village green and either stayed at the front of the marquee or were inside. There were one or two who saw something of interest, though..."

"Go on."

"I started by knocking on the doors of the houses just further down from the alehouse. The residents there have a good view of the area of interest ... or they would if they bothered to look out of the window. Unfortunately, half of them didn't."

"Get on with it, man."

"Yes, sir. The first house belonged to Mrs King. I remember her arriving at the fete, probably because I always feel rather sorry for her, with her being on her own and all that... Anyway, I asked if she'd noticed any comings and goings at the back of the marquee, and she had. She noticed Mr Hewitt examining what we believe was the damaged area, and then she saw me escort Mr Taylor and Mr Hobbs to fix the problem."

"We're aware of all that."

"But there's more. Shortly after we'd all left, she saw another man wearing a dark coat and hat. He approached the same area from the other side of the green."

"By Jove! Well done, Constable. Did she get a good look at him?"

The constable's chest deflated. "No. Apparently, he crouched down, and he kept the brim of his hat over his face."

Eliza turned to Connie. "I don't know how he managed that with all those ropes."

"I said that myself." Constable Jenkins seemed rather pleased with himself. "Sadly, Mrs King couldn't pass any comment because she'd not been that way herself."

"Did she think this man may have removed the tent peg?"

"She couldn't see, with it being so low down, but he appeared to be rummaging on the ground for something."

Inspector Adams looked up from his notes. "How long did he stay?"

"Not long, and once he finished what he was doing, he retraced his steps and disappeared the way he came."

"So, he could have sabotaged the marquee. I don't suppose any of you could hazard a guess who this man is?"

Eliza huffed. "Not from such a vague description. We could do with finding more people who saw him."

Constable Jenkins grinned. "I already have. Mrs King's next-door neighbour saw someone matching the same description, a couple of hours later."

Eliza's head shot up. "Shortly before the murder took place."

"Apparently, although she'd only nipped into the front room to open a window. As soon as she'd done that, she returned to the kitchen."

"So, she didn't see what he was up to."

"There'd been so many people milling around, she wasn't paying much attention."

"We need to find this man as our top priority." Inspector Adams put a large circle around his notes. "The chances are, he's our killer."

Connie caught Eliza's arm. "Do you remember when we spoke to Mrs Hartley? She said there was someone at the back of the marquee when she was on her way home."

"Yes! She thought it was Mr Steel, but he was helping with the prizes at that point, so we wondered if it was Mr Pitt."

"It would make sense if it was." Sergeant Cooper carried on as everyone stared at him. "He always wears a dark suit under his grocer's coat."

Inspector Adams grunted. "Is there a man in the village who doesn't own a dark jacket and hat?"

"No, but..."

Eliza cut across the sergeant as she turned to Connie. "I can't believe we didn't ask Mrs Hartley what the man was wearing when she saw him. Mr Steel always has that light-coloured jacket on in the summer. He'd have been instantly identifiable."

Constable Jenkins nodded. "He was wearing it on Monday."

"He was. Which brings us back to Mr Pitt." Eliza paused. "We need another word with him. His story never did make sense."

Inspector Adams tapped the end of his pen against his teeth. "It all sounds very plausible, but remind me of his motive."

Eliza's shoulders sagged. "We've yet to establish that."

"Do we have any reason to believe he knew Mr Hobbs before Monday?"

"No." *How did I miss something so basic?* "I fear we got a little excited about him going missing from the shop at the same time as the murder." *And I was relieved that he'd seen Henry.*

"We'll need to follow up with him."

"Let me do that." Eliza stood up. "I can't believe I missed it."

"If you must, but take Constable Jenkins with you. Sergeant, you can go to the flour mill to check that they made a delivery on a bank holiday."

"Yes, sir. It will be Monday now, though. I doubt they'll be open on a Saturday afternoon ... or tomorrow."

The inspector cursed under his breath. "All right. I suggest we spend the next day and a half going over our notes and reconvene on Monday once we've answered these questions." He checked his pocket watch. "There's no point me hanging around here. I'll go to London now and be back in time for our meeting. Midday sharp."

The two police officers stood up as the inspector left, but Sergeant Cooper hissed as the front door closed behind him.

"And good riddance. He's like a bear with a sore head."

Constable Jenkins grinned. "He was fine with me."

Eliza put an arm between them. "That's enough. We need to put any squabbles to one side and have the information ready for him on Monday morning. Maybe he has other problems we don't know about."

"I wish he'd leave them in London."

"He should, but..." Eliza looked at Constable Jenkins "... shall we pay Mr Pitt a visit now? Get it over with."

"I'm ready when you are." Constable Jenkins beamed at her but Connie hesitated.

"Would you mind if I don't join you? I'm getting a headache..."

"That's not like you."

Concern crossed the sergeant's face. "Are you all right? Would you like me to escort you home?"

"You can't leave the station unattended." Constable Jenkins glared at him. "I've been told to assist Mrs Thomson, so I can't stay..."

"It's all right, Constable." Connie drew a hand across her forehead. "Perhaps I could sit here until you get back. Would you mind, Sergeant?"

"N-no, not at all. I'll leave the front door open so we don't invite any tittle-tattle."

"Good idea." Eliza stood up. "Shall we go, Constable?"

Constable Jenkins gave Sergeant Cooper a backward glance as they left. "Are you sure we should leave the two of them alone?"

Eliza ushered him forward.. "Quite sure. Now, how do we tackle Mr Pitt? Why don't I start the questioning and you chip in as and when?"

"Right you are."

. . .

Mr Pitt was on his own in the shop when they arrived, but his smile faltered when Constable Jenkins followed Eliza through the door.

"N-no Mrs Appleton today?"

"No. She has a headache, so she's sitting quietly until it passes."

"That's annoying. Send her my regards..." He studied Constable Jenkins. "Are the two of you together?"

"We are. We're here to ask you more questions about the murder."

"I've just told Sergeant Cooper everything I know..."

"I'll be the judge of that..." Constable Jenkins stepped up to the counter, but his stance relaxed as Eliza glared at him.

"I'm sorry, Mr Pitt. We have a couple more questions. Did you, by any chance, know the dead man, Mr Hobbs?"

Mr Pitt shook his head. "I never laid eyes on him."

"Did any of the men erecting the marquee come into the shop?"

"No, not one of them. You'd think they would, but they didn't spend a thing. The skinflints."

Constable Jenkins moved to the counter. "So, you'd no reason to want him dead?"

"Don't talk nonsense. Why on earth would I?"

"Well ... you left the shop at precisely the right time to attack him. Why else would you do that?"

"Are you suggesting I'm a murderer, Constable?"

Eliza's eyes were fixed on Constable Jenkins. "No, he's not. Are you?" She kept her eyes fixed on him until he replied.

"No, but..."

Eliza held up a hand to stop him. "We needed to

eliminate you from our enquiries, and it was important to find out if you were acquainted with the dead man."

"You should have been able to do that already. I've told you I was meeting a delivery driver."

"You did, but it's strange he was working on a bank holiday…" Eliza let her sentence hang as Mr Pitt's face reddened.

"I-I don't know why he was. They may have been short of drivers and so they were making up for lost time. My usual driver was ill last week."

Eliza nodded. "It must be that, then. Thank you, Mr Pitt."

Constable Jenkins chased after her as they left the shop. "Is that it? We should have got a confession out of him…"

Eliza counted to three. "Patience, Constable. Sergeant Cooper hasn't been to the flour mill yet, so we don't have enough evidence to go in all guns blazing. We need to keep his trust so he continues to talk to us."

"Oh. Is that what you always do?"

"I try."

"Sergeant Cooper never does that."

Eliza smiled. "I'm hoping you'll realise that there's more than one way to interview someone. If you learn from all those around you, it will serve you better in the long run."

"If you say so … but can I arrest Mr Pitt when the time comes?"

"*If* the time comes, you'll need to arrange that with Sergeant Cooper not me."

"I'm not asking him. He'll want to take the glory himself when I've done most of the work."

Eliza grimaced. "Inspector Adams should do it, then. It's not worth falling out over."

CHAPTER TWENTY-FOUR

The following morning, as the church service ended, Eliza stood at the end of the pew waiting for those who'd been seated nearer the front to file past.

"Good morning, Mr Steel. Mrs Steel."

Mr Steel flashed her a broad smile. "Good morning, Mrs Thomson. Please, after you." He stepped back to let her and Connie into the aisle before joining Archie behind them. "Dr Thomson, I was hoping to see you. I wonder if you could come over to the house tomorrow to check on Mrs Steel. She seems as breathless as ever, even though I make sure she takes her medicine regularly."

Archie nodded. "I can manage that. Digitalis is a difficult drug to get the dose right, so we may need to adjust it."

Eliza turned to them. "Let me know what you need, and I'll drop it off for you."

Mrs Steel sighed. "That's very generous. I know I should come to the surgery myself, but walking here this morning was such a challenge, I fear I'll be in bed for the rest of the day."

"Oh dear. We can't have that." Eliza continued to walk with her. "You should have said something at the fete, if it was too much for you."

"I didn't mind. It was worth it to see all those smiling faces."

"You're right. It was a lovely afternoon. It was just a shame it was spoiled at the end. I don't suppose you noticed anything that might be relevant to the murder investigation?"

Mrs Steel shook her head. "I'm afraid I didn't."

"Neither of us did." Mr Steel joined them. "I've already told Sergeant Cooper what I saw, and Mrs Steel was with me for the whole time."

"Oh, I didn't realise."

Mrs Steel glanced up at him. "It wasn't quite like that, dear. We walked to the marquee together, but once you'd found me a chair, you went outside to talk to Mr Royal."

"But you were inside and not on your own for long before we handed out the prizes together."

"We did, but we should still be accurate."

Eliza paused as they reached the church door. Once she'd shaken hands with the vicar, she continued talking to Mrs Steel. "Did you notice Mr Hewitt examining the marquee by any chance? The area behind the flower displays."

"I can't say I did. I saw him several times over the afternoon, as you'd expect, but my chair was facing the entrance and with having rather stiff shoulders, I didn't turn around."

"That's a shame."

"You might be as well asking Mrs Royal. I was talking to her while our husbands were otherwise engaged, and she was looking towards the flower displays."

"Thank you, Mrs Steel. I'll follow up with her."

The walk to the path that cut across the village green was slower than Eliza expected as Mrs Steel continually paused for breath, but eventually, Mr Steel bid Archie farewell and took his wife's arm.

"Come on, let's get you home."

Mrs Steel waved to Eliza and Connie. "It was nice to talk to you. I'm sorry I couldn't be any more help."

"Not at all, you can only tell us what you saw." Eliza was about to leave but stopped and turned back to them. "Actually, before you go, may I ask who walked you home when you left the fete?"

"My husband. Why?"

"Mr Steel told us he hurried off to the bowling club as soon as the prize-giving had finished."

"I did. I went back for her." Mr Steel looked around his wife to stare at Eliza. "I knew she couldn't hurry, so I told her I'd be as quick as possible."

Eliza cocked her head to one side. "What time do you think you got back?"

He shrugged. "Ten, fifteen minutes after I left..."

"So, you weren't in the marquee when Mrs Petty discovered the body?"

"No. I thought I'd told you."

Eliza's cheeks flushed. "Yes, you did, but I wanted to check, given you said you'd been with your wife for the whole afternoon."

"I was with her for the time you consider the murder took place."

"Ah, I see." Eliza stepped away from the path to let them pass. "Have a good afternoon."

Eliza had no sooner turned towards the surgery than Archie caught her arm.

"What was that all about? It was as if you were accusing him of being our killer."

"Don't be silly. Some of his story didn't add up, and I wanted to check. That's all."

"Did you need to be so harsh? I've got to spend the afternoon with him."

She sighed. "I didn't mean to be. Will you apologise for me?"

"If he's still speaking to me."

"Of course he will be. He was just talking to you about taking over at the club. Again. He seems to have a bee in his bonnet about it."

"He can't think of anyone else suited to the job."

"If he's so concerned, he should carry on himself."

"You've seen his wife. He's going to need to spend more time with her."

"He should take her to the club with him."

Archie tutted. "You know it's men only."

"Until you take over. Have you told him you'll be allowing ladies in if you're in charge? There should be a benefit to all this extra work."

"I'll be doing no such thing. It won't even be my decision. Changes need to go to committee, and there are not many men who'd be happy for their wives to accompany them."

"They never complain when we come to cheer you on, or they want us to make afternoon tea."

"That's different."

"No, it's not. Either we should be allowed full access or none at all." She grinned at him. "We should withhold our labour. See how the committee like making their own sandwiches and scones."

Archie sighed. "Don't go getting ideas..."

"I'm only saying. Anyway, let's not argue. Connie's joining us for Sunday luncheon, so we need to be on our best behaviour."

"Aren't we always?" Archie looked across at Connie. "You've been quiet today."

"I'm sorry, I'm just tired. I've not been sleeping very well."

"Would you like me to give you something to help?"

She shook her head. "I'll be fine. I'm just worried about Sergeant Cooper."

"Is he all right?"

"It's nothing that Inspector Adams staying in London wouldn't solve."

Eliza looked at her husband. "The inspector's rather short-tempered at the moment, and he's taking it out on Sergeant Cooper."

"That's not like him. Do you know what's wrong?"

"No, he's not very talkative. Perhaps when he's here tomorrow, you could invite him to the alehouse. He may talk to you."

Archie laughed. "You'd better give me a list of questions."

"Frank's not even done anything wrong." Connie's voice shook as Archie held open the front door for them. "He's trying his best..."

Archie grimaced at Eliza. "Why don't you both go and take a seat in the drawing room, and I'll ask Iris to pour us all a sherry?"

"Don't you want me to speak to her?"

"There's no need. I'm going to the office to check Mrs

Steel's medication. She was worse than I expected, and I don't know why."

"All right, but be quick. Dinner will be ready soon."

Once they got to the drawing room, Connie sighed and flopped onto the nearest settee.

"Oh dear. That doesn't sound good." Eliza took the seat beside her.

"Frank was so down last night. I've never seen him like that before."

"Is it all to do with Inspector Adams, or is he angry with Constable Jenkins, too?"

"I'd say it's both. I mean, Constable Jenkins ... he's a constable. He should take his orders from his sergeant, not go off and do his own thing."

"Don't you think Constable Jenkins' initiative will reflect well on Sergeant Cooper in the long run? Especially if it helps to solve the case."

"How can it look good? It should be Frank taking the praise."

"But Jenkins must have learned what he knows from Sergeant Cooper. That should be something to be proud of."

Connie shook her head. "He won't see it like that."

"Then talk to him..." Eliza paused as Iris joined them. "Ah, Iris. Have you come to pour the sherry?"

"Yes, madam."

"Splendid. We won't wait for Dr Thomson."

Archie appeared at the door as she spoke. "You don't need to. I found what I needed on the top of my desk."

"So, all that disorganisation works, then."

He laughed. "Clearly."

Eliza accepted a glass of sherry and waited for Connie and Archie to get theirs. "Thank you, Iris. We should be ready in about ten minutes."

"Yes, madam."

Once they were alone, she turned to Archie. "One more question before luncheon. Do you remember when you arrived at the fete and I asked where you'd got to? You told me you were talking to Mr Steel."

"You're not still going on about that."

Eliza tutted. "I only want to know if his wife was with him."

"Not then, but he could have gone back to the house for her when I left him. Being at the fete for three hours may have been too much for her."

"I suppose so. I just wanted to check."

"Maybe you did, but that's enough. You're barking up the wrong tree. Mr Steel wouldn't harm anyone."

CHAPTER TWENTY-FIVE

E liza was in the dispensary the following morning when Archie strode through the door and headed to the counter.

"Where's the digitalis?"

"Here. Why?"

"I may as well go over to the Steels' now, while we're quiet. I'll take some more tablets in case she needs them."

"What if more patients turn up? You're not due to finish for another half an hour."

"It won't be urgent if they're only arriving now."

Eliza studied him. "That's not like you."

"I want to check on Mrs Steel. I'm concerned about her after the way she was yesterday. She used to go everywhere with Mr Steel, except the bowling club, obviously, but now it's as if she's housebound."

"She wasn't showing any signs of being overdosed with digitalis..."

Archie rolled his eyes. "And why would she be?"

"I'm only saying."

"Well, don't. You'd make a problem in an empty room if you could." Archie paused as a police carriage drove past the window. "It looks like Inspector Adams has arrived."

"I'd better get a move on, then. He wants to meet again at midday to see if we've come up with anything since Saturday."

"Is that why you were interrogating Mr Steel?"

"After the way the inspector was last week, I wanted to make sure we have answers to all his questions. I hope Sergeant Cooper's been to the flour mill this morning."

"Why would he go there?"

"To find out why they were making deliveries on a bank holiday, and to see if the driver can confirm Mr Pitt's alibi."

"Ah, well, I hope he's been too, if it puts a smile back on Mrs Appleton's face."

Eliza grimaced. "You and me both."

The inspector was in the office with Constable Jenkins when Eliza and Connie arrived at the station, and he grunted as he looked up. "Is there any sign of Sergeant Cooper out there?"

Connie's face paled. "No, why?"

Jenkins spoke. "He went out at about ten o'clock, but I've not seen him since."

"Oh goodness..."

Eliza put a hand on her arm. "I'm sure there's a perfectly reasonable explanation."

Inspector Adams turned back to his notes. "There'd better be. I don't have all day."

Eliza took a seat and looked across the table to Constable

Jenkins. "Why don't you update the inspector about our meeting with Mr Pitt?"

He beamed at her. "I already have."

"Ah."

"Which means the disappearance of Sergeant Cooper was completely unnecessary." Inspector Adams scowled at her. "Why didn't you tell him he needn't go?"

"We still need to check Mr Pitt's alibi."

"Not if he'd never met Mr Hobbs and has no motive to want him dead." The inspector stared at the constable. "Don't you two ever talk to each other?"

"I didn't want to upset the sarge…"

"Upset him! This is a murder investigation, not a playground tiff. What the…?" The inspector jumped to his feet and dived towards the counter as the front door clattered and Sergeant Cooper's voice echoed around the station.

"Get in there and stay there."

"What's going on?" Inspector Adams stared at Sergeant Cooper as he pushed Mr Pitt into the cell next to the office and slammed the door shut.

"Fraud. That's what. And more besides, I shouldn't wonder."

"I saved a few bob on flour … that doesn't make me a murderer…"

Mr Pitt's shouts faded into the background as the inspector pushed Sergeant Cooper into the office and slammed the door.

"What the devil's going on?"

Sergeant Cooper's face coloured when he noticed Connie, and he straightened his jacket. "I called at the flour mill and the owner told me they were shut last Monday and made no deliveries."

Connie gave a weak smile. "So, Mr Pitt's alibi was a lie?"

"It was, so I drove straight to the shop to confront the crook." He pointed through the wall to the cell. "It turns out that he knew the name of the delivery driver all along, a Mr Cox, and told me to check his alibi directly with him. He said that if Mr Cox had been up to no good, then he, Mr Pitt, knew nothing of it."

Inspector Adams stared at him. "Did you find this driver?"

"Eventually. I had to go back to the mill to get his details and find out where he was delivering. It was like a game of cat and mouse."

"So ... what did he say?"

"He admitted he'd loaded several spare bags of flour onto the carriage on Saturday afternoon, ready to deliver on Monday ... without the owner knowing."

Inspector Adams grunted. "Presumably, the owner wouldn't get the money, either."

"No. He'd arranged it with Mr Pitt that he'd get a twenty-five percent discount if he accepted the delivery on Monday."

"So, why's Mr Pitt in the cell, rather than this Mr Cox?"

Sergeant Cooper stared at the floor. "Because Mr Pitt is also a murder suspect, and he lied about his alibi."

"Did Mr Cox not arrive when he said he did?"

"He did ... but..."

"So, he's had his alibi confirmed."

"But they were up to no good..."

Inspector Adams gritted his teeth. "I admire your

enthusiasm, Sergeant, but I hope you haven't arrested Mr Pitt for the murder of Mr Hobbs."

The sergeant mumbled something under his breath.

"Speak up, man."

"I didn't officially arrest him."

"I'm glad to hear it. You can go out there and release Mr Pitt with a warning. Once we've finished here, try arresting Mr Cox instead. He seems to be the troublemaker here."

"Yes, sir."

"Constable, you seem to be managing slightly better. I'm putting you in charge of liaising with the police in Molesey. Find out whether they've found Mr Bedford yet."

Connie stamped her foot. "No!"

"I beg your pardon?"

There were tears in her eyes as the inspector glared at her. "Sergeant Cooper's done a good job of finding out what Mr Pitt was up to..."

Sergeant Cooper's cheeks reddened. "That's enough..."

"No, it's not. The inspector's treated you like a fool this last week, and I won't stand by and watch when you've been so helpful."

"Mrs Appleton!" The inspector's face was crimson as he looked at Eliza. "Take your companion home and don't bring her back. It would appear this investigation is getting too much for her."

Connie put her head down and reached for her handkerchief as Eliza nodded.

"I've nothing else to report at the moment, but I'll keep my eyes open. Will you be staying in Moreton for the week?"

"I hope not. I want this case settled within the week. I've other things to concentrate on."

"Very well. I'll see what I can do. If you want any time off tonight, Dr Thomson will be in the alehouse."

"I'll bear that in mind."

Eliza held the door for Connie, and they walked in silence until they'd passed the shop. Finally, Connie lifted her head.

"I'm sorry. I didn't mean to get us thrown out."

"Don't upset yourself. You were only trying to protect Sergeant Cooper."

"I've made it worse, though ... and he didn't even stick up for me."

"I don't think he dared, the mood Inspector Adams was in."

Connie put her hands to her face. "I feel such a fool."

"You must really love Sergeant Cooper."

"Love?"

"Don't you?"

"I like him ... a lot."

"Are you sure that's all it is?" When Connie didn't answer, Eliza continued. "There's no shame in it, you know. I've no doubt he feels the same way about you."

"After that outburst? I imagine he never wants to see me again."

"Don't be silly. It will have shown him how much you care for him. Men like that. I suggest you go home, wash your face and smarten yourself up. I've a feeling he'll come calling as soon as he can get away from the station."

"He won't. He'll be too embarrassed after the way the inspector spoke to him."

Eliza walked past the surgery until they reached Connie's front gate. "Don't be so sure. Now, do as you're told. I'll be around later, and we can go for a walk to pass the time."

. . .

Archie was still in his office when Eliza got home, and he frowned as she joined him.

"That was quicker than I expected."

"Things didn't quite go to plan. Sergeant Cooper found out that Mr Pitt was buying flour illegally and leapt to the conclusion that he was guilty of murder and arrested him."

"Ye gods." Archie put down his pen. "I'd have thought that would have taken longer to sort out..."

"It will, but Connie caused a scene when the inspector lost his temper, and I had to bring her home."

"Is she all right?"

"Not really. I tried to cheer her up by telling her Sergeant Cooper would visit as soon as he could, but she didn't believe me."

"Do you think he will or were you just saying that?"

"He will ... and if he hasn't called by the time I see her this afternoon, I'll go to the station and tell him to get round there."

Archie laughed. "Normally, I'd try to stop you, but maybe it would be for the best."

"Why Sergeant Cooper hasn't proposed marriage to her yet, I don't know. What more does a man need?"

"Don't you go telling him. It should be up to him."

"A little nudge..."

"No! He's a grown man."

"All right. If you say so." Eliza took the seat usually occupied by the patients. "The inspector gave the impression he has other things on his mind, which is why he's in such a bad mood. I told him you'd be in the Golden Eagle tonight if he'd like a break."

"So I can be the brunt of his temper?"

"So you can find out what's troubling him. How did you get on with Mrs Steel? Did you sort her out?"

"Yes, it was strange, though. I'd prescribed one tablet four times a day, but Mr Steel swore blind that I'd only told him one tablet a day to be taken at night."

Eliza's forehead creased. "Why would he think that? Do they have many medicines between them and he's getting confused?"

"They have a few, but none of the others are taken once a day. If she was only taking one at night, it's no surprise she had no energy during the day. Anyway, I gave them both instructions this time, so hopefully, she'll improve quickly."

"I hope so. I'll pay her a visit later in the week and see how she is."

CHAPTER TWENTY-SIX

Eliza glanced at the clock on the mantlepiece as it chimed for two o'clock. *No sign of Connie. Does that mean Sergeant Cooper's with her?* She emptied her cup and placed it on its saucer as Archie followed suit.

"I should go and check if Connie's all right, but I don't want to disturb her if Sergeant Cooper's arrived and they're having a heart-to-heart conversation."

"Can't you look out the window and see if they're sitting outside? That's what you usually do."

"I will." Eliza stood up and walked around the table before she pressed her face against the glass and looked to the right-hand side. "He's there. They look very serious, too. I wonder when he arrived."

"You should have been paying more attention."

"I know, but I was going over my notes again and got carried away."

"Why were your notes so important all of a sudden?"

"Mr Pitt was our key suspect, but now we know he's

innocent ... of murder, at least ... we need to think about things differently."

"Have you come up with much?"

Eliza crossed back to the table and closed her notebook. "No. Absolutely nothing. I'll go and ask Sergeant Cooper if they discussed anything else after we'd left the station."

"I thought you didn't want to disturb them."

"I don't, but this is rather important. I'll give them five more minutes and then go around. Sergeant Cooper will thank me if it gets Inspector Adams off his back."

Connie's face told Eliza all she needed to know when she arrived at the front gate to the small cottage next door.

"That's a welcome smile."

Sergeant Cooper hadn't seen her arrive and stood up as she spoke. "Mrs Thomson."

"Oh, sit down, Sergeant. I was hoping you'd come to cheer her up."

"I couldn't leave her upset."

"But what about you? How were you with Inspector Adams after we left?"

The sergeant gave a small chuckle. "He actually apologised and said he had other things on his mind."

"I suspected as much. Did you come up with any ideas on what to do next?"

"We took a full statement from Mr Pitt, and he admitted he'd only come over to the games stalls so that people would notice him. That was why he threw the sticks so badly. He wanted to be seen so that no one would suspect he was up to no good."

"And we're confident he was with this Mr Cox from twenty to four until five to?"

"We are."

"What did he do after that? He may still have been able to get to the marquee in time for the bells at four o'clock."

"He said he was busy putting the flour away before Mrs Pitt came home and found it. She'd have killed him if she'd known."

Eliza chuckled. "I don't doubt it. Can Mrs Pitt confirm there were no unexpected supplies of flour when she got home?"

"Correct. She knew nothing about the delivery until we started our investigations."

"So, he might not be our murderer, but the owner of the flour mill should be happy that Mr Cox has been found out."

"He doesn't know about it yet. Inspector Adams asked me to go to Over Moreton and tell him, given it was me who uncovered the fraud. I've to ask if he wants to press charges, too."

"I'm sure he will. Are you going there now?"

"I am, but I'd hoped the two of you might accompany me. There are people in Over Moreton we've not spoken to yet, who may be able to help. Could we split up and see what we can find out?"

Seeing Connie's eyes brighten, Eliza nodded. "We'd be delighted to."

The journey to Over Moreton only took ten minutes in the carriage, and Sergeant Cooper found the flour mill at the far side, beyond Mr Royal's premises.

Eliza studied the surrounding fields. "I don't think I've been to this part of the village before."

"Aren't we near the Manor? Lord Harrington-Smyth's estate." Connie peered into the distance on her left.

"I think we are, now you mention it. Slightly more to the west, I would say." She looked at Sergeant Cooper. "Has anyone spoken to Lord or Lady Harrington-Smyth since the fete? They were in the marquee at the presumed time of death, so they may have seen something."

The sergeant shook his head. "None of us dared…"

"They can be formidable, but they're not above the law. Could we pop over to speak to them once we've finished here? I've met them several times, so I can make the introductions, if that's necessary."

"Hopefully, it won't be, with the uniform and all, but it may help."

"We can cross that bridge when we get to it. Would you like us to wait here while you go into the mill?"

He looked unsure as he nodded. "If you don't mind. I'll be as quick as I can."

Eliza watched him disappear through the door of the building before she turned to Connie. "You seem happier."

"You were right. He said he hated to see me upset and came round as soon as he could."

"So, you've sorted things out?"

"We have. He's picking me up at six o'clock tonight and we're going to take a long walk."

"I'm glad." Eliza waved a hand in front of her face. "It's rather stuffy in here. Should we climb down to get some air?"

"Are the steps lowered?"

Eliza tentatively opened the door. "They are. Come on,

there's a bench a little further up the lane. Sergeant Cooper should see us before he realises we're not in the carriage."

The afternoon sun was warm on their backs, and once they'd settled in their seats, Eliza gave Connie a sideways glance. "Was Sergeant Cooper cross about you shouting at the inspector?"

"No. He said he was honoured. He didn't know I cared so much."

"There we are, what did I tell you?"

"I still feel a fool. Inspector Adams won't want me involved any more."

"That doesn't matter. If it's given Sergeant Cooper the kick he needs..."

"What do you mean?"

"Only that ... oh, he's here now." Eliza waved as Sergeant Cooper strode towards them. He grinned as he approached.

"You got too warm inside, did you?"

"Just a little. How did you get on?"

"The manager was furious, as you can imagine, but he'd suspected Mr Cox was up to something and had already told him not to bother coming into work again."

"Does he want to press charges?"

"He would, but given the man no longer has a job, the chances are he'll have left Over Moreton, so we're unlikely to find him."

Eliza rolled her eyes. "That's all we need, a second man to go missing. There isn't a chance he's our killer?"

"Not according to Mr Pitt. He said he'd watched him leave the village, because he didn't want the carriage to be around when Mrs Pitt got home."

"That's a relief. It should mean that we don't need to go on a wild goose chase looking for him. We need this murder investigation finished first."

"I wouldn't argue with that. Now, let me help you into the carriage, and I'll take us to the Manor to see His Lordship."

CHAPTER TWENTY-SEVEN

A butler in a dark morning suit and bow tie on a white shirt opened the front door of the Manor as their carriage pulled up in the centre of the large turning circle at the top of the driveway. Eliza didn't recognise him from that last time she'd visited, and he immediately greeted Sergeant Cooper.

"Sergeant." He bowed his head. "Is there something wrong?"

"Not as such, sir. We're investigating the murder at the Moreton fete on holiday Monday. Might Lord or Lady Harrington-Smyth be available?"

"You can't think His Lordship would do such a thing?"

"Not at all, but they were in the marquee for most of the afternoon, so we'd like to ask if they saw anything."

The butler nodded. "Very well. Follow me and I'll tell them you're here." He led them to the drawing room at the front of the house before he disappeared. The expansive room had large floor-to-ceiling windows on two sides overlooking the gardens, and bookshelves on the wall adjacent to the door.

Eliza studied the decor. "They've brightened this room up since we were last here."

"And got rid of some furniture." Connie turned in the middle of the room. "It doesn't seem quite so cluttered."

Sergeant Cooper wandered to the window, his helmet under his arm. "It's a lovely room, but does it need to be so vast? My whole house would fit in here."

Connie chuckled. "And mine. Still, it's big enough for me."

But might be a bit cramped for two. Eliza smiled to herself and studied the landscape, while Connie and the sergeant spoke in hushed voices. They all flinched when the door opened and the butler announced Lord and Lady Harrington-Smyth.

"Afternoon, Sergeant." His Lordship's voice boomed across the room. "Want to talk to us about this murder, do you? I wondered when you'd get here."

"You did?" Sergeant Cooper looked at Eliza, but His Lordship continued.

"Of course. We were in the tent for most of the afternoon, so I expect you need to know if we saw anything."

"And did you?"

"Not a thing. I was even looking. Not for a body, of course. At the marquee. We have one here that we needed erecting, and I was curious to see the workings."

"Ah, right..." Sergeant Cooper struggled for words, so Eliza stepped forward.

"Good afternoon, Your Lordship, Lady Harrington-Smyth. I'm Mrs Thomson, and this is my companion, Mrs Appleton. You may remember us..."

"From that other confounded murder. Yes, we do." Lord

Harrington-Smyth looked at his wife. "Damned strange business for women to be interested in."

"Language, dearest."

"Sorry, my love."

Eliza flushed. "I was going to say that I'm sure Mr Taylor and his men would be happy to help if you need a marquee."

"It's already sorted. I spoke to a chap at the fete who said he'd do it. He started on Saturday."

"Only one? I thought it needed a team."

"Apparently not. This fellow's been putting them up for years and said he could manage alone."

"May I ask his name?"

"Bedford, I think. The groundsman will know."

Eliza's mouth fell open. "We've been looking for him."

"Folks have wondered where he is, have they? Don't worry, he's perfectly safe here."

"I'm sure he is, but would you mind if we speak to him?"

"Only if you don't delay him. We need the thing up for Wednesday. Having a few people round..."

"We'll do our best not to slow him down, then. Thank you." Eliza grinned at Connie and Sergeant Cooper. "Before we go, may I ask Lady Harrington-Smyth if she recalls seeing anything unusual last Monday?"

Her Ladyship tutted. "I don't need his permission to speak, but my answer rather depends on what you consider unusual. People measuring the size of vegetables seems quite out of the ordinary to me..."

Eliza grimaced. *Poor Archie.* "What about anyone appearing out of place, or up to no good ... something like that?"

"It's hard to say with so many people being there. I didn't

know who should have been where. There was a man who struck me as odd, though. He had a heavy dark jacket on, which was quite wrong for the time of year. He had a rather furtive look about him, too."

"A man in a dark jacket?" Eliza glanced at Sergeant Cooper. "We've had reports of him already. Did he wear a wide-brimmed hat as well?"

"He did. So much so that I couldn't see his face. That's why it seemed strange."

Eliza's shoulders dropped. "Not even a glimpse? Did you by any chance notice the colour of his hair?"

"I'm not sure that I did. Or did I? Was it grey?" She looked at her husband. "Didn't you see him?"

"Can't say I did. It would be a safe bet to say he had grey hair, though, given that most men around here are over fifty."

"That's what I'm worried about. Did I imagine it?"

"What about his height? Was the man taller or shorter than average?"

"I couldn't say. He was outside when I saw him and he was stooping down, as if he was hiding from someone."

"Was this before or after the prize-giving?"

"After. We were just leaving the marquee when he darted from the back on our right."

Could that have been as soon as he'd killed Mr Hobbs? "That's very helpful. Did you hear the church bells when you were leaving?"

Lady Harrington-Smyth put her fingers to her temples and closed her eyes. "When we were still in the marquee. It must have been four o'clock."

"Splendid. Thank you. If you remember anything else, would you let us know?"

"I'll see what I can do. Oh, actually, there was something else. The shoes."

"I'm sorry?"

"For someone in a black jacket, I'd expect them to be wearing black shoes, but they weren't. They were brown."

"Brown shoes with a black jacket?"

"Exactly. It was plain wrong."

"Was he wearing black trousers, too?"

"No. They were navy. The man looked a fool. I ask you. Who wears black, blue and brown, all at the same time?"

Eliza smiled. "That, Lady Harrington-Smyth, is what we hope to find out."

After getting directions from the butler, Sergeant Cooper led the way along a path towards a large expanse of grass at the side of the house. The frame of a half-erected marquee came into view as they rounded a beech hedge, but at first glance, there was no one working on it. They hadn't walked much further when Connie nudged Eliza's arm and pointed to a bench at the far end of the garden.

"There he is."

Mr Bedford seemed preoccupied with his pipe as they headed towards him, but as soon as he noticed them, he jumped to his feet, his eyes darting around the edges of the garden. Before he could move, Sergeant Cooper raced towards him and swiftly cuffed his hands behind his back.

Connie bounced on her toes and clapped as Sergeant Cooper escorted his prey towards them. "Well done, Sergeant."

"Thankfully, there are no exits in that direction." He held Mr Bedford's arm as he looked at Eliza.

"Do you have any questions?"

"I do indeed." She studied the man before her. "Mr Bedford. It really isn't a good idea to disappear from home and work, shortly after a man you were furious with was murdered. What do you have to say for yourself?"

"How've I disappeared? I've been here all week."

"Without telling anyone?"

He sighed. "Look, I needed the money."

"You had a perfectly good job with Mr Taylor. Why would you leave that to come here?"

"I've not left, just taken time off."

"Mr Taylor isn't aware of that. Why didn't you tell him?"

"I was going to ... when I get back. I couldn't risk him taking over this job."

"Isn't it usual for a team of men to erect a marquee rather than one man?"

"I told you. I needed the money. If Mr Taylor had got wind of this, I'd have got my paltry wage, but as it is, I'll get all the money myself. I had no choice after Mr Hobbs died without paying me my twenty pounds."

Eliza shook her head. "You realise it will probably take four times longer for you to do this on your own, so you'll end up earning less than you would if you'd been part of the team."

He snorted. "You don't think Mr Taylor splits the money evenly? He takes more than his fair share... It's about time I got a fair day's pay."

"So, you took a job he would have got himself, and then expect to carry on working as if nothing's happened?"

"He needn't know…"

Sergeant Cooper tugged his arm. "That will be up to the inspector. I want him to hear the full story before we decide what to do with you. This way. We're going to the station."

Inspector Adams was nowhere to be seen when they returned to the police station, and Constable Jenkins insisted on keeping Mr Bedford in the cell.

Eliza gasped. "You can't do that. He's here as a witness, not a suspect."

"We need to keep him where we can see him, and we don't want him disappearing again before the inspector gets back."

"When will that be? Where's he gone?"

"He didn't say, other than it was urgent and he'd be as quick as he could."

Mr Bedford grunted. "I'll sit in here for now, as long as I get a cup of tea … and a biscuit … but I'm not staying all night."

Constable Jenkins glared at him. "You'll do as you're told."

"Constable." Eliza took him to one side. "We must assume he's innocent until proven guilty. He could get a solicitor…"

"I doubt it if he's short of money…"

"Sergeant, will you speak to him?"

"But he's right. What else are we going to do with him?"

Eliza raised her hands by her sides and dropped them again. "I give up. At the very least, I suggest you take a statement from him and then be hospitable until Inspector Adams returns, or you could be in trouble. We need to go."

Following a brief farewell, Eliza took Connie's arm, and they walked to the surgery. "You're more cheerful than you were at luncheon."

"I am. I just hope Inspector Adams doesn't spoil it when he gets back."

"If he's already apologised for earlier, I doubt he will." Eliza stopped as they reached the surgery gate. "Have a nice evening with Sergeant Cooper."

"I'm sure I will."

She waited until Connie reached her own front door before she stepped into the surgery. After removing her hat, she wandered into the drawing room, where Archie was waiting for her. "You've finished early today."

"I didn't have many home visits, so I thought I'd make the most of it. How was Mrs Appleton?"

"A lot better, thank you. She'd had chance to speak to Sergeant Cooper, and they were both smiling when I got there. He ended up asking us to go to Over Moreton with him while he visited the manager of the flour mill. As we were there, we realised we were close to the Manor, so called on Lord and Lady Harrington-Smyth to ask if they'd seen anything of note at the fete."

"And had they?"

"Her Ladyship had noticed the man in the black jacket and hat at around four o'clock, sneaking away from the marquee."

"Which may have been just after the murder was committed. Did she know who he was?"

"No. That's why I'm not as excited as I might be. She said he had the brim of the hat pulled down over his face and was bent over as he walked."

"All the descriptions seem to agree with each other, then."

"They do, although we have a few more details now. One thing that drew Her Ladyship's eye was that he was wearing navy trousers and brown shoes with his black jacket."

Archie's forehead creased. "A workman, then?"

"It could be, but we're happy enough with the marquee men's alibis."

"What about the one who disappeared?"

"Mr Bedford. We've found him! Can you believe he's putting up a marquee for the Harrington-Smyths?"

"On his own?"

"Apparently. He said he needed the money and wouldn't earn so much if he was doing it for Mr Taylor."

"And that was why he upped and left? Nothing to do with trying to get away?"

"That's what he told us, but Sergeant Cooper brought him to the station, anyway. Unfortunately, Inspector Adams isn't around, so the constable stuck him in the cell, not knowing what else to do with him. If I was him, I'd let him go. Lord Harrington-Smyth won't be happy if the marquee isn't up by Wednesday."

"So, you believe him?"

Eliza nodded. "I'm inclined to. I think we're better off concentrating on the man with the brown shoes."

CHAPTER TWENTY-EIGHT

Archie was waiting for Eliza at the breakfast table the following morning, and he put down his newspaper as she took her seat.

"I was beginning to think you weren't coming."

"I've not been that long. Did you meet Inspector Adams in the alehouse last night? Is that why you were late in?"

"I did as it happens, although he didn't arrive until about a quarter to ten. He's a lot on his plate."

"So I gathered." Eliza leaned forward. "Did he share any gossip?"

"No, and I'm glad he didn't. That way, I needn't lie to you."

Eliza tutted and helped herself to a slice of toast from the rack between them. "Did he tell you what they did with Mr Bedford?"

"They let him off with a warning and told him not to go anywhere without letting Mr Taylor know. He was of the same opinion as you, that Mr Bedford was probably telling the truth."

"So that leaves us looking for the mystery man. Did Inspector Adams know about him?"

Archie shook his head. "He didn't say, and I didn't ask. He'd come for a drink to get away from work, not dredge it all up again."

"That's a shame. I'll go over this morning and see what he thinks."

"You're not taking Mrs Appleton...?"

Eliza creased the side of her cheek. "Did he say something?"

"Only that he wasn't happy having his authority challenged."

"I can't say I blame him, although I don't like going behind Connie's back."

"I'm sure she'll..." Archie paused as Iris joined them.

"The postman's been, sir." She handed Archie a small selection of letters.

"It looks as if there's one from Mr Bell."

Eliza extended a hand as he offered it to her. "It may be about Henry." She waited for Iris to leave them. "Father said he was going to invite him over for dinner and find out why he wanted to speak to Dr Dunlop in such secrecy."

Archie raised an eyebrow. "Shouldn't that have been for me to do?"

"The chances of him coming here are slim, and I wasn't aware you had any plans to go to London in the next few days. Father thought he was helping."

Archie sighed. "All right. What does he say?"

Eliza sliced open the top of the envelope, pulled out the letter and skimmed over the opening pleasantries. "Henry joined me for dinner on Saturday evening... Apologised for not joining us on Friday... We had a long talk... Ah, here we are. He says Henry was reluctant to tell him what was on his mind, but finally admitted it was to do with a young lady."

"That's what we suspected. I don't know why you worry so much."

"Henry walking out with someone *is* something to worry about ... even more so when he feels the need to keep her a secret. Why would he do that?"

"He probably doesn't want you interfering."

"I've every right to, if he wants this woman to be his wife."

"We don't know that he does ... do we?" Archie leaned over and took the letter from her. "No. He's been walking out with her for a few months. It's far too early to jump to conclusions. That will be why he's said nothing."

"What's wrong with wanting to meet her?"

"He'll want to do things in his own time. You put too much pressure on him. Anyway..." he carried on reading "...it says here that Henry has promised to visit on his next day off."

"When will that be?"

"He doesn't say, but it shouldn't be long if he's worked every day since last Tuesday."

"I'd better decide what I'm going to say to him, then."

The rest of the morning was quiet, and once the early influx of people had disappeared from the surgery, Eliza wandered down to Archie's office.

"The waiting room's empty at the moment. Can you manage by yourself if I call at the police station?"

"I'm sure I can. Don't make a nuisance of yourself, though, if Inspector Adams doesn't want any help..."

"As if..." Eliza waved as she turned to leave. "I'll see you later. "

She hadn't left the surgery when the door opened and Inspector Adams strolled in.

"Inspector. I was about to pay you a visit."

He avoided her gaze. "After yesterday's to-do, I wasn't sure if you would, but I'd hoped to speak to you."

"Come through to the morning room. Would you like coffee?"

"That would be lovely, thank you."

After popping her head into the kitchen, Eliza opened the door to a small room next to the dining room. "It's pleasant in here at this time of day, before the sun swings around the house." She offered the inspector a chair. "I heard you let Mr Bedford go."

"I did. We had nothing to hold him on."

"I didn't think so. Can I presume Sergeant Cooper told you about Lady Harrington-Smyth's sighting of our potential killer?"

"He did, but we're at a loss as to who it could be. Have you any ideas?"

She shook her head. "Short of knocking on the front door of everyone in the village and asking to see their shoes and jackets, I'm afraid I don't."

"Even then, most men will have a black jacket."

"Her Ladyship was a little more descriptive than that. She said it was a heavy material that looked out of place for the weather."

"That could still apply to most men around here."

"And the brown shoes?" Eliza looked across to the

inspector, but Iris disturbed them when she brought in a tray of coffee.

"Will that be all, madam?"

"Yes, thank you." She waited for the door to close. "I've had a thought. The man in question was wearing a black jacket, navy trousers, and brown shoes. You wouldn't expect any self-respecting man to go out like that. That suggests he either dressed in a hurry, or he has no wife to lift his clothes out for him."

Inspector Adams nodded. "Or both."

"Quite, although, even if Archie was rushing, I wouldn't let him out looking like that."

"So, we could be looking for a widower or bachelor?"

"It would make sense."

"It would. It would also narrow down our potential suspects. Would you be able to draw up a list of those who fit the criteria?"

Eliza nodded. "I could, but the drawback is that there are not many of them. Other than the marquee men, the vicar, Mr Hewitt, Sergeant Cooper and Constable Jenkins, all the other men in the village have wives. There are a lot more women on their own."

"Your son and his friends had no lady companions."

Eliza's stomach flipped. "But none of them were wearing clothes matching the description. Besides, I thought we were happy with their alibis."

"We were when Mr Pitt was our prime suspect, but we'll need to look at them again. Don't forget, jackets are easy to change, and we never actually spoke to your son."

No. "I just don't believe he'd do anything like that."

217

"Then you'd better extend your list to those from Over Moreton."

"I'll need help with that. Mrs Royal may be the best person to ask. She'll know most of the people over there."

"If you could do that today, I'd appreciate it. I really could do with getting back to London."

Eliza handed him a cup of coffee. "It sounds serious. Have you another murder to investigate?"

"I wish it was that simple."

"Oh dear. Well, if you need any help, let me know."

"I'm afraid I need to sort it out myself."

Once Inspector Adams had bid her farewell, Eliza moved to the teak writing desk in the corner of the morning room and took out some paper. She didn't have many names on her list when Archie found her ten minutes later.

"I thought you were going out."

"I was, but Inspector Adams beat me to it and came here."

Archie glanced at the empty cups. "You could have told me."

"I'm sorry. We were talking about the investigation, or more particularly about this poorly dressed man, and got carried away. We decided that for a man to go out so uncoordinated, he must be without a wife."

Archie chuckled. "Trust you to think of that."

"It's true. No self-respecting woman would want her husband to go out looking like that. The problem is, there are not many lone men in Moreton, so I'll pay Mrs Royal a visit after luncheon and ask for her help with the Over Moreton contingent."

"I'll go through my records if you like, in case you miss anyone. The doctor in Over Moreton would probably do the same. Shall I ask when I go over there later?"

"If you wouldn't mind, although the inspector wants some names this afternoon. I'll finish the list for Moreton-on-Thames when I see Connie, and we can do our best for Over Moreton and tell him he can have the rest tomorrow. Checking the medical notes would take the guesswork out of it." She put the pen back in the inkwell and blotted her paper. "Before this came up, I was planning on paying Mrs Steel a visit to check how she's getting on with the right dose of her tablets. Do you have any objection to me calling?"

"No, it would save me a job, actually. I need to go to the shop."

Eliza stared at him. "When did you ever do the shopping?"

He laughed. "I didn't say I was. I'm going to visit Mr Pitt. Apparently, since Sergeant Cooper locked him up, he's been waking in the night in a cold sweat. Mrs Pitt called and asked if I could give him a tonic."

"Poor Mr Pitt. As much as I like Sergeant Cooper, I sometimes wonder about his policing methods. Not that you're ever allowed to repeat that in front of Connie."

Archie held up his hands. "As if I would."

CHAPTER TWENTY-NINE

The Steels' maid opened the door when Eliza called twenty minutes later, and she showed her into the morning room where Mrs Steel looked up from her writing desk.

"Mrs Thomson, how lovely to see you. Please, take a seat. Is this a social visit?"

"After a fashion. I wanted to check how you are now you've increased your tablets."

"Oh, much better, thank you. I couldn't believe how lethargic I'd become. So quickly, too."

"It was strange that Mr Steel got the dosage wrong. Could he have got mixed up with some other tablets?"

Mrs Steel sighed. "I suppose he could, bless him. He won't admit it, but he's trying to do too much at the moment, and I've not been able to help."

"Is that why he'd like to hand over the running of the bowling club to someone else?"

"He doesn't want to, but I've insisted he must. He's

spending more and more time there, keeping the place looking its best. I hardly see him."

"That's why I worry about Dr Thomson taking over. Mr Steel told me he was painting the fence on the day of the fete. My husband couldn't do that, even if he didn't have a full-time job."

"I've tried to tell him, but he says that having Dr Thomson in charge will bring some prestige to the club."

Eliza smiled. "That makes a change. So many people used to look down on him for being a doctor. My father included."

"That's nonsense. Look at how improved I am compared to Sunday. He should be applauded."

"And I'm very pleased. Hopefully, you'll be able to resume your outings soon."

"Oh, I hope so, although my husband isn't one for going out when it's just the two of us."

"I'd heard you regularly went out together."

"Only if I insisted on going with him, but I've not been able to recently."

"But now you're feeling better..."

"Oh, it's not just that. Since he left work, he's become so attached to bowling I hardly see him."

"Oh dear. Is that something else for me to worry about? It sounds as if we should find someone else to take over." Eliza sighed as she stood up. "Anyway, you're clearly busy, so I won't take up any more of your morning. I'll tell Dr Thomson you're feeling better."

"It's no problem. Thank you for calling." Mrs Steel pushed herself up from her desk. "Let me see you out now I have the energy..." She glanced around the room. "Where's my cane? Not that I really need it, but when I'm on my own, it makes me feel safer."

Eliza groaned. "You've just reminded me. I took some walking canes from the bowling club cloakroom last week and I've not returned them. I should do that sometime soon."

"Do you go into the club? I've always been told I'm not allowed."

"Not as a rule. I only called last Monday, when we needed to make some refreshments for the police and witnesses."

"Ah, that makes sense. I'd be most disappointed if I was the only one who couldn't go in."

Eliza sighed. "I've told Dr Thomson that if he becomes chairman, he needs to change the rules to let us all in. I don't know why we should only be welcome when they want us to make afternoon teas."

"I quite agree with you. It sounds like Dr Thomson would make a splendid chairman, despite your doubts."

"We'll see." Eliza paused as she reached the door. "Is there a time Mr Steel isn't at the bowling club? I probably shouldn't call with the walking canes while he's there."

"He's always home for luncheon between one and two o'clock, so you could try then. Or go round six o'clock when he's here for dinner."

Eliza nodded. "What time does he usually arrive in the morning?"

"Not until about eleven o'clock. He likes to read the paper before he goes out."

"That would work better. I'll nip over first thing tomorrow before surgery starts."

. . .

Connie tapped her fingers on her dining table as she and Eliza stared at the sheet of paper in front of them.

"I've never considered how few single or widowed men there are around here."

Eliza didn't look up. "It just goes to show they can't live without us. If they did, their houses would be a mess and their children probably malnourished."

"I'm sure Sergeant Cooper's house isn't untidy ... not that I've been in recently."

"There are always exceptions, but on the whole, you can tell if a house has no woman in charge. I shudder to think of how Henry lives. I doubt his wage would cover a housekeeper."

"Not on his own, but they could split the bill between the four of them."

Eliza nodded. "I suppose so. I really should ask. Ooh, I almost forgot, I had a letter from Father this morning, and he said it was trouble with a young lady that was causing Henry angst while he was here."

"There you are. We said there would be a reasonable explanation."

"I know, but I still worry what she'll be like. Still, at least there'd be someone to take care of him if he were to marry her. Not that marriage is likely just yet. They've only been walking out together for a few months."

"There's a bright side to everything." Connie smiled and looked back at the list. "Should we walk around both villages and check the state of the houses to be sure we've identified everyone? The curtains are often a good giveaway."

"They are, but we don't have a lot of time. I'm not sure I have the energy, either."

"No, me neither."

Eliza folded the paper in half. "That will do for now. I'll pop next door and see if Archie's found anyone else in his records, and then I'll nip up to the station to give this to the inspector."

"On your own?"

"It's for the best after what happened. I'll come straight back, and we can go for a walk."

Connie's lip quivered. "I've spoiled things, haven't I?"

"It wasn't your fault, and I'm sure it will pass once the inspector deals with whatever problem he has in London."

"I hope you're right." She stood up. "Shall I put the kettle on?"

"Why not? I'll be as quick as I can."

Archie had very little additional information when she returned home, and so, with a spring in her step, Eliza hurried to the police station.

Sergeant Cooper was at the counter when she went in, but his face dropped. "Are you on your own?"

"We thought it would be better if Connie stayed away. For now, at least."

"I fear you're right. I presume you're here to see Inspector Adams?"

"I am. Is he here?"

The sergeant took a step backwards and pushed open the office door. "In there."

The inspector stood up as she joined him. "Mrs Thomson. Excellent. Do you have something for me?"

"I do, but I'm afraid it's not much to go on. Dr Thomson checked his medical records, but we've already identified everyone around here. He's going to ask the doctor in Over

Moreton to do the same, but so far, the only single or widowed men we've come up with over there are the doctor himself, Dr Wark, the vicar, the bank manager, and several workers at Mr Royal's manufactory. There may be workers at the Manor, too. The butler and the like, although I doubt they'd have been at the fete."

"At least it's a start. When will Dr Thomson be able to confirm the full list?"

"By tomorrow, he hopes, but I'll warn you, I wouldn't expect to find many more. As I said earlier, there are more widows than widowers around here."

"Isn't that the case everywhere?" He retook his seat. "I'll send Constable Jenkins to Over Moreton this afternoon. I'm going to write to your son, advising him I need to speak to him."

"You're going to London again?"

"I don't mind where I meet him, either here or in London, but it needs to be this week."

"You may be in luck. I had a letter from my father earlier and he said Henry was planning to visit Moreton on his next day off."

"When will that be?"

"I'm afraid I don't know, but it should be this week."

"Very well. I'll still write, but I'll ask when we can expect him. This has gone on for long enough."

The kettle had boiled, and the tea was brewing when Eliza returned to Connie's cottage, and they carried their cups of tea out to the shade of the front garden and took seats on opposite sides of the table.

"Did the inspector have anything to say?"

"Not a lot, but he looks like a man with the weight of the world on his shoulders."

"Do you know what the problem is?"

"No, he won't tell me, but I've been thinking. If the situation in London is as bad as all that, why stay here?"

Connie slouched in her chair. "He must think Frank isn't up to the job."

"I doubt it. It's only been a week since the murder, and many take a lot longer than that to solve."

"Could he be staying out of the way of someone?"

"It had crossed my mind, but why would he keep saying he has to get back?"

"Maybe he *should* go, but he doesn't want to."

"That's a possibility. I was going to delay dinner tonight and call at the bowling club to return the walking sticks we borrowed, but I think I'll leave it until tomorrow morning and let Archie go to the alehouse instead. The inspector may stop by for a drink, so I'd hate to miss an opportunity. While I'm on my own, I'll go through the newspapers again to see if I missed any news about the goings-on in London."

"Is that possible?"

"Since we were in Brighton, I've not had chance to sit and read them properly. If there really is something of importance, it should be in *The Times*."

"You'd expect so, although Inspector Adams may not be involved in it. Perhaps he has a lady friend of his own who's causing him sleepless nights."

"That's a thought." Eliza looked at Connie. "I'd assumed it was work related, but maybe it isn't."

CHAPTER THIRTY

It was turned eight o'clock when Archie left for the alehouse and Eliza wandered into the kitchen as Cook and Iris were finishing the dishes. Iris jumped when she saw her.

"Madam. What are you doing in here? May I get you something?"

Eliza waved a hand. "I'm absolutely fine, but I wonder if you still keep the old newspapers in here. I'd like to look through some of them."

Cook smiled. "We throw nothing away." She bustled over to a cupboard near the back door. "They should be in order. I add the new ones to the top and take them from the bottom if we need any. Do you want the local paper or *The Times*?"

"*The Times*, please. Do you have them back to July when we went to Brighton? I've not had much time to read since we got home."

"I can manage that." Cook rummaged through the pile before pulling out a stack. "Here we are. They go as far as the twenty-ninth of July. We didn't get any while you were away."

"Of course. I'd forgotten that. Never mind. Hopefully, these will do."

Iris watched as she headed to the door. "Are you going to read them all tonight?"

"Gracious, no. It will take me a week to do that. I hope that a quick scan of the headlines will help with what I'm looking for."

"Then I wish you well. Shall I bring your cocoa in at ten o'clock, as usual?"

"Yes, please. I'll have had enough by then. Oh, and I'll be in the dining room. It will be easier to read them on the table."

"Very good, madam."

It seemed as if the heat of the summer and the light evenings had reduced the number of crimes in London and as the clock struck quarter to ten, Eliza sat back in her chair. *That was a waste of an evening.* Her eyes flicked to the remaining newspapers. *Not many left. Keep going.* She checked the date on the next in the pile. *Wednesday, 9 August. Almost a week ago.* With nothing of interest on the front page, she turned past it and ran her finger down each column on the subsequent pages. Petty thieving, drunkenness, vandalism... Nothing of note. *Keep going.* She turned the page and repeated her actions but stopped halfway down the second column. *Oh my.* She leaned closer to the newspaper, her hands suddenly perspiring. *How did I miss that?* The story took up less than an inch of the column, and she reread it several times. *I doubt it's the cause of Inspector Adams' worries, but it would have been nice if he'd mentioned it. I can't believe he didn't know.*

She looked up from the paper when there was a knock on the door and Iris joined her.

"Here you are." She put down a mug of hot chocolate milk. "Did you find what you were looking for?"

"No, unfortunately not. There are some interesting things here, though." She closed the paper she'd been studying and put it to one side while she collected up those she'd finished with. "Would you take these back to the kitchen for me? I've not finished with the rest, so I'll look at them tomorrow."

"Certainly. Will that be all? It's time for my bed, if you don't mind."

"Of course I don't. I'll see you in the morning."

Eliza was at breakfast early the following day, and Archie studied her as she sat down.

"Is everything all right?"

"Yes. Why wouldn't it be?"

"Because I've usually finished here before you arrive. It's not like you to follow me down."

"I'm keen to hear what Inspector Adams had to say last night."

Archie sat back as Iris put a plate of kippers in front of him. "He didn't say anything, because I didn't see him."

"You didn't? I thought he was staying there."

"He could have gone straight up the stairs ... or may have stayed late at the station. He said he'd been busy the night before, and so I assumed he was tired."

"Did you stay until closing time?"

"I did. I thought you'd be asleep when I came in, but you looked restless."

"I did some research last night to see if the reason for Inspector Adams' agitation was in the newspaper."

Archie rolled his eyes. "I'm sure he'd tell us if it had anything to do with us."

"It doesn't matter if it has or not, I'd still like to know what's troubling him. It's not like him to be so offhand."

"Did you find anything?"

"Nothing that would impact the inspector, but there was something of interest. I'm surprised you didn't spot it."

"What's that?" Archie helped himself to a slice of bread and butter as Eliza retrieved the newspaper.

"There, halfway down the second column. Lord Lowton's being released from prison."

"Oh, I did see that. I must have forgotten to mention it."

"You forgot…" Eliza's mouth opened and closed with no further words coming out.

"It's nothing to worry about. We knew he'd be out sooner or later, and it doesn't affect us. I think you were entertaining Mrs Hartley when I read it, and it slipped my mind."

"How can you be so flippant after all he did?"

"He didn't do anything."

"Not to you." She put the newspaper to one side. "I wonder if that's why Henry's weekend at Lowton Hall was cancelled."

"Quite possibly. I doubt His Lordship would want a house full of people when he got home."

"The paper doesn't actually say when he's being released."

"I expect he'll be at Lowton Hall by now, given it was in the news last week."

"You're right. I'll ask the inspector when I see him. He's bound to know. In fact, I'll call at the station with the list you got from Over Moreton. Do you have it with you? You didn't give it to me yesterday."

He reached into his inside pocket. "I'd hoped to pass it to the inspector last night."

Eliza straightened it out on the table. "It's not much longer than the list we had for Moreton."

"We didn't expect it to be."

"No." She read the names. "Are you acquainted with the men listed?"

"A few of them. Those that come to the bowling club. There are some that don't. Why?"

"Would you vouch for any of them, or say any were more of a priority than others to talk to?"

"I don't know them that well. If you're going to visit Mrs Royal, I'd have a word with her."

"I'll have to make some time this afternoon. I wanted to go to the bowling club this morning, to return those walking canes before Mr Steel arrives."

"You shouldn't be going in there."

"I won't go in properly, only to the cloakroom."

"Even so. If anyone sees you…" Archie sighed. "I'll be walking past later. I'll take them."

"That would be a help, thank you. If you're doing that, would you be able to arrange the carriage for me to go to Over Moreton? I won't have time to walk."

Archie glanced over his shoulder into the front garden. "It won't be until after surgery. There's a queue forming already."

. . .

The Royals' house was an attractive detached, double-fronted property at the far end of a quiet cul-de-sac and Eliza admired the ivy climbing the walls as the carriage came to a stop. The coachman rolled down the steps and helped her onto the footpath.

"Thank you. I don't expect to be long."

A housekeeper answered the front door moments after she knocked, and after a brief exchange, she showed her into the drawing room. "I'll let Mrs Royal know you're here."

Eliza studied the portraits around the room but turned quickly as the door opened. "Mrs Royal. Thank you for seeing me."

"Not at all. You'd like to talk about the fete, I believe. I was expecting the police to call."

"Normally, they would, but they're rather busy with their being so many people to talk to, so I offered to help. I'd also like your opinion on a list of suspects we've drawn up."

"My opinion? How can I possibly help?"

Eliza smiled. "We've had several sightings of a man at the fete who we believe could be the murderer. Unfortunately, he wore a hat with a wide brim and none of our witnesses saw his face."

Mrs Royal screwed up her eyes. "I still don't know how I can help. I don't recall seeing anyone like that."

"I've spoken to Mrs Steel, and she told me that during the fete, while you were talking to each other, you were facing the flowers at the back of the marquee. Did you notice any disturbances while you were there?"

"There was a breeze that ruffled the material once or twice, but other than that..."

"A breeze?" Eliza cocked her head to one side. "I thought the air was calm."

"It was, for the most part, but I noticed a few ripples."

"When would that have been?"

"Ooh ... close to four o'clock, I should say. We'd finished the prize-giving, and I was saying farewell to Mrs Steel."

"That was the time of the murder ... or at least, we think it was. Is it possible there was a person on the other side of the material rather than a breeze?"

"Now you put it like that, I suppose it could have been, but if it was, I didn't see them."

"Was your husband with you at the time?"

"No. He'd gone outside to look for Mr Steel."

"So, both men were outside."

"Apparently, Mr Steel wanted to open up the bowling club for the evening, and my husband wasn't sure if he'd left or not. He wasn't gone for long before he came back, saying he couldn't find him."

Eliza groaned under her breath. "I should have asked your husband this when I spoke to him, but do you know if he checked around the back of the marquee? Or even the bowling club?"

She shook her head. "He didn't say, but I doubt he went as far as the club, because he wasn't away for long enough. He didn't mention anything if he did."

"I'll call and ask him on my way home, but before I go, I've a list of names I'd like to share with you. I told you that the man we suspect wore a wide-brimmed black hat, along with a heavy black jacket with navy trousers and brown shoes..."

"No!"

"I'm afraid so. I wondered if this meant the man had no wife to dress him."

"Well, if he does, she must have been asleep that day. Men are hopeless if they're left to their own devices. Have you any idea who you're looking for?"

"That's where I'm hoping you can help." She offered Mrs Royal the sheet of paper. "This is a list of men who are either bachelors or widowers. Is there anyone on that list who might be more likely than the others to hold a grudge against Mr Hobbs?"

Mrs Royal shook her head as she studied the names. "I can't say there is. All the gentlemen listed are perfectly pleasant. I'd be horrified to think any of them would do such a shocking thing ... never mind kill anyone."

Eliza chuckled. "I must admit, I've never seen anyone looking so poorly dressed before. And you can't think of anyone we've missed..."

"No. You've done very well." She handed the list back to Eliza. "I'm sorry I can't help."

Eliza folded the paper and stood up. "Never mind. It was worth a try."

"It was no trouble at all." Mrs Royal rang a small handbell at her side. "I'll ask the housekeeper to show you out."

CHAPTER THIRTY-ONE

E liza was finishing her cup of tea after luncheon when Connie knocked on the door and let herself in.

"Where've you been?"

Eliza placed her cup carefully on its saucer. "I wanted a word with Mrs Royal, so I nipped to Over Moreton."

"Why didn't you tell me? We always go together."

"It was only to show her the list of names we drew up, so it wasn't worth troubling you. I'm hoping you'll come with me to visit Mrs Hartley this afternoon."

Connie's back stiffened. "Why do you need to see her again?"

"While I was talking to Mrs Royal, I realised two things. One was that I hadn't asked Mr Royal if he'd gone around the back of the marquee when he was looking for Mr Steel, and the other was that we'd forgotten to ask Mrs Hartley more about the man she saw near the bowling club."

"We're going to Over Moreton again?"

"No, I called in on Mr Royal on my way home, and he

said he'd only wandered to the front, surveyed the people milling around the games area and gone back inside."

"So, you spoke to the Royals on your own, but saved Mrs Hartley for me?"

"Come on, don't be like that. She was perfectly civil the last time we saw her. Besides, I thought you'd want to visit Oak House again."

"You mean you would."

"And I want you to come with me."

Connie's smile was slow to return. "Very well. Are you ready to go?"

Eliza emptied her teacup. "I am now. I've something else to tell you on the way, too."

"That sounds intriguing."

"*I* think it is, but Archie's been quite dismissive about it."

"Now I'm curious."

Eliza said nothing until they were on the path leading across the village green.

"You know I said I was planning to go through some old newspapers last night to see if I could work out why Inspector Adams is so touchy this week?"

"Did you find something?"

"Nothing that relates to Inspector Adams, but there was a small piece about Lord Lowton."

Connie's eyes widened. "What about him?"

"He's been released from prison."

Connie yelped. "He can't have been."

"We knew he wouldn't be in there for long, so I suppose four years was as much as we could hope for."

"You don't think he'll come after us, do you?"

"It did cross my mind, but Archie's not concerned. He says His Lordship will have other things to worry about."

They paused to let a carriage pass before crossing the road on the other side of the green and taking the lane to Oak House.

"I've been wondering if Lord Lowton's return home was the reason Henry's weekend was cancelled at such short notice."

"Why wouldn't he tell you, if it was?"

"Perhaps he didn't want to worry me."

"It should be Lord Albert who's worried. Is he still planning on marrying that commoner?"

"I've not heard that he isn't." Eliza shuddered as they reached the gates to Mrs Hartley's driveway. "I'm just glad I wasn't there for the homecoming."

Eliza had to knock on the door twice before Mrs Hartley arrived wearing a soft cream dress.

"Good afternoon, ladies. This is a pleasant surprise. Are you here investigating, or is it a social call?"

"We'd like to ask a couple more questions about the fete, if we may."

"Come in, then." She smiled as she stepped back, and they joined her in the hallway. "We'll go into the drawing room. It's lovely in there at this time of day."

Eliza nodded. *I remember.*

"May I get you some tea?"

Eliza looked at Connie, who shook her head. "No, thank you. We've not long since finished luncheon, and this is only a quick visit." They followed Mrs Hartley up one flight of stairs and turned left into a large, brightly decorated room overlooking the front drive. "You mentioned last time we spoke that you'd seen a man behind the marquee as you walked home from the fete."

"The man I thought was Mr Steel, but it couldn't have been, because he was handing out prizes."

"That's the one. I forgot to ask earlier, but do you remember what he was wearing?"

Mrs Hartley stared into the corner of the room. "He was in dark clothes. Black, I would say, but the trousers were a different shade..."

"Could they have been navy?"

"Possibly. I was too far away to say with any certainty."

"And did he wear a black hat?"

"No. That was the strange thing. He wore no hat."

Eliza stared at Connie. "That's most unusual."

"He looked as if he was adjusting his jacket too, as if he'd just put it on."

"Really?" Eliza's mouth fell open. "If he got changed, it could have been almost any man at the marquee."

Connie gasped. "And it wouldn't matter if they had a wife or not. She wouldn't have seen him."

"That's true. How on earth do we narrow down the list of suspects now?" Eliza studied Mrs Hartley. "Have you been out into the village since the fete?"

"Not since I came to the surgery. I've had no need."

"Would it be possible for you to join us for a walk?"

"Now?"

"If you don't mind. I'd like to take you to the shop, the churchyard, along the river, and anywhere else where we may meet a few men. I'm hoping you'll recognise one of them as the man you saw."

Mrs Hartley paused as she stared through the window. "Why not? I've nothing else to do."

"Splendid."

"Would you mind if I brought my daughter? I'm trying to encourage her to get out more often, too."

"Not at all. Was she at the fete?"

"No. She said the crowds would be too much for her. But a walk may suit her better. Would you give me a few minutes to speak to her?"

"Of course."

As Mrs Hartley left, Eliza wandered to the window and gazed out at the old oak tree. "It's a shame we can't call at the alehouse or bowling club. That's where most of the older men will be."

"We can sit and watch them play bowls."

"That's a good idea, although we should leave that until we need to rest our feet."

The sun was warm as they set off, and Mrs Hartley carried a cream parasol over her shoulder as they left the churchyard and walked along the road towards the river.

"I'm so cross that Jane wouldn't come with us. How she hopes to find a husband when she won't venture from the house, I don't know. She's already far too old to be a spinster..."

"We should have given her more warning."

Mrs Hartley sighed. "It's no excuse. Not that there are many men out this afternoon. I imagine they're all at work."

"Either that or at the bowling club. We can stop to watch a match at the end of our walk. I think we should go to the shop first and then the river."

Mrs Hartley hesitated. "The shop?"

"I'd like you to take another look at Mr Pitt. When you first told us you'd seen someone behind the marquee, we wondered if it was him, so it would be helpful to either rule him in or out."

Mrs Hartley took a deep breath. "Very well."

Eliza put a hand on her arm. "Don't look so worried. I'm going to ask for a jar of jam, so you won't need to do anything other than study him."

"Right."

Mr Pitt glowered at them as they went in. "Ladies."

Eliza smiled. "Good afternoon, Mr Pitt."

"Are you here on that investigation?"

"No, not today. I'd just like some jam, please."

He grunted. "I'm glad to hear it."

"I'm sorry about what happened, but I believe Sergeant Cooper has apologised."

"Not well enough, he didn't. Cheek of him, thinking I'm a murderer."

Connie's cheeks coloured. "You did give him reason to be suspicious…"

"Nothing that warranted being locked up. I'm a laughing-stock around here now."

Eliza approached the counter. "I'm sure you're not, and for the record, I've not heard a word against you. Sergeant Cooper was only doing his job, so I hope there's no harm done."

"No, well... Think on before you start interrogating people."

"We will." Eliza pursed her lips as she studied the shelves behind Mr Pitt. "Do you have any of Mrs Pitt's jam? It goes particularly well with scones."

"It does that. What flavour would you like? We've only got damson or blackcurrant."

"Ooh, there's a choice. I'll tell you what, why don't I take one of each?"

"She'll be pleased with that." He put the jars, with their brightly coloured paper lids, onto the counter.

I hope you are, too. "Thank you. Will you add them to the bill? I'll send Iris in to settle it tomorrow."

Eliza slipped the jam into her bag and, with a cheery farewell, led Mrs Hartley out of the shop. "Well?"

"It wasn't him."

Eliza released her breath. "I can't say I'm sorry, but it doesn't help with the investigation."

"No." Mrs Hartley grimaced. "He wasn't happy to see you. Is it true he was arrested for the murder?"

"It was a misunderstanding, but he didn't take it well. Not that I blame him." Eliza sensed Connie stiffening beside her. "Shall we go to the river?"

"Do many people walk along the bank?"

"It depends on the weather, but it's a nice way to get to Over Moreton if you've the time and energy. Didn't you go that way on the afternoon of the fete?"

"I did, but it was quiet. Everyone was otherwise engaged."

"They would have been." Eliza glanced over to the bowling club as they passed. "Do any of the men over there look familiar?"

Mrs Hartley stopped as she peered at those playing. "I recognise some of them from the village, but the man from behind the marquee isn't there."

"That's annoying."

Connie leaned across. "Maybe the players will have changed when we get back."

"I hope so." Eliza turned to the church clock. "It's time for tea, so some may have gone in early. Let's keep going. Are you all right for time, Mrs Hartley?"

"I am for another hour or so."

"Splendid. If we have no joy this afternoon, would you care for a drive to Over Moreton tomorrow and take a stroll around the village? There are more shops there ... and a different group of men."

Mrs Hartley hesitated before she nodded. "Yes. I need to get out more."

"Excellent. I'll ask Dr Thomson to arrange a carriage for us. It may be enough notice for your daughter, too."

"I'll invite her, thank you." Mrs Hartley suddenly stopped, her gaze towards the bowling club on her left. "That's him. That man over there. He's the one I saw behind the marquee."

CHAPTER THIRTY-TWO

Eliza stared at Mrs Hartley before following her gaze. "You're sure?"

"Almost certainly. He's about the right height and girth. And has the same style of hair..."

Connie's forehead creased. "Why would he want Mr Hobbs dead?"

"That's a good question. And one we need an urgent answer to." Eliza's pulse raced as she glanced around them. "We probably should report him to the police, but they won't arrest him unless we can give them a motive."

"But they must." Mrs Hartley looked at her. "We can't work that out on our own."

"Mrs Thomson's very good at these things." Connie gave Mrs Hartley a knowing look as Eliza shot her a glance.

"I'll do my best, but help is always welcome." She jumped as the church bells struck the hour. "Why don't we go to the surgery and go through our notes to see if we can piece something together before we visit the police?"

Connie stared at her. "Mrs Hartley as well?"

"If she wants to."

"I don't want to intrude…"

"You'll be doing nothing of the sort. Will she, Connie?"

Connie lowered her eyes. "No."

"Good. Shall we go?"

Mrs Hartley hung back as Eliza ushered Connie ahead of them. "Does this mean our trip to Over Moreton is off tomorrow?"

Eliza paused. "It needn't be, if you'd like to go."

"I think I would, now I've got used to the idea."

"Splendid. In the meantime, let's see what we can work out."

Eliza opened the door to the surgery and followed Connie and Mrs Hartley inside. "Go through to the drawing room and I'll tell Iris we're here." She glanced down at the umbrella stand as she passed. *Confound it. Archie forgot to take those canes. I'll walk over with Mrs Hartley when she leaves and return them myself. I'll just have to hope Mr Steel doesn't see me.*

The teacups and cake stand were empty when Eliza sat back in her chair.

"The murder looks as if it was premeditated, with the tampering of the marquee used to get Mr Hobbs on his own, but why on earth would our suspect want him dead?"

"Assuming it was him." Mrs Hartley twisted her fingers. "We still can't be sure that the man I saw was the killer."

"Not for certain, but looking at the times more closely, perhaps he did have the opportunity."

"Even so, if he had a motive, we may never know what it was. Mr Hobbs can't tell us, and I doubt the killer will."

"You're right, but in these situations, it's usually one of three options. Either Mr Hobbs knew something that the killer didn't want revealing; Mr Hobbs was blackmailing him; or Mr Hobbs was up to no good and the killer wanted to stop him from doing whatever it was."

Connie studied the notes that were spread out over the dining table. "But Mrs Hartley's right. If it was between the two of them, we'll never find out what it was. Unless the police get a confession."

Eliza nodded. "Annoying as it is, that might be the best we can hope for." She collected up the sheets of paper. "I'll write all this up before I speak to the inspector." She stood up and cleared the table. "I hate it when things are left hanging."

Mrs Hartley smiled. "You've done incredibly well. I expect the police will be delighted."

"The problem is, I usually tell them who the killer is, the motive and how the murder was committed. As it stands, we've not even identified the murder weapon. Maybe I'll think about it overnight and speak to them tomorrow."

"Will we still go to Over Moreton?"

Eliza nodded. "There's no reason we shouldn't. The case is almost solved, so there isn't much more we can do. Shall we say two o'clock?"

"I'll be here."

"Splendid." Eliza stood up. "I need to pop into the bowling club with some walking canes we borrowed, so Mrs Appleton and I will walk part of the way home with you."

Connie's mouth fell open. "Mr Steel will be there."

"He may be, but I'm tired of his silly rules. If he catches me, I'll just hand them to him."

The outer door of the bowling club had been left ajar, and Eliza popped her head into the vestibule before peering through the glass of the inner door.

"I think they're all outside." She looked back at Connie. "You wait here. I'll only be a minute."

She scurried along the hallway to a door on the right hand-side, marked 'Capes and Coats'. *How quaint. It's time they brought that up to date.* The small room was dull, but the light from the rectangular window above the hangers was all she needed to slip the canes in amongst the others. *Doesn't anyone ever take these home?* She was about to leave when her hand caught a particularly large handle. "Ouch." *What on earth was that?*

She pulled out a cane with a handle in the shape of a hammer and was surprised by its weight compared to the two she'd returned. *It must belong to a large gentleman, but why leave it here?* She was about to replace it when she noticed a mark on the metal. *Blood? Surely not.* She peered out of the door and into the corridor. *All clear. No one should miss this for a couple of hours.*

Connie was waiting by the steps and immediately noticed the cane. "Why did you bring out another one?"

"Because I want a closer look at it. Come on, let's get away from here."

They hurried across the village green, not stopping until they reached the safety of the surgery. Once inside, Connie looked at her.

"What was that all about?"

Eliza held the handle of the cane at eye level and pointed to the dull red mark. "What do you think?"

"Blood?"

"I'm guessing so, but I'd like Archie to confirm it. Not that he'll be happy about where I found it. Now, where is he?"

She wandered to the office, but when he wasn't there, she went into the drawing room. Archie was sitting beside the window.

"What are you doing here?"

"I live here."

"I didn't mean that. Why are you so early? You said you were busy this morning."

"I was, but I had a visit from Mr Steel, and it rather unsettled me."

"What did he want?"

Archie indicated for them both to sit down. "It was about the murder. He told me he knew who'd done it."

Eliza's mouth opened and closed several times before she spoke. "Who?"

"Mr Bedford."

"B-based on what?"

"He said he'd been following the case and had worked it out."

"Has he been to the police?"

"Not yet. He asked me what I thought he should do."

"What did you tell him?"

"I tried to stall him until I'd spoken to you and said he needed to be certain before he made such a serious accusation."

"Does he have any evidence or witnesses?"

"He said *he* was a witness."

Eliza gasped. "He saw what happened? Why on earth is this the first we're hearing about it, then? And why did he need to work it out for himself if he saw it?"

"He hadn't been sure of what he'd seen and was hoping someone else would confirm it."

"And have they?"

"He didn't say as such, but he said the man was wearing a dark hat and jacket... Is everything all right? You've gone very pale."

Eliza gazed into mid-air. "We thought we'd identified the killer ... and it wasn't Mr Bedford. I need to rethink this ... and pay Inspector Adams a visit, too. I've a horrible feeling that if we don't, someone else may be killed."

Constable Jenkins smiled as Archie held open the door of the police station for Eliza and Connie.

"On your own, Constable?"

"I will be all evening. Inspector Adams needed to go to London, and he asked Sergeant Cooper to accompany him and pay your son a visit."

"He's gone to London?" Connie's yelp was drowned out by Eliza's.

"Henry? Why?"

The constable glanced between the two of them. "The sarge said he'd be back later and would call on Mrs Appleton when he arrived. He went because the inspector's fed up with waiting for young Dr Thomson to turn up here."

"He only wrote to him yesterday."

"That doesn't seem to matter. This business in London is

clearly troubling him. He's been like a bear with a sore head again today."

"Oh." Eliza's shoulders dropped as the constable continued.

"Is there anything I can help with?"

Eliza looked at Archie, who shook his head. "No, thank you. What time will he be back?"

"Around midday, tomorrow. Shall I tell him you called?"

Archie took hold of Eliza's arm. "If you wouldn't mind. Thank you, Constable."

Eliza ate her dinner in silence, but once finished, she looked across at Archie.

"You look as thoughtful as me."

"I'm just mulling over what you told me. I can't quite believe it."

"Do you agree it's likely to be blood on the end of the walking cane, and it would have been heavy enough to be the murder weapon? Have you seen the bruise on my hand? I didn't hit myself terribly hard with it?"

"I can't argue with that, if the killer wielded it correctly."

"Which they obviously did."

Archie smoothed his moustache. "It suggests that someone knew what they were doing. Someone who's used to manual labour..."

"Mr Bedford, you mean?"

"It would make sense."

"Would he have gone into the bowling club, though?"

"He wouldn't have needed to if the owner had taken it to

the fete and he'd *happened upon it*. We should ask Mr Steel if he knows who it belongs to."

"No." Eliza calmed herself. "Not until we've spoken to Inspector Adams..." She paused as the front door slammed. "Who's that at this hour of the night?" She stood up and peered into the hall. "Henry. What are you doing here?"

"Didn't Grandfather tell you I'd be visiting?"

"He did, but he didn't say when. Sergeant Cooper's gone to London to speak to you. Did you see him?"

"No." Henry walked into the dining room and looked in the serving dishes as he joined them at the table. "Evening, Pa. What did Sergeant Cooper want?"

Eliza retook her seat. "You're one of the few people who was at the fete who hasn't given them a statement."

"Oh, is that all? Is there any meat left?"

"I daresay there is, but you seem very blasé about this murder. Do you know more than you're telling us?"

"Not at all. I believe Toby told you we'd gone for a walk to Over Moreton and missed the whole thing. I've nothing else to add. Would you ask Iris for a plate? I've not eaten since midday."

Eliza stood up, but the maid joined them before she'd reached the door.

"Ah. There you are, Iris. We have an unexpected visitor. Could you do a plate of meat for him and some gravy? We've enough vegetables here."

"Certainly. I thought I heard someone. Will he be staying the night?"

Eliza looked at Henry. "How long will you be here?"

"Two nights."

So don't upset him in the first ten minutes. "Could you freshen his room for him?"

With a nod of the head, Iris disappeared towards the kitchen as Eliza returned to the table.

"So..." *Don't rush in.* "How's life in London?"

"Busy. I've been working fourteen-hour days for the last week, so it will be nice to catch up on some sleep while I'm here. If Sergeant Cooper was looking for me, can I assume you haven't caught your murderer yet?"

"We're getting close. We'd hoped to speak to Inspector Adams about it this afternoon, but he's in London, too."

"He's worried about Lord Lowton, I imagine."

Eliza's head jerked up. "Is that what this is about?"

"Didn't you know?"

"Only from the newspaper. Why didn't you tell us he was being released? I presume that's why Lord Albert cancelled his bachelor party."

"It's only postponed while he makes it clear to the old man that he'll marry who he chooses ... just like he did. He expects to hold it next month, a week before the wedding."

"So, he's going ahead with it..." *Wait a moment.* "Sorry, before you answer that, why is Inspector Adams worried about it?"

"He's not spoken to you?"

"No. Why should he?"

Henry stared out of the window but then sat back with a smile as Iris arrived with a half-full plate of braised beef. "Lovely, thank you. May I have a cup and saucer and a fresh pot of tea, too?"

Henry helped himself to mashed potato and emptied the vegetable dishes as Iris cleared the table, but he waited for her to leave before he spoke again. "It's not my place to gossip if he's trying to keep it from you."

Eliza didn't have to speak as she glared at her son.

"All right... There's nothing certain, but when Lord Lowton was released, it was clear he was angry with those who'd put him in prison. The police are worried he might do something stupid."

Eliza yelped. "What does that mean ... and does it include us?"

"It's difficult to say, but they believe Inspector Adams will be top of the list. They've set a police guard outside Lowton Hall to watch His Lordship's comings and goings."

Archie shook his head. "Ye gods."

"You told me it was nothing to worry about."

"Because I knew no more than you. Will you let this be a lesson to keep out of other people's affairs?"

"He needed to be brought to account..."

"Not if it puts us at risk. He moves in powerful circles..."

Henry scooped up a forkful of potato. "I expected there to be extra police around the village. Have you seen any?"

Eliza and Archie shook their heads.

"I'd mention it to the inspector, then. You can't be too careful."

CHAPTER THIRTY-THREE

The dispensary was quiet the following morning and Eliza spent as much time as she could at the window watching for Inspector Adams' carriage. By eleven o'clock when the last patient left and there was no sign of him, Eliza hurried to Archie's office.

"He's still not here."

"We didn't expect him to be. Constable Jenkins said he wouldn't arrive until about midday."

"Given the situation, I'd hoped he might be early. I don't know what I'm going to tell Connie."

"I wouldn't tell her anything. She'll only panic."

"But she's on her own in that house..."

"All the more reason not to worry her. The bigger question is, what do we do about Mr Steel and Mr Bedford? Is it worth a drive to the Manor to speak to Mr Bedford?"

"I doubt he'll be there. Lord Harrington-Smyth said the marquee needed to be ready for Wednesday and then it would stay up for a week or two, if not longer."

"So, Mr Bedford may be in Molesey?"

"If he's gone back to work with Mr Taylor, he could be anywhere, although I expect he'll be in the alehouse in Molesey each evening. Not that I'll be able to go looking for him."

"You can't, but I can. I'll ask Henry if he'll come with me. Have you seen him this morning?"

Eliza shook her head. "No. I wondered if he was staying out of the way until we'd finished surgery."

"Or because he doesn't want to talk about this young lady he's walking out with. With all the fuss he created last night, she never got a mention."

"Somehow it didn't seem important. Do you think he did it on purpose?"

"Probably, knowing Henry."

Eliza huffed. "I'll go and see if he's around. I want to find out what he's up to before he goes back to London. Oh, I nearly forgot. Would you ask for the carriage to be ready at about two o'clock? I offered to take Mrs Hartley to Over Moreton."

"What did you do that for?"

"I wanted her to identify the man she saw behind the marquee and thought we'd have to look there."

"You said she's identified him."

"She did, but I suggested the outing beforehand and she was looking forward to it. I could always use it as an excuse to look for Mr Bedford."

"No." Archie stared at her. "That needs to be left to Inspector Adams now."

"If he ever arrives."

Henry's bedroom was empty when she went upstairs, and

she followed the sound of humming until she found Iris polishing one of the windows.

"I'm sorry to disturb you, Iris, but have you seen Henry this morning?"

"He came down for breakfast at about ten o'clock, then went straight out."

"I don't suppose he told you where he was going?"

"I'm afraid not."

"Never mind. I'm sure he'll be back when he's hungry. I'll be in the dining room if you need me."

"Very good, madam."

Once downstairs, Eliza spread her notes out on the table, but after a cursory glance, she turned to the window. *Come on, Inspector. Where are you?* She didn't wait long before his carriage appeared, and she hurried to the door when it stopped outside and the inspector climbed out.

"Inspector, how nice to see you. We were going to call..."

"We? You and Mrs Appleton?"

"Dr Thomson, actually. Would you care to come in?"

"I will, thank you. I was hoping to speak to both of you."

"About Lord Lowton?"

The inspector stared at her. "Who told you that?"

"Henry. He arrived home last night."

"Had he spoken to Sergeant Cooper before he left London?"

"No, it appears they missed each other. I believe His Lordship has you in his sights."

The inspector sighed. "We don't know that for sure. I'm more bothered about who else he may be angry with. We're keeping an eye on him, just to be on the safe side. Not that we can do that indefinitely. We're hoping he'll calm down now he's home." He studied her. "Is that why you wanted to see me?"

"Actually, no. Come through to the surgery. Dr Thomson will explain."

Archie stood up as Eliza held open the door. "Inspector, thank goodness you're here. Has my wife told you our dilemma?"

Eliza answered for him. "I've not said anything. I'll leave that to you."

"Ah, right. You'd better take a seat, then. Can we get you a tea or coffee?"

"No, thank you. I need to get to the station and tell Sergeant Cooper about the situation with Lowton."

"So, he doesn't know?"

"We were trying to keep it contained and deal with it discreetly, but Lord Lowton's carriage was seen in Richmond..."

"Richmond! Is father all right?"

"He's fine. I spoke to him last night and we've posted a police officer at his address."

"We must invite him here. I can't have him on his own if Lord Lowton's looking for him."

"And we will, but at the moment, we've more pressing business for the inspector." Archie pointed to the door. "Will you close that, Eliza? We don't want anyone overhearing..."

Inspector Adams was pacing the room with the walking cane in his hand, and as Archie finished, he paused, resting his hands on the back of a chair.

"What's your opinion of this Mr Steel? Would you say he's a reliable witness?"

"I've known him for over five years, and he's always been of excellent character."

"But we interviewed Mr Bedford and had no reason to doubt his alibi. Have you changed your mind about him, Mrs Thomson?"

Eliza shook her head. "I can't say I have. I've gone through my notes again, and I really don't see how he can be our killer."

"But you've no proof, or even a motive for your alternative suggestion."

"It's within our grasp. I know it. If you'll just humour me, I'm sure we'll find the evidence we need…"

"All right." The inspector checked his pocket watch. "It's half past twelve now. Tell me what you want me to do. If we can get this sewn up this afternoon, I'll be a happy man."

Mrs Hartley and her daughter arrived at the surgery as the church bells rang for two o'clock, and Iris showed her into the morning room.

"Good afternoon, Mrs Thomson, Mrs Appleton. You remember my daughter, Miss Dalton."

"We do indeed." Eliza stood up from her seat near the fireplace. "I'm afraid we've had a change of plan for the afternoon."

"Oh." Mrs Hartley's face dropped. "Has our outing been called off?"

"Not if you'd still like to join us, but Mrs Appleton and I have to visit the Manor while we're in Over Moreton. We may also need to go elsewhere, although I don't know where that may be just yet. If you'd prefer to postpone it until another day, we'd quite understand."

"Is this to do with the murder?"

"It is. I'm afraid there's been a development we need to follow up."

"Then I'd like to come with you, as long as I'm not in the way. It's a lot more exciting than sitting at home, and now that Jane's with me..."

Her daughter flushed. "We don't have to go."

"But I'd like to. If Mrs Thomson will have us."

"Of course I will. Shall we go?" Eliza glanced out of the window. "The carriage is here."

Eliza and Connie took the seats with their backs to the horses, and as they pulled away, Eliza studied the bowling club. *I hope Inspector Adams finds what he's looking for.* As they left Moreton, Mrs Hartley interrupted her thoughts.

"The Manor seems a strange place to go for the investigation. You don't suspect Lord Harrington-Smyth, do you?"

"Not at all. I want to speak to one of the men who erected the marquee. He was working there earlier in the week, and we're hoping someone could tell us where his next job was."

"Ah. That explains why we may go further afield." Mrs Hartley patted her daughter's hand. "Isn't this exciting!"

"It would be if there wasn't a killer on the loose. We'd be far better off at home with the gates locked..."

"And where's the fun in that...?"

Eliza gave the young woman a sympathetic smile. "I don't expect we'll come across him this afternoon."

"Do you know who it is?"

Eliza nodded. "I have my suspicions. We just need to prove it. That's why we want to find the marquee man." She glanced around as they turned into the driveway of the Manor. "I'll go to the door and ask the butler if he knows anything about Mr Bedford's whereabouts, or if he can give us the name of anyone who does."

Connie looked at her. "You're leaving me here?"

"It will only be for a minute."

The butler had the door open by the time Eliza clambered from the carriage, and she smiled as she approached.

"Good afternoon. I wonder if you can help."

"I'm afraid His Lordship is out for the afternoon…"

"That may not be a problem. I'm actually looking for the man who put up the marquee, Mr Bedford. Might you know where he was due to work once he left here, or could you point me in the direction of someone who would?"

"I can do better than that. A rope securing the marquee was coming undone and so I called Mr Bedford to attend to it. He's here now."

"Really. That's fortuitous." *Although very bizarre that they've had the same problem with both marquees.* "Am I able to take the carriage around the side of the house instead of walking?"

"Certainly." The butler walked with her across the driveway and gave the coachman directions to the lawn. Eliza was settled in her seat by the time they were ready to leave, and the butler rolled up the steps and closed the door.

Connie waited until they moved off. "Where are we going?"

"To the marquee. As chance would have it, Mr Bedford's here repairing the frame."

"Another one?" Connie huffed. "It makes you wonder how good these men are if they need to repair them all the time. Isn't there anyone else around here who could do the job better?"

Mrs Hartley shook her head. "I don't think there is. I remember when we had ours, there wasn't a lot of choice."

"Then perhaps there should be. That would keep them on their toes..."

Eliza twisted in her seat to get her first view of the marquee, but immediately pulled on a cord attached to a bell. Connie stared at her as the carriage stopped.

"What's the matter?"

"Over there. Look." She pointed to a man wearing a black jacket and dark-brimmed hat.

"Oh, my... What's he doing here?"

Eliza's stomach churned as she opened the door. "I've a feeling he's the reason Mr Bedford was called here this afternoon."

"You can't get out without the steps..."

"But we need to catch him red-handed."

Miss Dalton leaned forward. "How do you know who it is? You can't even see his face."

Eliza's voice was barely a whisper. "He's the man I suspect is our killer..."

"But you said..."

"Jane! That's enough. Leave this to Mrs Thomson."

Connie grabbed Eliza's arm as she dangled a leg from the carriage. "What are you doing? We can't confront him."

Eliza sighed as the coachman rolled down the steps. "You're right, but the driver can."

"What would you like me to do, madam?"

Eliza pointed across the grass. "See that man over there...?"

He turned to follow her gaze, but at that moment, the suspect caught sight of them and fled to the other end of the field.

"Shall I go after him?"

"No, you'd better not. We need to get back to Moreton with the utmost haste."

Connie gasped. "We can't let him get away..."

"We can't do much about that now ... besides, it would be too dangerous to approach him."

"What about speaking to Mr Bedford?"

"That's a good point." She looked at the coachman. "Would you be able to run across to Mr Bedford, the man working on the marquee, and ask him to go to the bowling club in Moreton for four o'clock? Tell him to bring his colleagues, Mr Taylor and Mr Gilbert. If he can find them."

He checked his pocket watch. "Four o'clock will be cutting it fine if he has no carriage."

Why is there always a problem? "Could he borrow one from the Manor? I'm sure His Lordship wouldn't mind. I need him in Moreton as soon as possible."

The driver stepped away from them. "Let me speak to Mr Bedford first. He can sort that out while I get you to Moreton."

CHAPTER THIRTY-FOUR

The village was quiet a quarter of an hour later when the carriage arrived outside the police station, and the coachman helped Eliza and Connie onto the footpath.

"May I do anything else for you, madam?"

"If you wouldn't mind, once you've taken Mrs Hartley and Miss Dalton home, would you park somewhere near the edge of the village and watch who arrives from Over Moreton?"

"Am I looking for anyone in particular?"

"The man we saw in the black coat and hat, although there's every chance he'll have changed his appearance by the time he arrives."

"Then how will I know him?"

"You won't, but if you take a note of everyone you see, it may help confirm our suspect's identity. I'm going to the bowling club as soon as I've spoken to the inspector. Could you join us at four o'clock? I'm fairly certain the man in question will be in the village by then."

"Yes, madam."

Mrs Hartley leaned forward. "Are you sure we can't help? It's been rather fun."

Eliza studied her. "I don't know that fun is the right word, but now you mention it, you may still be needed. I daren't invite you into the station, but you come to the bowling club for four o'clock, as well. Mr Steel will let you in by then."

Inspector Adams was in the office when Sergeant Cooper showed them in, but there was no smile on his face.

"Good afternoon, ladies. Did you have any joy with Mr Bedford?"

"More than our fair share. And, I'm guessing, more than you had."

"How do you know?"

"Because the black hat and jacket I sent you to look for hasn't been in Moreton this afternoon. We saw it being worn while we were at the Manor."

The inspector sat up straight. "Did you see who was wearing it?"

"Unfortunately not. Before we could approach the suspect, he'd made a run for it."

Inspector Adams groaned. "So, we're no further on?"

"Oh, but we are. Mr Bedford had been called to the marquee to repair a broken joint. The same problem we encountered here shortly before the murder of Mr Hobbs."

"Are you suggesting the murderer deliberately sabotaged the marquees to entice his victims there?"

"That's exactly what I'm saying. Thankfully, Mr Bedford was oblivious to what was going on, other than wondering how another of his knots had come undone. He was with a gardener when the coachman spoke to him, and it was agreed that he'd borrow one of Lord Harrington-Smyth's carriages so he could collect Mr Taylor and Mr Gilbert, if he could find them, and bring them here as soon as possible."

"Did you speak to him?"

"No, I was eager to get back, and I still want to get to the bowling club in case Mr Bedford is early. Will you join me to welcome our guests?"

Eliza was pacing in front of the bar of the bowling club when there was a commotion at the door and Mr Steel barged in.

"What's going on here? Get these women out. This is a gentlemen's club..."

Eliza scanned the room where the marquee men sat alongside Mr Hewitt, the Pitts and Mrs Hartley. "I don't see anyone else complaining?"

"Because it's not their club... Now, out, all of you..."

Sergeant Cooper extended his arms to the side, trapping Mr Steel against the door. "Inspector Adams has invited some people for a chat. Now, are you going to sit down and be quiet, or do I have to cuff you?"

Connie bit her lip as she watched from her place beside the bar, but Eliza strode towards Mr Steel, her eyes narrow.

"Please sit down, Mr Steel. My husband will join us shortly, and I'm sure you'd rather not make a fuss while he's here." She flinched as he glared at her.

"Don't think we'll allow women in here, even if he takes over. I'll still be on the committee."

"You should look for another chairman, then."

Mr Steel flopped into a seat in the far corner of the room as Archie, Henry and the coachman arrived with Constable Jenkins. The constable grinned at his sergeant.

"Sorry we're late. We had one or two loose ends to tidy up."

"Well, hurry up and get in." Inspector Adams glanced around the room. "Are we all here?"

Constable Jenkins checked the faces, his gaze lingering on Mrs Hartley. "I would say so, although there seems to be more here than necessary."

"That's perfectly all right, Constable. I've vouched for all those here. You stand at the back and keep an eye on everyone. Sergeant Cooper, you guard the door to make sure there are no unexpected visitors." Inspector Adams paced the room with his hands clasped behind his back as the constable took up his position. "Before I begin, I'd like to thank you all for coming. I believe you all have an interest in identifying the person who murdered Mr Hobbs, and I'm hoping that by the time you go home tonight, the culprit will be in custody."

Mr Steel smirked at Archie before he pointed at Mr Bedford, but Inspector Adams appeared not to notice.

"If you cast your minds back to bank holiday Monday, the fete was almost over when Mrs Petty looked beneath the flower table to find Mr Hobbs' body lying beneath it."

There were nods all around.

"It quickly became clear that the cause of death was consistent with the victim being hit on the side of the head by a heavy object."

Eliza ran a thumb over the bruise on her hand. *Very heavy.*

"The post-mortem determined that the time of death was roughly between three and four o'clock, and so the dilemma we faced was that the murder couldn't have taken place inside the marquee. There were too many people around. So how did Mr Hobbs end up lying beneath said table? And more importantly, were there any witnesses?" Inspector Adams scanned the room, holding the gaze of each person present. "After days of speaking to yourselves, and your fellow villagers, it became apparent that no one witnessed the crime. Instead, we've had to rely on those who may have known Mr Hobbs to determine a motive."

The inspector paused as Eliza stepped forward. "Fortunately, my son, Dr Thomson Junior, was in the Golden Eagle at the start of the fete and was aware of a man in the opposite corner of the snug who had a steady stream of callers while he was there. It turned out that the man in the snug was Mr Hobbs, and those who spoke to him formed our list of suspects."

Eliza looked around the room. "Mr Taylor, Mr Bedford, Mr Gilbert, Mr Hewitt and Mr Steel were all identified as visitors. Not that they were the only ones under suspicion. Mr Pitt had some explaining to do, but thankfully for him, he had no motive, and he had an alibi for the time of the murder."

Mr Pitt stared at the floor but said nothing.

"On top of that, it was discovered that one of my son's friends, Dr Dunlop, had a motive for disliking Mr Hobbs, but we were able to dismiss him as a suspect, as he'd left the village before the murder was committed."

Mr Steel snorted. "I don't know why you're going around in circles. I told your husband I saw the murderer with my own eyes."

Eliza smiled. "You have, and we'll come to that, but first things first. Why would anyone want Mr Hobbs dead? And which of the gentlemen here is our killer?"

"It wasn't me. I hardly knew the man."

Eliza ignored Mr Steel as she carried on. "Our

investigations uncovered that all the men I've mentioned, except for Mr Hewitt, had argued with Mr Hobbs. Firstly, there was Mr Taylor. The hard-done-to employer who had a worker who wasn't pulling his weight and who, through his careless acts, was costing the business money. Mr Taylor has been unwilling to share the reasons he was unable to fire him, but still, it must be a huge relief to have Mr Hobbs out of the way."

Mr Taylor stood up. "I've told you why I couldn't get rid of him. Besides, I was at the front of the marquee for the whole time, waiting for everyone to leave."

"You told us that you hadn't dismissed him because you'd worked with him for too long, but is that really a good enough reason to keep someone employed, especially if they're causing problems?" Eliza raised an eyebrow. "Perhaps it had more to do with the fact that Mr Hobbs was blackmailing you when he found out about some thieving several years ago."

"No! Who told you that? I ... I didn't kill him..."

"Then why lie? It really doesn't pay to mislead the police during a murder investigation." She turned her gaze to the man next to him. "Mr Gilbert, you'd also worked with Mr Hobbs for a long time, and it soon became apparent that you, too, had reason to want him dead."

"Not dead! I just wanted him to leave my wife alone."

"But he wouldn't, would he? He demanded money from you before he'd cooperate."

"I had none to give him."

"So the fact he's no longer with us must be very helpful..."

"That doesn't mean I killed him." He stared at his colleague on his left.

"You may well look at Mr Bedford. He knows rather a lot

about Mr Hobbs' greed and the various ways he upset everyone."

Mr Bedford turned to his colleagues. "They already know I had nothing to do with the murder. Why would I kill him when I'm still angry about it? He owed me money that I won't get back."

"And that's the difference between these three suspects. Mr Hobbs owed Mr Bedford money, while the others were indebted to him. But they weren't the only ones." Eliza paused as she studied her audience. "There's someone else in this room who owed Mr Hobbs money, and rather a lot of it. Isn't that right, Mr Bedford?"

Mr Bedford nodded.

"Would you point out the man in question?"

Mr Bedford stood up and turned to the back of the room before raising his right arm. "There he is."

CHAPTER THIRTY-FIVE

The room fell silent as Mr Bedford stared at Mr Steel.

"He owed Hobsy over twenty pounds."

Mr Steel jumped to his feet. "That's preposterous. I did nothing of the sort."

"But you knew Mr Hobbs rather better than you cared to admit?" Eliza raised an eyebrow.

"He was a business acquaintance, that's all, and what we were doing was perfectly legal. It had nothing to do with the police and was no motive for wanting him dead."

"Is that why you were so keen to find his killer for us?"

"Yes..."

Eliza noticed Archie's surprise but kept her eyes on Mr Bedford. "I believe you disagree with Mr Steel. Would you tell those in the room what you've just told Inspector Adams?"

Mr Bedford remained on his feet, his dark eyes piercing Mr Steel. "He met Mr Hobbs at the bank..."

"I told them that..."

"But did you mention that you gave Mr Hobbs special treatment when you noticed he was placing rather a lot of

money into his bank account? Money he'd won on the horses."
Mr Bedford turned back to Eliza. "To cut a long story short,
Mr Steel enjoyed a flutter himself, but had run into trouble
with his wife when she found out he was spending so much
money. It was agreed that Mr Steel would meet Mr Hobbs
once a week, so he could give him details of his chosen horses
and his betting money. Mr Hobbs would then place the bets
for him. That's the *business partnership* he's on about. If he
won, Mr Hobbs would return any winnings, minus a small
fee. If he lost, Mr Steel would still have to pay the fee. As he
hadn't won for a number of weeks, his debt was mounting."

Mr Steel glared at him. "What utter nonsense. You're
only saying that to save yourself. I saw you murder Mr Hobbs
with my own eyes."

"That's a lie..." Mr Bedford clattered through some chairs
as he headed to the back of the room, but Constable Jenkins
caught his arm.

"That's enough." He pushed Mr Bedford backwards.
"Get to your seat before I put the cuffs on you."

Mr Bedford glared first at the constable and then at Mr
Steel. "You won't get away with this..."

"Mr Bedford..." Inspector Adams' voice bellowed around
the room. "Sit!"

Mr Bedford grunted but returned to his chair as Inspector
Adams turned his gaze on Mr Steel.

"You said you witnessed Mr Bedford attack Mr Hobbs.
Would you care to elaborate?"

"There's not much more to say. I'd nipped to the bowling
club and there was a man in a black jacket and wide-brimmed
hat wielding a heavy-looking walking cane. A moment later, I
heard a thud, and the man ran away."

"Did you see the man's face?"

Mr Steel pointed. "It was him."

"No, it wasn't. I don't even own a wide-brimmed hat..."

Inspector Adams called for silence as Eliza stepped forward.

"Mr Steel. Could you tell us when the attack took place?"

"When?" He glanced around, his gaze avoiding Archie's. "You said the death was between quarter to four and four o'clock, so it must have been then."

"Was it after you finished the prize-giving?"

"Clearly. I'd gone to open the bowling club."

Eliza looked at Inspector Adams. "That gives us a dilemma, does it not?"

"What do you mean?" Mr Steel's eyes were like bullets as he stared at her.

"We didn't consider you as a suspect when this investigation started, given you were handing out prizes at the estimated time of death, but if you say you saw someone bludgeon Mr Hobbs, then that changes everything. You could just as easily have done it yourself."

"What nonsense!"

"Then how do you explain your presence outside the marquee so close to the end of the prize-giving?"

"I-I didn't leave until we were finished."

"Are you sure? We have a witness who saw you." Eliza addressed Mrs Hartley. "Can you confirm that this is the man you waved to on your way home?"

Mrs Hartley nodded. "I can."

"When Mrs Hartley first suggested she'd seen you, we didn't believe it could be you. You had the perfect alibi, and Mrs Hartley assumed she must be mistaken because you didn't respond to her. But now, based on your own admission, can we assume you slipped out of the marquee before Mr Royal awarded Mrs Appleton her prize? That would have given you time to be at the scene at four o'clock when the church bells rang."

"You can't prove anything."

"I also wonder if it's a coincidence that you've just confirmed our suspicions about the murder weapon." Eliza reached into an alcove in the wall. "We've not breathed a word about it to anyone, but I'm assuming this is the walking cane you were referring to."

His face paled as Eliza continued.

"As big and heavy as it is, it wouldn't have been obvious if you'd seen the murder from a distance."

"I have very good eyesight..."

"As have many of our witnesses, including someone who can place you at the Manor this afternoon while Mr Bedford was repairing another problem with the marquee. Did you sabotage it on purpose so you could end Mr Bedford's life, too?"

"What?" Mr Bedford got to his feet, but Eliza interrupted.

"Please sit down, Mr Bedford. When we called to see you earlier, there was a man loitering in a dark jacket and wide-brimmed hat, remarkably like the one we'd had reported at the fete. We know it wasn't you because you were working on the repair, oblivious to the man who shot off as soon as he spotted us."

Mr Steel pushed Constable Jenkins to one side as he strode to the front of the room. "I was at the bowling club all afternoon..."

Eliza looked at Inspector Adams. "Is that true, Inspector?"

"No, it isn't. I called around two o'clock, to ask Mr Steel why he hadn't reported seeing the murder sooner, but he was nowhere to be found."

"Possibly because he was out of the village."

"I was here…"

Eliza's eyes narrowed. "Then why do we have a report of you returning to Moreton shortly after three o'clock?" She looked at the coachman. "Isn't that right?"

"Yes, madam. He was in a carriage looking rather flustered."

"Was he wearing the dark hat and jacket?"

"No, he was not."

Eliza looked over to Sergeant Cooper. "Would you do us the honours, Sergeant?"

"Where's he going?" Mr Steel made to go after him, but Constable Jenkins grabbed his arm. "My office is down there. It's private…"

"Sit down, Mr Steel, before I cuff you."

Mr Steel trudged back to the corner of the room but remained on his feet until Sergeant Cooper finally returned, holding a black jacket in one hand and a wide-brimmed hat in the other.

"I believe these are what we are looking for."

Eliza smiled as Mr Steel stared at them. "Would you like to tell us where you found them, Sergeant?"

"Folded into a bag at the back of a cupboard in Mr Steel's office … behind several other boxes."

Eliza stared at Mr Steel. "Would you care to tell us how they got there?"

"How do I know…?"

Mr Bedford stood up and spun on the spot. "Because you

put them there. Did you want to kill me off because I knew too much? Or so you wouldn't have to pay the debts Mr Hobbs left behind? He wouldn't have owed me any money if you'd paid what you owed. Even if you go to the gallows, I want that money before you leave."

"All right, Mr Bedford." Inspector Adams pointed to Constable Jenkins. "Put the cuffs on Mr Steel. We've enough to charge him with the murder of Mr Hobbs."

"No ... I'm not hanging for this." Mr Steel bolted for the door, but when Sergeant Cooper stepped in front of him, Mr Steel grabbed his arm. "Out of my way."

"Mr Steel!" Sergeant Cooper regained his composure. "I'm arresting you for..."

"You're arresting me for nothing. Get out of the way." Mr Steel pulled the sergeant to one side and punched him in the jaw, knocking him sideways. Mr Steel leapt backwards as Sergeant Cooper fell, but before he could open the door, Constable Jenkins was on him.

"Not this time, sir. You're going nowhere."

CHAPTER THIRTY-SIX

Once Inspector Adams had taken Mr Steel to the police station, Eliza walked across the village green with Mrs Hartley towards the road and Oak House beyond.

"Thank you for everything. I don't know that we'd have solved it without you."

"I'm sure you would, but it was nice to play a part, anyway ... so soon after returning to village life, too. I'm just sorry that Sergeant Cooper got injured."

"Not as sorry as Mrs Appleton, but thankfully, he'll be fine. Dr Thomson said the worst he could expect is a bruised chin for a week or so."

"At least she'll be there to look after him. It must be hard for her knowing what a dangerous job he has."

"It's not usually a problem around here. Thank goodness."

Eliza stopped as they reached the road and she heard her name being called. She crossed the road as Mrs Petty hurried towards her.

"What's been going on? I couldn't help noticing you all going to the bowling club. Have you identified the killer?"

Eliza smiled. "We have, thanks to Mrs Hartley. It was Mr Steel."

"No!" Mrs Petty's eyes widened as she stared at Mrs Hartley. "How did you know?"

"I saw him. Not that we realised it was him at the time. We assumed it was someone else because he should have been awarding the prizes."

Mrs Petty shook her head. "Why didn't I think of that? I saw him sneak off as soon as he'd given Mrs Steel my prize. He slipped down the side of the marquee behind everyone. I took no notice, because he's always been such a gentleman ... and I was delighted to be the centre of attention, if only for a minute."

"Don't blame yourself. We all dismissed him for a while. In the end, it turned out he was rather too keen on betting on the horses, and it clouded his judgement."

Mrs Petty's forehead creased. "But he killed a workman. How did he even know him?"

"From the bank where Mr Steel worked. They had an arrangement where Mr Hobbs put bets on for him so Mrs Steel didn't find out."

"Tut tut. What a shame. How did Mrs Steel take it?"

"She wasn't there. Inspector Adams will pay her a visit once Mr Steel is securely locked up."

"The poor love. She'll be devastated. She used to go everywhere with Mr Steel when he wasn't at the club. If only she'd been with him on the afternoon of the fete."

"Gracious, Mrs Petty. You've probably just explained why Mr Steel gave her the wrong dose of some of her tablets."

"I have?"

"Yes ... and it wasn't a mistake, after all. By deliberately giving her a low dose, he knew she wouldn't be able to follow him. He must have been planning this for weeks."

"I'm glad I could help. Not that it makes things any better for Mrs Steel. I'll call on her tomorrow."

"I'm sure she'd appreciate that. It's going to come as a shock to her."

"It is." Mrs Petty's sullen expression suddenly brightened again. "What happened to Sergeant Cooper? I saw Mrs Appleton helping him from the club."

"Unfortunately, he took a blow to his jaw. Nothing serious, but he'll need to rest for a few days."

"Well I never. It goes to show that you really don't know people at all."

"It certainly does." Eliza flinched as the church clock struck six. "I'd better be going. Dinner will be ready soon."

Mrs Hartley smiled at her. "I can make my own way from here if you need to go. Please call in for afternoon tea at any time. Mrs Appleton, too."

"We will. Thank you."

Eliza left her companions talking as she put her head down and strode to Sergeant Cooper's house. The front door was open when she arrived, but she knocked and waited on the doorstep.

"May I come in?"

When there was no answer, she stepped inside. "Connie, are you here?"

A second later, her friend appeared, tears streaming down her face.

"My goodness. What's the matter? Is Sergeant Cooper all right?"

"H-he's fine, but ... he's asked me to marry him."

"Oh, Connie ... congratulations!" Eliza threw her arms around her shoulders. "I'm so pleased for you." She suddenly took a step backwards. "You did say yes?"

Connie laughed through her tears. "Of course I did."

"Then why are you crying?"

"Because ... I'm happy ... excited ... scared..."

"Scared?"

Sergeant Cooper appeared, the swelling on his jaw already noticeable. "I told her about Lord Lowton." He squeezed Connie's shoulder. "I can't let her stay in that house on her own any longer. I'd never forgive myself if anything happened to her."

Connie's voice squeaked. "Why didn't you tell me?"

"I only found out last night and don't have many details. Besides, I didn't want to worry you."

Sergeant Cooper's cheeks coloured. "I hope I've not done that, but I couldn't leave anything to chance."

"I'm sure she'll be fine with you looking out for her." Eliza took Connie's hands. "Have you set a date for the wedding?"

Sergeant Cooper puffed out his chest. "Two months today ... assuming the vicar agrees. We don't want to wait any longer."

"I'm very glad to hear it. You've already been together for far too long without making her an honest woman."

Connie wiped her eyes with the backs of her hands. "You don't mind?"

"Why on earth would I mind?"

"Because Frank will take care of me from now on."

"Which is how it should be. Now, I'm going to go home and tell Archie that he needs to buy a new suit."

A sherry was waiting for Eliza when she walked into the drawing room, and she remained standing as she raised her glass to Archie and Henry.

"Good health."

"Good health." Archie took a sip of his drink as she sat beside him on the settee. "How's Sergeant Cooper?"

Eliza tutted. "I didn't actually ask him, but I'd say he's fine. He's asked for Connie's hand in marriage."

"That's nice... About time, too."

"I said that. They're not hanging around either. They plan to marry in two months' time."

Henry looked at her from the settee opposite. "Why the rush?"

"Inspector Adams told the sergeant about Lord Lowton, and he doesn't want Connie to be on her own while he's a threat."

Henry stared down at his drink. "I doubt he'll trouble Mrs Appleton."

"What makes you say that?"

"He has other people in his sights."

"Like Inspector Adams?"

"Amongst others."

"What aren't you telling us?"

"He's not happy with Lord Albert, either, for obvious reasons. And then there's me..."

"You?" Eliza stared at Archie and then twisted round in her chair as Henry stood up and walked behind her to the window. "I might as well tell you. The young lady I've been walking out with is Lady Alice ... and ... and I've asked her to marry me."

Eliza gasped as she gaped at her son. "Marry ... Lady Alice..."

"We're hoping to be married in the spring ... as long as Lord Lowton does nothing stupid in the meantime."

"But surely you'll need his permission."

Henry shook his head. "We'll be married whether he likes it or not. The only difference is whether he agrees to a society wedding, or we elope."

"Is that what the telegram was about?"

Henry sighed. "It's not what you think. I just wanted to tell her I was here so she wasn't worrying about me."

Eliza turned back to Archie. "Are you listening? Our son could be putting his life in danger ... and if he elopes, there won't even be a proper ceremony. You must stop him."

"I'll do no such thing. And neither will you. Lady Alice is a lovely girl, and there's no way her mother will see her married without half of London being invited. We should be delighted for them." Archie stood up and raised his glass to his son. "Congratulations. I hope you'll both be very happy together."

THE NEXT BOOK IN THE SERIES

The Calling Card Murders

September 1905: A shopping trip to London leads to disaster, but it doesn't end there...

Eliza and Connie face their most difficult challenge yet. Can they discover the killer, before the killer finds them?

Visit my website for details of retailers:
https://www.vlmcbeath.com/

Sign up to a no-spam newsletter for further information and exclusive content about the series.

Visit
https://www.subscribepage.com/eti-freeadt

Further details can be found at **www.vlmcbeath.com**

Have you read all the books in the series?

The full series:
A Deadly Tonic (A Novella)
Murder in Moreton
Death of an Honourable Gent
Dying for a Garden Party
A Scottish Fling
The Palace Murder
Death by the Sea
Murder at the Marquee
The Calling Cards Murders
A Christmas Murder (A Novella)

AUTHOR'S NOTE AND ACKNOWLEDGEMENTS

As I've worked my way through the series, each book has been a standalone story with the only overarching theme being the relationship between Connie and Sergeant Cooper.

For this book, and the next one, I decided to break that mould.

I came up with the idea of linking the books when a reader wrote to me asking some follow up questions about the relationships in *Death of an Honourable Gent*. Most notably about Henry and Lady Alice.

To be truthful, I hadn't given it a lot of thought, but the idea of developing their storyline and bringing back the Lowton family had its appeal. If you've yet to read *Death of an Honourable Gent*, I hope I didn't give away too many spoilers. I tried not to.

If you've read the whole series, I hope you remembered the Lowton's, as well as other characters who've previously made an appearance in the books. These include: Mrs Petty, Mr Hewitt, and Mr and Mrs Pitt. Those who've been less prominent are Mrs Hartley and her daughter, who were in *Dying for a Garden Party,* Mrs King from *The Palace Murder,* and Mr Royal from way back in *Murder in Moreton.* I decided to reintroduce them given that the story was set in Moreton, and most of the familiar characters were likely to be present at the village fete.

This book will clearly lead into the next one as I'm sure you'd like to know if Connie does finally marry Sergeant Cooper. On top of that, I thought I'd spice it up with Henry's betrothal to Lady Alice. Will they actually tie the knot, or will Lord Lowton have something to say about it?

As I write this author's note, I don't actually know how it will end! It's always one of the fun parts of writing to find out what the characters want to do. I hope you enjoy whatever I come up with!

As always, I'd like to thank my friend Rachel and husband Stuart for their support with this book and for giving early feedback. I would also like to thank my editor Susan Cunningham, and my team of advanced readers who helped to make sure the final version was as good as I could make it.

Until next time...

Val

ALSO BY VL MCBEATH

Historical Family Sagas Inspired by Family History...

The *Ambition & Destiny* Series

The full series:

Short Story Prequel: *Condemned by Fate*

Part 1: *Hooks & Eyes*

Part 2: *Less Than Equals*

Part 3: *When Time Runs Out*

Part 4: *Only One Winner*

Part 5: *Different World*

A standalone novel: *The Young Widow*

The *Windsor Street Family Saga*

The full series:

Part 1: *The Sailor's Promise*

(*an introductory novella*)

Part 2: *The Wife's Dilemma*

Part 3: *The Stewardess's Journey*

Part 4: *The Captain's Order*

Part 5: *The Companion's Secret*

Part 6: *The Mother's Confession*

Part 7: *The Daughter's Defiance*

To find out more about VL McBeath's Family Saga's visit her website at:

https://www.valmcbeath.com/

FOLLOW ME

at:

Website:
https://valmcbeath.com

Facebook:
https://www.facebook.com/VLMcBeath

BookBub:
https://www.bookbub.com/authors/vl-mcbeath

Printed in Great Britain
by Amazon

35917059R00169